**She hadn't seen him for years, and now that he'd surfaced again, danger seemed to follow her everywhere...**

"No." She shook her head and held up a hand to stop any excuses that might roll off his tongue. "There are no reasons. The minute you walked out that door like a thief in the night—Ha, that's good one. Thief in the night. That's exactly what you are, isn't it? Chief Inspector Burnell very kindly regaled me with all your exploits. Do you know that you're quite infamous all over Europe?"

"I'm sure old Oliver had a jolly time doing so. The police cannot prove anything. Nothing. They're just a gaggle of old biddies who have nothing better to do than to sit around coming up with farfetched theories."

"You're a thief and a liar. Charles is my friend and he needs my help. I'm going to help him." She took a step closer to Gregory and poked him in the chest. "You can't stop me. No one can. It's called loyalty. Something you know absolutely nothing about. Now, I'm going to walk across the campo and into my hotel. Go do whatever it is that you do. I'm sure there must be some jewels lying around here somewhere that you can steal."

The salty tears streaming down her cheeks blurred her vision as she entered the hotel lobby. She impatiently wiped them away with the back of her hand and kept her gaze downward as she asked for her key. She took the lift up to the fourth floor. There was no one in the corridor when the doors opened. Her room was just around the corner to the right. She fumbled with the key in the lock. Why did she allow him to get to her like this? *Why*? She thought she had put it all behind her, that she was stronger. Now, out of the blue, Gregory walked back into her life and everything was topsy-turvy. She finally opened the door. "Oh, my God," she gasped.

**A journalist, a jewel thief, and a Russian spy...when their paths cross, it's murder.**

Journalist Emmeline Kirby hasn't laid eyes on her former lover Gregory Longdon, a jewel thief, in two years. But she literally tumbles into his arms, after she witnesses two men attempt to murder her friend and fellow journalist, Charles Latimer, in Venice.

When Charles is ultimately killed, Emmeline is determined to bring his murderer to justice. But as she and Gregory delve deeper, they become ensnared in a hunt for a Russian spy in the British Foreign Office, who has his sights set on keeping his identity a secret at all costs—as Charles found out too late.

# KUDOS for *Lead Me into Danger*

In *Lead Me into Danger* by Daniella Bernett, reporter Emmeline Kirby attends a party in Venice, where she meets an old friend who tells her he's in danger. When he is later killed in her own flat in London, she is determined to investigate and solve his murder. As she does, dark secrets are uncovered and she finds her own life is in danger. Bernett's characters are well developed and intriguing. Her plot is strong and well thought out, the action fast-paced and exciting. You'll have a hard time putting this one down. ~ *Taylor Jones, Reviewer*

Lead Me into Danger by Daniella Bernett is a clever mystery involving espionage and spies. Our heroine, journalist Emmeline Kirby, is in Venice when she runs into an old friend. He begins an intriguing conversation with her, but breaks off suddenly when he sees someone across the room. When he is later murdered, Emmy is determine to get justice for him and to find out what it was that he knew that got him killed. As she and her former lover, a jewel thief, follow the clues, she discovers corruption and treachery on a major scale, leaving her unsure of whom she can trust. *Lead Me into Danger* is a fast-paced, page-turning mystery that will hook you from the very first paragraph. This one's a keeper, folks. You will want to have it close to read again and again. ~ *Regan Murphy, Reviewer*

# ACKNOWLEDGEMENTS

I would like to thank the Mystery Writers of America New York Chapter for its strong support and a wealth of good advice. In particular, I would like to thank Chapter President Richie Narvaez, and Sheila and Gerald Levine.

I also would like to thank New York Times bestselling authors Tracy Grant, Susan Elia MacNeal, and Lauren Willig for remembering how hard it was at the beginning and helping a struggling fellow writer.

I have one small note on the story that follows here. For those of you familiar with London's Holland Park neighborhood, you know that there is no park in the square near Stafford Terrace. The one in this book is purely my creation and is intended to propel the story.

# LEAD

# ME INTO

# DANGER

Daniella Bernett

*A Black Opal Books Publication*

*To my parents and my sister Vivian for their
unconditional love and support.
My life is enriched because I have you.*

# CHAPTER 1

## London

*February 2010*:

He turned up the collar of his overcoat against the thickening fog. The damp chill seemed to permeate his leather gloves, so he dug his hands deeper into his pockets. His footsteps echoed hollowly as he walked along Kennington Road in Lambeth. He turned into Fitzalan Street, where the bare tree branches cast eerie shadows upon the square, like the ghouls and goblins in a children's story. He stopped in the middle of the block in front of Number Thirty-Two, one of those nineteenth-century mansions that had long ago been converted into flats. The steps were still slick from the rain earlier in the evening. He searched the names of the tenants listed on the intercom panel beside the door. He pressed several buttons, hoping that someone would buzz him in.

The intercom crackled as a disembodied female voice broke the silence. "It's about time you showed up, Derek. I'd nearly given up on you. I've been waiting for over an hour." There was a loud buzz and a click as the door was unlocked.

He smiled to himself as he walked into the hall and silently thanked Derek—whoever he was—for being late. He took the lift up to the fourth floor. Number Five was down the corridor to his right. As luck would have it, there was no one about. His pick slipped easily into the lock, a couple of twists and, within seconds, the door was open. The thin beam from his torch bounced quickly over the living room.

From the layout of the flat he had memorized, he knew that the study was down the short hallway next to the bedroom. Once he found it, he crossed the room and turned on the desk lamp. He sat in the swivel chair and began methodically going through all the drawers. After half an hour without any success, he began riffling through the paperbacks and leather-bound volumes in the two bookcases along the opposite wall. He was beginning to lose his patience. *Nothing.* Where would he have hidden it? But his thoughts were interrupted, when he heard someone unlocking the front door.

He quickly turned off the desk lamp and waited. "Mr. Latimer, is that you? You're back early. I thought you'd be in Italy until Monday," a woman's voice called out. "Are you hungry, Mr. Latimer? Would you like me to fix you a light supper?"

Damn, he thought. Mrs. Saunders, the old busybody who came in twice a week to cook and clean for Latimer. Maybe she'd go away.

"*Mr. Latimer?*"

He heard her coming down the hall toward the study. She hesitated. "Mr. Latimer, are you in there?"

She slowly opened the door and flicked on the switch. She saw a heap of books on the floor and papers strewn all over the desk. "Dear, oh dear. What's been happening here?"

Mrs. Saunders took a step into the room. The last

thing she would ever hear before her neck was snapped was the door closing behind her. She crumpled to the ground. One minute alive, the next dead. It had happened so quickly she didn't have time to struggle or cry out.

His search had yielded nothing, so there was no point for the assassin to hang about any longer. He didn't have to worry about fingerprints because he was wearing gloves.

He opened the door into the corridor a crack. It was empty. Quietly, he hurried toward the stairs. He didn't want to wait for the lift and risk being seen. In five minutes, he was outside and was immediately swallowed up by the fog. He retraced his steps up Kennington Road, walking at a steady pace so as not to attract any undue attention. He crossed Lambeth Road and continued along Kennington until it turned into Westminster Bridge Road.

The assassin crossed Westminster Bridge. Once on the other side of the Thames, he pulled out his mobile and called a certain number in the Russian embassy.

He heard the phone ring twice. He hung up and dialed again, allowing it to ring two more times. The signal. This time a male voice with a heavy Russian accent answered. "Yes?"

"It was not in the flat. Latimer must have it with him."

"I see," the voice at the other end of the line said.

"The housekeeper came while I was there."

"And?"

"I dealt with her."

"I see. Is there any way to connect it to you?"

"No."

"Good. Your job is done. Your money is waiting for you in a locker at Heathrow."

The assassin heard a click and then silence. He tossed the mobile over the parapet and it disappeared into the murky depths of the Thames with a soft splash. He had stolen it that afternoon from an unsuspecting businessman exiting a taxi on Regent Street. There was no way to trace him to the call to the embassy.

He whistled as he descended the few steps into the Westminster tube station. Within seconds, he was lost amid the crush of commuters hurrying home.

Soon afterward, a call was made on a secure line from the embassy in Kensington Palace Gardens to an apartment on Via Veneto in Rome. "It was not in the flat. Latimer has it."

"We'll take over from here." The line went dead.

# CHAPTER 2

## *Venice*

The Corteo delle Nazioni was one of the city's main Carnival attractions. The event began with a gondola ride down the Grand Canal from the City Council's Palace near the Rialto Bridge to the opulent Ca' Vendramin Calergi, the Renaissance-style palazzo that was home to the casino. Everyone dressed in period costumes for the event, which honored Venice's traditions and its consular corps.

Emmeline was among this year's three hundred enthusiastic participants, who hailed from the forty countries with consulates in and around Venice. Her friend Philip in the Foreign Office had managed to wangle an invitation for her, when he discovered that she would be in the city during Carnival. She had laughed when he said it was a lavish party everyone should experience once in his or her lifetime. And now, here she was, dressed in a cobalt-blue Renaissance velvet gown with a froth of lace and seed pearls across the bodice. Her dark eyes peered out from a gold mask tied with a black ribbon that was lost in her short, dark, curly hair.

A sigh escaped her lips as she listened to the romantic strains of Vivaldi, Telemann, and Albinoni swirl round and round. She wended her way through the throng of partygoers. *Venice.* Bewitching siren, jewel of the Adriatic, who seduced the soul—and stole the heart. It was both heaven and torture to be back in this lovely city. The last time Emmeline was here had been two years ago. *Was it only two years ago?* When she had been excited and eager to see Venice for the first time. When she had been with Gregory. Handsome, charming Gregory. Oh, never mind. It seemed so long ago, so much had changed. That was another life—another self—when she still entertained naïve dreams about love and happiness.

Despite all the colors and the festive mood about her, Emmeline felt alone. Tears pricked her eyelids. It was too much to be back here. She had the urge to run out of this beautiful palazzo and lose herself in the quiet streets of this city, whose architecture had not changed in four centuries. Emmeline checked her watch. Nine o'clock. Perhaps she would stay for another half an hour and then she'd politely make her goodbyes.

The chamber orchestra began playing a Strauss waltz. All around her people were dancing. Suddenly, Emmeline felt a tap on her shoulder. "May I have the honor of this waltz, Miss Kirby?"

Emmeline turned and her face broke into a wide smile at the sound of the familiar voice. "Charles? Charles Latimer, I haven't seen you in ages."

The man bowed gallantly. He took off his mask and pulled her into his arms to give her a kiss on the cheek. He held her hands as he stood back. "It is good to see you, darling."

"And you, too, Charles." They began to sway to the music. He hadn't changed in the year since she had last seen him. He still oozed sex appeal and playfulness. Perhaps, there were a few more fine lines around his inquisitive blue-gray eyes, but this only seemed to enhance his attractiveness. As usual, his chestnut hair shimmered with golden highlights, now mixed with one or two strands of gray. However, not one of those strands was out of place. She knew many female colleagues who had fallen hard for Charles. After all, how could they help themselves? He was six-foot-two, lithe and graceful. He also had a razor-sharp intelligence and wit. It was no wonder Charles had received so many awards for his work. At fifty-three, he was one of the best investigative journalists in the business.

The piece ended and Charles guided her by the elbow to a quiet corner. "Emmeline, darling, I must admit that our meeting tonight was not a chance occurrence."

"No?"

"No." He shot a quick glance around them to make sure no one was listening. "Philip told me you would be here tonight. You're the only one I can trust."

Emmeline placed a hand on his arm. Something in the tone of his voice sent a shiver down her spine. "Charles, what is it? You know I'll do anything for you."

"Yes, I know. I'm working on a big story, really big. It is so explosive that it will rip Whitehall apart or, at the very least, it could take years to recover from the repercussions."

Emmeline tilted her head to one side. He had piqued her interest. "I'm intrigued. You know I always love a good story."

Charles searched her deep brown eyes and rested his hands on her shoulders. "Darling, I don't want to frighten you, but I must warn you that there is an element of danger involved."

For a second, he saw that her cheeks blanched. "I'm game. Now, tell me everything and what I can do to help."

Charles flashed one of his most engaging smiles.

"Good girl. I knew you wouldn't let me down." He lowered his voice. "It all started about a month ago. I was going to meet Philip for dinner."

"For dinner or to pump him for Foreign Office gossip?"

Charles grinned. "Ah, it is sad to see such skepticism in one so young."

"I'm not a child, Charles. I turned thirty in May. And my work is just as respected as yours."

"Yes, sorry. I didn't mean to imply anything to the contrary. That's why I came to you. Because of your instincts, skill, and persistence in seeking out the truth. Now, as I was saying. Philip and I had planned to have dinner. He was running a bit late, so he asked me to meet him at the Foreign Office. That's when I saw him..." His voice trailed off.

"Saw who?" Emmeline prompted, but he wasn't looking at her. She turned to follow the direction of his gaze. She saw the Russian consul, Dimitri Petrov, and an older man, probably a member of the consular staff, across the room. They were deep in conversation.

"Emmy, this was a mistake. We can't talk here. There are too many people about," Charles said hurriedly.

"What's going on?"

"Look, it's nine-thirty," he whispered. "Meet me in an hour in front of the church of San Bartolomeo near the Rialto Bridge."

"But—"

"I promise I'll tell you everything. Until then, I don't think it's safe for you to be seen with me." He gave her a distracted kiss on the cheek and disappeared into the crowd.

Emmeline was left standing there alone. She accepted a glass of champagne from a waiter. Her gaze slid sideways as she took a sip.

Petrov and the older man were gone.

℘⅋℘⅋

Music and laughter floated up the curving staircase of the palazzo, as he crossed the long corridor and slipped into the master bedroom at the far end. His footfalls had been lost in the thick crimson runner with the elaborate floral pattern that graced the cool marble floor. But he need not have worried. The hundred or so guests down below who had come to celebrate Carnival and Signora Talamini's thirtieth birthday were more interested in the wine, the music, and the food to take any notice of him.

The door closed with a soft click behind him. Long, tapered fingers of silvery moonlight spilled from the balcony window and lovingly caressed the bed, the carpet, and dressing table before disappearing into the dark shadows dozing in the corner of the room. The bed, already turned down by the maid, quietly awaited the master and mistress to retire for the night. The thief smiled to himself. Judging by the festivities downstairs, this would not be for many hours yet. However, he still had to work quickly.

He pulled out a pencil torch from an inner pocket beneath his cape and walked over to a bucolic landscape painting hanging on the wall to the right of the dresser. After carefully feeling around the edges of the frame, his gloved fingers found the catch. He pressed it and the painting swung away from the wall to reveal a safe. The thief directed the thin beam of light on the tumbler and slowly turned. Right thirty, left eleven, right twenty-two. Click. The safe was open. He ignored the two stacks of euros and reached for a square, black-velvet box. He opened the lid. Involuntarily, he sucked in his breath. Even in the half gloom, the flawless seven carat diamond pendant sparkled with an inner fire. "Sorry to have kept you waiting, darling. I'm afraid I was unavoidably detained."

The thief gingerly lifted it out of the box to admire. Its myriad facets caught and reflected the moonlight. He wished he could stay to see the reaction on Signor Talamini's face when he presented an empty box to his wife later on this evening. Alas, you couldn't have everything in life. He would have to satisfy himself with the diamond.

"Not a bad bargain," he murmured to himself.

There was no time to waste. He slipped the diamond into his pocket, replaced the box, and closed the safe. He gave the tumbler a spin before putting the painting back in place. The thief took one last glance around the room to make sure he had not disturbed anything. Nothing. He opened the door a crack to see if there was anyone in the corridor. It was quiet. He slipped his white *bauta* mask over the upper part of his face. The mask, which had been worn almost constantly by people in the eighteenth century, also consisted of a black veil that concealed the hair, ears, and neck. A black tricorn hat and a black cape, known as a *tabarro*, completed the costume.

The thief tiptoed along the corridor and down the stairs. No one noticed him as he rejoined the party. He accepted the flute of golden champagne that a passing waiter offered. He took two sips and stood back to muse over the outrageous costumes of some of the guests. He began chatting in fluent Italian with an older gentleman, who had a full head of crisp white hair and wore a simple mask that only covered his deep-set dark brown eyes.

"Lovely party," the thief said.

"Oh, yes. Look at Giovana. How beautiful she looks this evening. *Bellissima*, don't you agree?" the older man asked.

The thief nodded as he cast an appreciative glance over the shapely figure of their hostess. There was a lot to admire indeed. A heart-shaped face with a smooth, olive complexion and shiny blue-black, shoulder-length hair. When she pulled her mask down to take a sip of wine or kiss a guest, he saw that she had round, jet-black eyes.

"And Paolo," his companion said. "Have you ever seen a man more in love? They make a handsome couple."

The husband, on the other hand, was a different story. Yes, the dusky, angular face behind the mask appeared to be extremely good looking, too. Paolo Talamini exuded confidence and arrogance. He was probably around thirty-five, slender with broad, muscular shoulders and a narrow waist. A few streaks of silver could be seen in his dark hair, which was parted to the right over his forehead. However, his hazel eyes held a coldness that belied the smile upon his lips. Here was a man who had something to hide.

But the thief turned to the older man and smiled. "I have never seen him look happier."

"Ah, then you know him well?"

"Oh, yes," the thief lied easily as he took a sip of champagne. "We've known each other for years."

"Friends. It is always nice to have old friends on special occasions such as this."

"Not friends. More like friendly business rivals."

"Ah, well. It is good that you do not allow your rivalry to get in the way of such a festive evening. By the way, my name is Nicolò Crespi."

The thief extended a hand. "A pleasure to meet you, signore. I hear Paolo has a very special present for Giovana this evening. He will make a big presentation after dinner."

"Really? How nice."

The thief finished his champagne and placed the empty glass on the tray of a passing waiter. "Well, I hope you enjoy the party, Signor Crespi."

He made to go, but Crespi put out his hand and pulled at his sleeve. "Surely you are not leaving now, signore?"

"I'm afraid I must. I have a prior engagement. I told Paolo I could only stay for a little while. If you'll excuse me, I must go and say goodbye to them."

"Of course. Of course. I hope to see you again in the future, signore."

But his last words were drowned out by the murmur of voices around him. The thief would be halfway across the room before Crespi realized he had never told him his name.

If the thief would have turned around, he would have seen that several of the ladies were trying to catch his eye as he made his way toward Signor and Signora Talamini. He made a dashing and enigmatic figure in his costume. He was nearly six feet tall and slim. If he took off the *bauta*, the women would see that he had dark wavy hair and a mustache. But what really drew one toward him were his eyes. They were like two pools of liquid cinnamon warmed by the summer sun and seemed to bore right through you. Sometimes, it was as if he could guess what you were thinking.

Only five more minutes and he was home free. Brashly, he went up to the host and hostess. "Paolo, Giovana, dear friends. It is good to see you again after so long." He took Giovana's hands in his own and kissed them gallantly. "You're stunning tonight, darling." Then, he turned to Paolo and gave him a kiss on each cheek, in the Italian fashion. "I hope to see you both the next time I am in Venice."

"You're leaving already?" Surprise laced Paolo's voice.

"I have to catch an early flight for Rome in the morning. I did tell you."

"Yes. Yes, of course you did. I'll have Stefano call a taxi for you. I will be back in a moment." Talamini went out into the hall and pulled the butler aside.

The thief was left alone with Giovana. Surprisingly, she was very shy for such a beautiful woman. She held her mask to her face and did not look him in the eye while her husband was not with them. There were long pauses in their conversation. Her posture relaxed, revealing her relief when Paolo returned and slipped an arm around her waist.

"It is all taken care of. The taxi is waiting outside."

"Thank you, old friend. We will have more time to catch up the next time I'm in Venice."

Paolo smiled and gave him a hug. "Thank you for coming. It meant a great deal to Giovana and me that you managed to come for a little while."

The thief smiled as his hand brushed the pocket beneath his cape. "You don't know what a pleasure it has been for me."

They followed him outside and waved as he got into the water taxi. They watched until the taxi disappeared at a bend in the Grand Canal.

Paolo kissed his wife's cheek as they walked back up the steps to rejoin their guests. "Paolo?"

"Yes, *amore mio*?"

"I was so embarrassed. I forgot your friend's name. What is it?"

Paolo stopped in the doorway. "*Cara*, he's not my friend. I thought he was a friend of yours."

"I have never met that man before in my life."

Husband and wife were left staring at one another, as

the thief settled himself into the water taxi and directed the driver to take him to the casino. He checked his watch. Nine o'clock. A couple of hours at another ball would be amusing. Who knew what little baubles he could pick up there?

# CHAPTER 3

Emmeline pulled her cloak tightly around her shoulders as the February night wrapped her in its moist embrace. A few flurries had started to fall as she stepped out of the water taxi at Rialto. It was only a five-minute walk from the bridge to Campo San Bartolomeo, where the sixteenth-century church stood.

Emmeline checked her watch. It was 10:15. She was early, so she took her time along the winding streets. She stopped on a humpbacked bridge for a moment and closed her eyes, listening to the velvet hiss of the canal as its waters gently lapped against the *fondamenta* and the gondolas below. A world of watery enchantment, in which one couldn't help but be swept away by Venice's rich history. Indeed, the very air seemed to be imbued with elegance, romance, and mystery.

A whisper of a breeze trickled down Emmeline's spine, causing her to shiver slightly. Her costume and the thin cloak did nothing to keep her warm. Or was it something else? Emmeline opened her eyes. All of a sudden, she was afraid.

The snow was getting a bit harder. She missed a turning and now she was lost. She started to walk in what she thought was the general direction of the church, but she wound up at a dead end. All the *calle* looked the

same. There was no one else about, which was strange for
Carnival. She tried to keep calm, to distract her mind by
thinking about Venice's past and what she loved about
this city. Unfortunately, as luck would have it, her
thoughts strayed to political murders and other intrigues
from centuries past. "Stop it," she chided herself. "Stop
being silly. Panicking will not help. You'll be there in
another minute."

Up ahead, Emmeline thought she heard voices. Or
was it only her mind playing tricks on her? She stopped
and listened. No, she definitely heard something and, by
chance, she happened to find herself in Campo San Bartolomeo.

Emmeline quickened her pace. Across the square,
there seemed to be three figures in the shadows by the
side of the church. She heard male voices. One voice was
raised in anger. They were speaking English, but she
couldn't make out what was being said. She thought one
of the men had an accent, as if English was not his native
tongue.

A scuffle seemed to be taking place. She heard a
grunt and a small cry. Emmeline huddled in a doorway. A
shiver slithered down her spine. She heard slow, hesitant
steps.

"Charles, is that you?" She sucked in her breath.
"You're hurt."

He swayed for a moment and then sank to his knees.
He grabbed Emmeline's wrist and pulled her toward him.
She screamed when she saw the knife protruding from his
rib cage. Blood was everywhere.

"*Charles?*" His eyes fluttered closed. She fumbled to
untie the strings of her cloak and tore it off to try to
stanch some of the blood. She bent down close to his ear.
"Charles, can you hear me?"

His blue-gray eyes opened wide. He squeezed her

hand so hard she thought he would break her fingers. "Emmeline." It was a hoarse whisper.

"Yes, I'm here. Who did this to you?"

"I r—recognized h—him—from Moscow. I—it's the same m—man. I'm s—sure now."

"Who? You're not making sense. *Who*?"

He looked up at her without seeing her and then his eyes closed. His grip loosened and his head slumped to the side. He was dead. *Dead.*

Emmeline was trembling.

Everything seemed to happen so quickly. Two men came running toward her. She stared at them for a second and then began to run back the way she had come. She was running blindly. All she knew was that she had to get away. She heard them behind her. They were getting closer. She darted down an alley to her right. Her breathing was coming in big gulps now. She thought her heart would explode in her chest. If only she could make her way to Piazza San Marco, there were always people at the cafes in the square. She could summon a police officer. Someone. *Anyone.*

Emmeline leaned against a wall for a minute. "Oh, please, God. Please help me." She closed her eyes. She thought her legs would buckle under her and the two men would find her. She heard their heavy footsteps again. They seemed quite close. The moon reappeared through the thinning fog. She began to run. Every few seconds she glanced over her shoulder to see if they were catching up. She stumbled, her legs becoming entangled in the long skirt of her costume.

Completely rattled already, she looked down and saw the ground rising to meet her.

That was when a hand suddenly reached out and grabbed her.

# CHAPTER 4

Emmeline gasped as she was shoved against a wall by a man. Her dark eyes widened when he lifted his *bauta* mask and she saw his face. "*Gregory*." It was a stunned whisper. That's all she had time to say.

"Shh," he hissed.

The next thing she knew, he was kissing her. He blocked her with his larger body as the two men who had been chasing her passed by and into Piazza San Marco without even a glance in their direction. After all, they were merely two lovers stealing a moonlight kiss at Carnival.

He pulled away, but he still shielded her in his arms. "It's all right. I think we've given them the slip."

Emmeline reached up and slapped him hard across the face. "How dare you?" She sliced him to pieces with a single, icy look. "How dare you take advantage of the situation?"

Gregory laughed as he rubbed his stinging cheek. He took off his mask and tricorn hat. That laugh she remembered so well. That laugh teased her and made her even angrier.

"Now, love, is that way to speak to the man who has just saved your life?" He leaned in closer and pinned her to the wall. She felt his warm breath as he murmured against her curls. "How about another kiss to show me how much you've missed me?"

She turned her face away to avoid his kiss. "Bloody cheek. I have not missed you." She glared at him defiantly. "I have more important things to think about these days. And, I'll have you know, I was perfectly fine." She tried to push him away.

He laughed again and let her go. "I always liked your fiery passion when you were upset. So why were those nice, friendly chaps chasing you?"

In her surprise at seeing him again, she had nearly forgotten about Charles. She shuddered, remembering his eyes staring up at her and the blood. For a second, she felt as if she might pass out.

Gregory grabbed her arm. "Are you all right, Emmy? You're awfully pale. Here take my cape or else you'll catch your death of cold."

"Gregory, they murdered Charles Latimer. That's why I was running. He fell at my feet. It was awful. There was a knife a—and blood. It was horrid."

The shock was beginning to set in. She felt the tears rolling off her eyelashes and slowly down her cheeks. He pulled her into his arms, without any protests this time. She clung to him, glad of his warmth and strength.

When she had calmed down, he asked gently, "Do you think that you'd be able to find your way back there?"

She was silent a moment. "Yes," she whispered. "He's in Campo San Bartolomeo. I left poor Charles lying there and I just ran."

"It's all right. Let's go find a *carabiniere.*"

There was a police station in a quiet campo off Riva degli Schiavoni near the San Zaccaria *vaporetto* stop. After being ignored for nearly ten minutes by the two officers behind the desk, a third officer appeared from the nether regions of the station and finally inquired if he could help them. Succinctly, Gregory explained the situation in Italian. The officer, an older man who looked tired and annoyed, asked skeptically, "*Morto*?" Dead.

"Yes, Officer…"

"Cavalcante. Antonio Cavalcante."

"Yes, Officer Cavalcante. Miss Kirby lost her way and stumbled across the murder."

"Humph." Officer Cavalcante grunted and glanced over at Emmeline again. "And you, signore? Signore what, by the way?"

"Longdon," Gregory replied. He was fast losing his patience as the officer wrote their names down in his notebook, as if they were the suspects.

"Signor Longdon, you believe this story Signorina Kirby told you? Perhaps you and she had a…what do you *Inglesi* call it…'a lover's spat' and she wanted to make you feel sorry for her? To make you jealous with a story about another man. When you English get into the Italian sun, it boils your blood and makes you mad."

Gregory gritted his teeth and clenched his fists at his sides. "First of all, Officer Cavalcante, if you hadn't noticed it is February and it is wet and cold. Secondly, I can assure you that Miss Kirby is not some flighty female. She is a well-respected journalist back in London. Thirdly, we just came across each other by chance. Neither of us knew that the other was here in Venice."

"Journalist?"

At this, the officer's ears pricked up. Gregory rolled his eyes. The bloody man probably thinks his name in the paper will get him a promotion.

"*Allora*, Signor Longdon, Signorina Kirby." He touched his cap and gave a curt nod in Emmeline's direction. "Take me to this body."

"Officer Cavalcante, it is not 'a body.'" Emmeline's

voice cracked, as she tried to swallow her tears. "That was my friend, Charles Latimer. A British journalist."

"Yes, of course. Forgive me, signorina. Please." He pointed toward the door.

It was midnight by now. An occasional wisp of cloud drifted across the full moon, which shimmered like a creamy pearl against the indigo sky. Strands of moonlight traced a path for them to the spot where Emmeline had encountered Charles and his murderers.

She stopped. "I can't—" She swallowed hard. "I can't look at him again. He's around the corner." She pointed vaguely in the direction ahead. "I'll wait for you here."

Gregory gave her shoulders a squeeze. The officer's brow lifted, but he shrugged and said, "*Bene.*"

Cavalcante returned after five minutes. "Signorina Kirby, I do not know the laws in England. But, I am sure that the officers there do not appreciate it when you waste police time."

"*What*? What do you mean?"

"What do I mean? What do I mean?" With each word, Cavalcante's voice rose an octave. He took off his cap and wiped his brow with a handkerchief. "I mean that there is no body, *niente*. I am going home to my bed, where I would have been an hour ago if I had not listened to you crazy English." He started to walk away, but then came back. "Signorina Kirby, I advise you to leave Venice in the morning before you are charged with obstruction of justice."

Emmeline stared at his retreating figure. Gregory was by her side again. He didn't say anything. She pushed past him and went around the corner. The square was empty.

She squinted into the darkness. She bent down in front of the doorway, where she had stood. There was nothing. No blood. No knife. Nothing. She heard Gregory behind her. "How can this be?" She turned to face him. "I saw him die tonight. I wouldn't make up a story like that. You do believe me, don't you? Don't you?"

She could hear the sniveling whine of desperation in her own voice. And she hated herself for it.

"Yes, love. Yes, I believe you." He put his arm protectively around her shoulders. "But someone went to a lot of trouble to hide what happened here. The question is why."

"It must have something to do with the new story he was working on. I'm sure of it. He started to tell me about it at the party this evening. Then he changed his mind and said it was dangerous because there were too many people around. That's why he wanted to meet me at the church. He said that he would explain everything, only he never got the chance."

"Did he say anything at all?"

"Something about a man he recognized from Moscow."

"Moscow?"

"Charles was the BBC's Moscow bureau chief for five years."

"That's all?"

"Let me think." She closed her eyes. Her mind pictured the party again. "Yes, there was something else. He started to mention something about the Foreign Office, but he stopped talking when he saw Dimitri Petrov and another man across the room."

"Petrov? The Russian consul?"

"Yes."

"It's all very curious. Did you get a good look at the two chaps who were chasing you? Would you be able to recognize them, if you saw them again?"

"I could never forget them. One was the older man

Petrov was talking to at the party. He's short and wiry with broad muscular shoulders. The other man was tall and heavy-set. He moved a little slower. I think he had a slight limp. I can't be certain, though."

"Well, that's a start. I'll walk you back to your hotel. Where are you staying?"

"Hotel Ala in Campo Santa Maria Zovenigo."

"I'm at the Danieli."

"The Danieli. Naturally. Only the best for Gregory." Suddenly she remembered she was angry with this man who she had not seen in a little over two years.

"Why don't you come back with me? We can arrange a flight home for you in the morning? In the meantime, you could get some sleep for what's left of the night."

Her laughter echoed harshly in the alley. She pinned him with a cold, hard stare. "In your room, I suppose? I don't think so."

He flashed her one his most engaging grins. "Why not? I could protect you."

"Protect me? That's a laugh. You're nothing but a thief and a liar. A common criminal." She started walking away from him.

"Darling, you wound me deeply. I take great offense at that remark. Criminal I may be, but common—never. I like to think of myself as an altruist. I like to help—"

She turned and spat at him. "Ha."

"—people who have more money than is good for them," he continued as if she hadn't uttered a word.

"So you steal their jewels and whatever else you can get your grubby hands on to line your own coffers?"

He clucked his tongue at her. "Grubby, another vulgar word. I must say, this new side of you is not very attractive."

"Uhh." She threw up her hands in exasperation.

"That's it. Good night, Gregory. I'm going back to my hotel and I hope I never see you again."

Emmeline stalked off and left him chuckling to himself. He watched her until she disappeared into the darkness. He always knew which buttons to press to get her riled up. "Oh, my darling, Lady Luck was smiling upon me when she dropped you back into my life. But I'm back to stay and there is nothing you can do about it."

Gregory patted his pocket and felt the hardness of the Talamini diamond necklace against his chest. He dug his hands deep into his pockets and whistled to himself as he headed toward his hotel.

ตจตจ

Two men emerged from the nearby shadows, one had a limp.

"Hotel Ala," the older one said.

"Yes, tomorrow we will have to pay a visit to check out the accommodations."

# CHAPTER 5

Emmeline woke at six the next morning. She showered and donned an elegant crimson suit with a black velvet collar and a cream silk blouse. She slipped into black pumps with a slight heel. She ran a brush through her dark curls and fastened a delicate cameo broach to her lapel. Finally, she finished off the ensemble with the delicate gold bracelet she always wore.

She fingered the bracelet. The bracelet Gregory had given her.

"Oh, damn that man. I should just chuck this into the rubbish." But she knew that she wouldn't—that she couldn't. "Damn him," she said again as she slammed the door to her room.

She took the lift downstairs. She crossed the lobby and went down the few steps into the dining room. After a quick breakfast, she returned to her room to grab her notebook and the press kit. She would catch *Vaporetto* Number 1 from the nearby Santa Maria del Giglio stop and take it to San Zaccaria, where she would switch to Line Twenty to go across the lagoon to the island of San Servolo, where the international trade conference was being held. Emmeline checked her watch. She had plenty of time.

Once on San Servolo, Emmeline showed the security guard her press pass and was directed to a room down a long corridor where other journalists were gathering. When she entered, she saw several faces she recognized. Jonathan Morton of the *Financial Times*, David Greer from CNN, and Claude Hubert of *Le Monde* were all chatting together. She waved at them and made her way across the room to greet her old friend, Vittorio Franzetti of *Corriere Della Sera*, one of Italy's oldest and most respected daily newspapers.

"Vittorio, *come stai*?" How are you?

He put his espresso down and kissed her on both cheeks. "Bella Emmeline, how wonderful to see you after so long. It does my old eyes good to see you."

"Old? Who's old? Certainly not you. You're still as handsome as ever. I bet you have to fight off the women."

He chuckled. "I will be sixty-three in September. An old man."

"Nonsense, you look at least ten years younger."

She was right. His tanned, oval face was relatively free of wrinkles and his large hazel eyes were full of intelligence and curiosity, like an eager schoolboy. Only his thick head of salt-and-pepper hair belied his youthful demeanor. "Ah, *cara*, you flatter an old man, but I will allow you to do it." They both laughed. He tucked her arm into the crook of his elbow. "Now, tell me what has been happening with you?"

"Well, actually, something rather disturbing happened yesterday." She pulled him into a corner and briefly explained the events of the previous evening. Except the part about meeting Gregory again. "The police think I made the whole thing up. But if Charles didn't die, where is he? He couldn't have gone far with that stab wound. He was bleeding heavily."

"I did not even know he was in Italy. Obviously, he did not want anyone to know what he was working on. Or at least not right away. Did he give you any hint what it might be about?"

"It was all so confusing. He was not making much sense."

"Perhaps, it was merely a robbery gone wrong."

"Then why would they move the body? And where is the body?"

"Yes." Vittorio rubbed his chin. "It is very puzzling."

They didn't have any more time to mull over the possibilities because they were being ushered into the conference hall. They found seats in the middle of the room, close to the podium. Emmeline took notes as she flipped through the biographies of the speakers in the press kit.

She stopped and stared at the face on the fourth sheet. Emmeline nudged Vittorio with her elbow. "That's him. That's the man who was talking to Petrov at the party."

"*What?* Anatol Zobrinsky? Are you sure?"

"Yes. Why?" She looked down at the bio. "It says he is a member of the Russian trade delegation in London."

"That's just a cover. Everyone knows it. He's former KGB. He is Putin's man in London."

"Are you saying he's a spy? Then why doesn't the British government kick him out?"

Vittorio smiled and patted her hand. "*Cara,* don't you know that, in diplomatic circles, spying is a thing of the past since the Berlin Wall came down and the Cold War ended?"

"But if everyone knows that he's a spy—"

"Emmeline, everyone knows and everyone turns a blind eye. The other side is just as guilty. It's the same game, just another variation on the original rules."

She stared at the face on the sheet in her lap. Anatol Zobrinsky was rather ugly. She hazarded a guess that he was probably in his late fifties. He had curly gray hair that framed a broad forehead. His face was all sharp angles. A tiny scar showed above his left eyebrow. His cold and unsmiling jet black eyes hinted at a ruthless nature. She could well believe that this man could commit murder without any qualms or regrets afterward.

e/se/s

Emmeline was only half-listening to the panelists. They were discussing the importance of loosening EU trade restrictions. There was nothing new in their discussions and projections.

She was turning over in her mind the enigma of Anatol Zobrinsky. What did he have to do with Charles? And what happened to Charles's body? Why hadn't his death been reported yet?

She was contemplating this last thought, when the moderator was introducing the next speaker: Anatol Zobrinsky. Her head snapped up. In the same instant that he stepped up to the lectern, Zobrinsky's eyes locked on hers.

He held her gaze for a long moment before turning his attention to his speech. She reached out and squeezed Vittorio's hand. She felt certain that if she had been alone, instead of in a crowded room, Zobrinsky would have finished what he had started last night in Campo San Bartolomeo.

There was no way she could leave the hall without disturbing the speakers. She was trapped until the morning session came to an end. At least she had Vittorio. He would help her.

The next speaker was a tall, good-looking man in an

exquisitely tailored, dove gray suit and sky blue tie. "Good morning, ladies and gentlemen. My name is Paolo Talamini and today I would like to discuss—"

The rest of his words were lost. Emmeline was concentrating on Zobrinsky as he left the stage. She followed his progress as he walked to the back of the room. He had a hurried conversation with a tall, heavy-set man with gray hair and a dark beard. She was sure he was the other man that had been chasing her the previous night. Now, they both turned and looked directly at her. She felt the color drain from her cheeks. She tried to remain calm. The taller man listened a minute longer and nodded his head. Then, he went and stationed himself at one of the doors. Zobrinsky was leaning against the other door with his arms crossed, ready.

She was trapped. Other than the stage, those were the only two ways of ingress and egress. She had no choice but to pass through one of the doors. "Vittorio?" She inclined her head and indicated with her eyes what the situation was.

He patted her hand. "Don't worry, *cara*. We'll get you out of here. You're safe as long as you're not alone. They wouldn't dare try anything in a room full of journalists."

"I hope you're right."

She tried to concentrate as the last speaker took the podium. Giles Hayden, an orphan from a little town somewhere in Devon who wouldn't let anything stand in the way of his driving ambition, which had propelled him through Oxford and into a career in the diplomatic corps. He was something rather high up in the Foreign Office now.

She would have to ask Philip, when she got back to London. *If* she got back to London.

A prospect that was looking rather bleak at the moment. She dropped her notebook on the floor. She took a quick glance at the doors as she bent down to pick it up. Zobrinsky and the other man were still there and Hayden was just concluding his speech. How would she get out? They wouldn't dare try anything here. If she could only get out of the hall and outside to the *vaporetto*, she'd be all right.

Everyone was applauding. Emmeline joined in, still trying to figure out how to make her escape.

"Thank you, ladies and gentleman," Hayden was saying. "I'm told there is a lovely luncheon planned for you in the dining room."

People were starting to leave. As she gathered up her handbag and notebook, she heard Giles Hayden laughing at something a reporter had said.

"Of course," she said under breath. "The stage."

She tapped Vittorio on the arm. "It was smashing to see you again. You must come to London soon. I'll have to introduce you to Gran. She'd adore you."

"What are you up to? Those two are still there."

"I know. But they'll have to catch me first, won't they? And they didn't do a very good job last night. *Ciao, amore.* Now go." She kissed his cheek and gave him a gentle push. He shrugged his shoulders in resignation.

When she was the only one left in her row, she saw Zobrinsky start to walk toward her. The other man followed suit from the opposite direction. However, she was quicker than either one. She made her way into the aisle, before they could reach her.

"Excuse me, Mr. Hayden."

Hayden turned. "Yes?"

"Emmeline Kirby, the *Times*. I was wondering whether you could spare a few moments. I have one or two questions for you."

"Well, yes. Of course, Miss Kirby. Your reputation

precedes you. I admired that series you did last year on the art forgeries."

"Thank you."

"If you would follow me this way."

"Certainly, Mr. Hayden." Out of the corner of her eye she saw Zobrinsky shake his head at the other man.

"Friends of yours?" Hayden asked.

"What?" She was surprised he had noticed.

"I've always been an observant bloke. For the last half hour, I've been wondering what such a pretty young woman could have done to cause Zobrinsky and that Neanderthal chap to stare daggers at you."

He smiled as he took her elbow and led her off the stage.

She started laughing. "It's a long story. You probably wouldn't believe me, if I told you."

"I'm a good listener. Try me."

She smiled and extended her hand once they were in the corridor and there was no sign of Zobrinsky and his friend. "Actually, Mr. Hayden, you've been more than kind, coming to my rescue. I think it would be best if I skipped the luncheon and returned to my hotel."

"Don't dash all my hopes like that, Miss Kirby. I was going to invite you to join me at my table for lunch. Now, I'll have to sit with all those boring chaps who gave speeches this morning."

She giggled. "I'm sorry. You were very kind."

"You've said that already. Look, I'll let you go only if you promise to have dinner with me one night in London. I'll give you a ring when I get back on Saturday. Is it a deal?"

"It's a deal, Mr. Hayden."

They shook hands on it. His handshake was firm and confident, but curiously cool.

# CHAPTER 6

The clock in Piazza San Marco was just striking noon as Gregory slipped into the shadows of the arcade. A few doors down from Florian's, one of the piazza's most famous eighteenth-century cafes, was Morelli & Son jewelers.

A bell tinkled as he opened and closed the door. There was no one in the shop. "One moment, please," a male voice said in Italian from behind the maroon curtain. A small, plump man with a balding head bustled out from the back. He was rolling down his sleeves. "You must excuse me, signore. I was—" He stopped when he looked up and saw Gregory. The old man's face broke into a wide grin that touched his soft brown eyes. "Gregorio." He came over and gave Gregory a hug and a kiss on both cheeks. "It is good to see you. It's been a long time."

Gregory returned the hug with the same intensity and warmth. "Tomasso, it's wonderful to see you, too. How are Sylvia and Gianni?"

"*Bene, bene.* Come in the back with me and have some espresso. Gianni will be here in a little while."

Gregory followed his old friend through the curtain and into his office, where there was a small stove. The delicious aroma of bubbling espresso tempted his nostrils.

"Please, sit down."

Gregory did as he was bid and, for five minutes, watched as Tomasso set out two demitasse cups and filled them with the rich, steaming black coffee.

"*Zuchero?*" Tomasso asked, but Gregory shook his head. "No, you never take sugar. Ah, I have some biscotti that Sylvia left for me this morning. They are from our local bakery. Please."

Gregory politely accepted one of the small almond cookies and dipped it in his espresso. They both savored their first sip of the espresso.

"Ah, *bene*. Now, we can talk. Why didn't you tell me that you were coming to Venice? How long will you be here?"

"It came up unexpectedly. I'll probably be here only a couple of more days."

"I see. You are here on a job?"

Gregory smiled. He fumbled in the pocket of his suit jacket and carefully pulled out a rather lumpy object wrapped in a handkerchief. He put it on the desk between them.

"What's this?"

"Open it."

Tomasso held his gaze for a long moment and then began unwrapping the object. He gasped when he saw the beautiful diamond pendant lying on a piece of onyx velvet. He gingerly held it up to the light, allowing the diamond's inner fires to wink mischievously at them.

"*Bellissima*, Gregorio." Tomasso put on his glasses to examine the pendant more closely. "The stone is exquisite and the setting is perfect."

"I thought you'd appreciate it."

"I recognize a master's work when I see it." Tomasso took off his glasses and fixed his brown eyes on Gregory. "*Allora*, from whom did you steal it?"

"Paolo Talamini."

"*Talamini?*"

"It was the least I could do after what happened with Romina."

They were both silent as they thought about Tomasso's lovely daughter, who fell madly in love with Talamini several years ago. He was merely toying with sweet, innocent Romina. He got her hooked on heroin and soon got bored with her. She was so devastated when he dumped her after six months that she committed suicide. Poor Tomasso came home early one afternoon and found her in the bathtub. She had slashed her wrists. She was only twenty-two.

Gregory clapped his friend on the shoulder. "It will not bring her back, but it makes life a little less comfortable for Talamini. Isn't it funny how he hasn't reported the diamond missing? Why do you think that is?"

Tomasso gripped Gregory's arm hard. "He will kill you when he finds out. He has very powerful friends. There are rumors that he is involved with the Mafia and arms dealing."

"Don't worry. I've always been able to take care of myself. Besides, there were over one hundred people at his party last night. Any one of them could have taken it. Now, is there anyone you can trust to get rid of this for me?"

"I've retired. I'm an honest businessman these days."

"Yes, but you still have contacts from the old days."

Tomasso fingered the diamond, but Gregory knew what he was really seeing was his daughter's face. It was a long moment before he said, "Leave it with me. I think I know someone. He is very discreet."

"Excellent." Gregory finished off his espresso and stood up. "I'm afraid I must go."

"So soon. Perhaps, you could come to dinner tonight? Sylvia would love to see you."

"I'm sorry, old friend. I'd love to see her, too, but I can't. There's someone else in Venice who needs my help right now, even though she doesn't realize it."

"Emmeline?"

Gregory smiled. "Yes, she's here and she's gotten herself into a bit of a mess."

"I understand." Tomasso saw him to the door. "Gregorio—"

Gregory clasped his friend's hand. "Shh, there's nothing to say. Nothing." Then, he walked out without a backward glance.

⌒⌒⌒

As the *vaporetto* pulled away from San Servolo, Emmeline could see Zobrinsky and the other man outside the entrance to the building. At first, she thought they were looking for her, but they couldn't see her because a very tall German was in front of her at the railing, blocking her from view. She turned up the collar of her coat and took a step forward, making sure to keep him between herself and the railing.

Zobrinsky was smoking a cigarette and pacing. He seemed to be waiting for someone. He checked his watch and said something to the other man. A minute later, the door opened and Paolo Talamini, one of the conference speakers, walked out. Zobrinsky threw his cigarette on the ground and stubbed it out with his toe. The three men appeared to be having a heated discussion.

"Now that's very interesting," Emmeline murmured to herself. "What would one of Italy's most influential industrialists be talking about with a Russian spy?"

# CHAPTER 7

## *London*

Chief Inspector Oliver Burnell took off his glasses and rubbed his eyes. They felt like sand paper. He'd been up for the last thirty-six hours on the Wilkinson murder. He closed the file in front of him. His team finally cracked the case this morning and the magistrate was issuing a warrant for the arrest of Wilkinson's wife.

Burnell's shoulders ached and there was a knot the size of boulder in his lower back. He dropped his head between his hands and closed his eyes. He heard the door open. "What do you want, Peters?" he said without moving.

"Sorry to disturb you, guv."

Burnell sighed and sat back in his chair. He fixed young Peters with a weary stare. "Yes, yes. What is it?"

"A call just came in. Apparently, some old woman has been found murdered in Charles Latimer's flat in Lambeth."

"Latimer's flat?"

"Yes, sir. A neighbor went to investigate when she saw the front door ajar. She was concerned because she knew Latimer was away in Italy on assignment."

Burnell pushed his hefty frame out of the chair and put on his jacket. "All right, Peters. Get Sergeant Finch. Tell him what's happened. I'll meet him downstairs in the car park."

"Yes, guv."

Burnell walked down the hall and jabbed the button for the lift. He dug one hand deep into his pocket and distractedly smoothed his beard with the other.

Two young constables hovered at the other end of the corridor, cursing the sight of Burnell. They were still reeling from the dressing down he had given them that morning about proper procedures. They had hoped to steer clear of him for the rest of the day. But here he was again. He was an imposing man, even when he was lost in thought as he was now. Not only was he tall, but he was big as well. His stomach protruded a good few inches over his belt. His clothes were not Savile Row, but as a rule they were always clean and neatly pressed, except if he was up all night on a case. At the moment, though, he looked decidedly rumpled. His round face, which normally retained a slightly ruddy complexion from the odd pint of beer in which they knew he liked to indulge, today was drawn and gray. Even from this distance, they could see that his bright blue eyes were bloodshot. Taking all of these signs into consideration, the constables wisely decided they needed some exercise so they quickly headed toward the stairs.

"Latimer," Burnell murmured to himself. He didn't like this development one bit. The chief inspector knew there was trouble brewing a month ago, when Latimer asked to meet him. As a rule, Burnell disliked the press. There were only one or two journalists for which he made an exception, Latimer being one. God knew why he liked the man. He was arrogant and damned full of himself,

especially where women were concerned. But he was a
great journalist who believed in the truth. For that, Burnell admired him. They could not be considered friends.
No, friends would be too strong a word. However, they
respected each other's work and from time to time they
were able to help one another.

Now, Latimer had gone and gotten himself entangled
in something dangerous and deadly. But what? The reporter hadn't told him what he was working on, only that
it was the biggest story of his career. Then the damn fool
went off to Italy promising to fill him in when he returned.

That was Friday. It was now Wednesday. There was
no Latimer, but Burnell did have a dead body on his
hands.

☙❧☙

The medical examiner and the forensics team were
already at work on the flat by the time Chief Inspector
Burnell and Sergeant Finch arrived on the scene.

"We're questioning everyone, flat by flat, Chief Inspector," a police constable reported.

"Good. Did anyone see or hear anything?"

"One woman. A Miss..." The constable consulted
his notebook. "Miss Belinda Richards in Number Two on
the second floor said that at about seven-thirty last night
someone pressed the intercom panel and she buzzed the
person in. She thought it was her Derek. He was late and,
when the intercom rang, she simply assumed it was him.
When Derek never materialized, Miss Richards thought it
had probably been someone for one of the other flats. She
didn't think anything of it, until today when we ques-
tioned her."

"All right, Constable. Carry on."

"Yes, sir."

Burnell and Finch took a look around the living room. Nothing seemed to have been touched here. It was an elegant room, yet comfortable. The design on the Persian rug echoed the burgundy of the leather sofa and armchairs. The low coffee table was made of cherry and gleamed in the soft light of the nearby lamp. There were a couple of week-old magazines on the table. Three landscape paintings graced the cream-colored walls. There was a drinks table in the corner next to the window. Burnell crossed the room and pulled the curtain back. The room looked out onto the square.

"I don't think we'll find anything in here, Finch."

"No, sir. The kitchen, the bedroom, and the bathroom are pretty much the same. The killer seems to have known what he was looking for. He went directly to the study. Unfortunately for Mrs. Saunders, she arrived a bit early and surprised him."

"Yes," Burnell said as he stroked his beard meditatively. "Let's go see the study."

The study was a far different story. There were books pulled from the shelves and piled in heaps on the floor. The desk was a mess. Drawers were left half open and papers were everywhere. In the middle of it all was poor Mrs. Saunders. She was a small, plump woman, probably not much over five feet.

Dr. Meadows, the medical examiner, was crouched down next to the body.

"Well, what can you tell us, John?"

The doctor stood up. "Hello, Oliver. Her neck was broken. She probably died instantly. Professional, I'd say. He surprised her from behind."

"Time of death?"

"I'd put it at between eight and nine last night."

"I know it's wishful thinking, but any fingerprints?"

Dr. Meadows pulled off his latex gloves and shook his head. "I'm afraid not. The majority of the fingerprints in the flat are Latimer's. We've found some belonging to Mrs. Saunders. In the bedroom—" He coughed. "In the bedroom, we found a few fingerprints that were not Latimer's. We also found some long, blonde hairs in the bed and on the carpet. The neighbors say that they'd seen Latimer swanning about with a gorgeous blonde on and off over the last couple of months. She sometimes spent the night."

Burnell clapped the doctor on the back. "We'll follow up on that. Thanks."

"I'll have the toxicology report to you in a couple of days." He closed his bag and left, his job here done.

The forensics team had finished taking pictures and was preparing to remove the body. Burnell sat down at Latimer's desk and flipped through some of the papers. Bills were mixed with some notes to old stories. No laptop. Nothing.

Damn Latimer and his secrecy. Where was the bloody man, and what had he gotten himself into?

"Sir?" Finch had come back into the room.

Burnell swiveled the chair around to face his sergeant. "Yes?"

"Latimer's lady friend is a model. Her name's Jocelyn Montgomery-Massingbred."

"Very posh. Where can we find this Miss Montgomery-Massingbred?"

"She lives in Mayfair."

"Mayfair, how nice."

"Apparently, her father is very well-to-do and bought her the flat."

"Bully for her. All right, Finch." Burnell pushed himself to his feet. "Off you go to see Miss Montgomery-Massingbred. I doubt that she'll be of much help, but you never know. Try to see if she can tell you what Latimer was working on."

"Yes, sir."

"Ring me on my mobile. I'm going home to shower and change. I'll see you at the station later."

It started drizzling as Burnell walked out of the building and waited on the pavement for one of the constables to give him a lift to his flat in Battersea. He turned up the collar of his coat and stamped his feet. The cold dampness had seeped into his bones. He shivered involuntarily. His mobile phone rang as the police car pulled up. "Burnell," he answered as he got into the car.

"Chief Inspector?" The voice sounded weak and out of breath.

"Latimer? Where are you? You've a hell of a lot of explaining to do. I've just come from your flat. Your housekeeper is dead and your study is in shambles." There was a long pause.

"He tried—to kill me. He knows I found out—"

"Who, man? *Who?* It's about time you dispense with all this cloak-and-dagger. I can't do a bloody thing unless you tell me what this is all about."

"He's after—Emmeline. My fault. You must help her. You must—"

The line went dead. "Latimer? *Latimer?*"

Burnell snapped his phone shut and slipped it back into his pocket. Then he slammed his fist against the dashboard.

"Trouble, sir?" the constable asked as he maneuvered his way through the traffic.

"Oh, I don't know, Davenport. Latimer's off gallivanting somewhere in Italy on a story and I have a body on my hands. I'd say the situation is a little troublesome, wouldn't you?" He slammed his fist again. "I'm going to wring Latimer's bloody neck."

But it sounded as if someone had already tried to do that and very nearly succeeded. And now, Emmeline Kirby had been dragged into this whole mess, whatever *it* was.

# CHAPTER 8

*Venice*

Gregory was deep in thought as he left Tomasso's shop. He despised men like Talamini, who thought people were expendable and could be tossed aside when they were no longer useful. The only things that mattered to such men were money and power, the more the better. Nothing was ever enough for them. However, this was also their weakness. Gregory smiled. Greed, whether for power or money, was all consuming and that was when your enemies could pounce. Talamini had not suffered nearly enough for what he had done to Romina. Gregory just had to discover his other weaknesses.

"Signore?"

Gregory turned around and found himself face to face with the older gentleman he had chatted with at the Talaminis' ball.

"Ah, yes, it is you," the man said in Italian. "I wasn't sure at first because you were wearing a mask last night, but I recognized the way you walk." He extended his hand. "Nicolò Crespi. We met at the Talamini party."

Gregory smiled. "Of course, Signor Crespi. I remember you well."

"I thought you said you were leaving for Rome this morning, Signor...Forgive me, but we were not properly introduced last night."

"Longdon. Gregory Longdon. My trip was cancelled and, as you can see, I'm still in lovely Venice for a few more days."

"Ah, *Inglesi*." Crespi switched to English, with only the merest hint of an accent. "Please join me for an espresso, Signor Longdon. I'm delighted your plans have changed."

Crespi ushered Gregory into Caffé Florian. They were immediately enveloped by luxurious warmth as they were swept back three centuries. Golden light from the sconces was reflected off the Baroque mirrors, making the tiny salon appear larger than it was and enhancing the beauty of the medallion oil paintings on the walls and the ceiling.

They settled themselves onto the plush red banquette at a table looking out over Piazza San Marco. Gray clouds had completely obliterated the watery sunshine of the morning. However, the weather did not stop the crowds, milling about in the square, from enjoying the spectacle of Carnival.

"*Allora*, Signor Longdon, you are my guest," Crespi said when a waiter appeared. "What would you like? A coffee or perhaps a glass of wine?"

'I'll have a cappuccino."

Crespi ordered two cappuccinos. "*Due cappucini, per favore.*"

"*Si, signore.*" The waiter nodded and quietly left them.

"Now, tell me, Signor Longdon." Crespi fixed Gregory with his onyx eyes. "How do you come to know Paolo and Giovana? I had the impression last night that you were not on friendly terms with Paolo. Not that I am surprised. Our Paolo does not inspire goodwill, quite the opposite."

Gregory smoothed his mustache and sat back. He stared at Crespi, trying to determine what this elegant stranger wanted from him. Who was he? Did Talamini send him as a warning? With his perfectly coiffed white hair and custom-tailored charcoal suit, Crespi did not look like one of the Mafia types that Talamini generally consorted with, nor did he look like an influential political figure. He looked more like an aging playboy. He was a charmer all right. And yet, there was more to Signor Crespi. Something not quite right. What secrets lay behind those dark eyes?

The waiter brought their coffees. Gregory took a sip from the steaming cup, while Crespi stirred sugar into his and smiled.

"You intrigue me, Signor Longdon."

"Do I? Now why is that?"

"It is obvious we are both men of the world. Therefore, I think you'll forgive me for being blunt." Crespi put his spoon down on the saucer and looked up at Gregory. "But I think that you are not quite what you seem."

"Funny, Signor Crespi, that's exactly what I was thinking about you."

࿇

It had started to rain again as Emmeline disembarked from the *vaporetto* at San Zaccharia. She opened her umbrella and hurried along the Riva degli Schiavone toward Piazza San Marco. As she entered the square, she stopped a moment by the Doge's Palace.

Emmeline never ceased to marvel at this exquisite

confection of white limestone and pink marble. It rose above a double Gothic colonnade graced with filigree carvings of medieval beasts and flowers. The palace was truly one of the world's architectural jewels. Next to it stood the Basilica of San Marco, a heady mix of Byzantine, Gothic, Renaissance and Moorish styles. Even on this gray day, the church's impressive golden domes sparkled and the four bronze horses standing over its doors looked as if they would break free of their reins and leap into the square.

The rain had chased away the big crowds, but the hardy souls persevered and stayed dry by walking around the square beneath the arcade. Emmeline followed suit. She shook her umbrella free of excessive water droplets and rolled it closed. Something caught her eye as she looked up. What was it? An object? A movement? A person? It hovered on the edge of her subconscious. She scanned the crowd up ahead and then she saw him. He moved quickly, almost furtively. He glanced once over his shoulder. Then he ducked behind a column and melted into a group of tourists.

"It's impossible," Emmeline whispered to herself. "Impossible. I thought he was dead." She pushed past several tourists and received dirty looks in response. It was no use. He was gone. Could it have been him? Or had the events of last night and this morning so addled her brain that she was seeing conspiracies everywhere she turned? She stopped. No. As a journalist, she was trained to notice things and she knew her eyes had not deceived her.

She was still standing in the middle of the arcade contemplating this new development, when a boy of about seven or eight tugged on her sleeve. "Signorina Kirby?"

She looked down and smiled. "*Sì?*"

The boy smiled back, revealing two missing front teeth. *"Per lei."* For you, he said as he handed her a folded note and scampered away.

She looked down at the note in her hand. "Wait," she called after him.

But, he was already out of earshot. Her dark eyes widened as she opened the note and recognized the handwriting.

> *Emmeline,*
> *Forgive me for involving you in this mess.*
> *You're the only one I can trust, but you must*
> *leave Venice immediately. It's not safe. All the*
> *answers are in London now.*
> *Charles*

"Thank God. He's alive," she mumbled under her breath. "Thank God."

"Talking to yourself? That's the first sign of senility, you know."

She swung around and found Gregory smiling down at her.

"Hello, love," he said. "Fancy a late lunch?"

She crumpled the note and stuffed it into her coat pocket. "What are you doing here? Are you following me?"

"No, darling. I was just having a cappuccino with a rather interesting chap I met last night."

"Oh, really? One of your underworld cronies, no doubt," Emmeline said as she started to walk away from him.

"Actually, he's a painter."

"A painter? I don't believe it."

"It's true. Nicolò Crespi is a bit of a character, I grant you. He doesn't paint anymore, though. He's retired now.

But he must have been fairly successful, judging by his clothes and the fact that he has a villa on Lake Maggiore and another one in Nice."

"He sounds too good to be true. In any case, I don't care nor do I have the time to stand here chatting with you. I must get back to my hotel to pack."

In one stride, he was at her side again. "You're leaving Venice?"

"Yes. Not that it's any of your business. We have nothing to say to one another."

She increased her pace, but he grabbed her arm and pulled her back.

"Hold on, Emmy. I'm not the enemy."

"There are two schools of thought on that."

"Has something else happened?"

She stared into his warm cinnamon-brown eyes. He always seemed to know what she was thinking. *Damn*, she thought to herself. *He has no right, absolutely no right, to look so handsome.* For a moment, all the memories came flooding back. All their lovely times together. All the things they whispered to one another in the dark, before they fell asleep wrapped in each other's arms. But that was the past. They were two different people now and nothing could bring back—

She felt tears sting her eyelids and averted her face. Seeing him again was too much. But she wouldn't allow herself to cry in front of him.

"Leave me alone. Just leave me alone." She shook herself free of his grasp and turned her back on him. In doing so, the note from Charles fell out of her pocket.

Gregory bent down to pick it up. He caught up to her on the little humpbacked footbridge just before the quiet campo where her hotel was located.

It had started to rain again and she had stopped to open her umbrella.

"So he's alive. What were you going to do? Rush off and pick up where he left off and get yourself killed in the process?"

He grabbed her shoulders and shook her. He was angry at her recklessness. An older couple turned around and stared at them.

"Shh. Keep your voice down," she hissed and dragged him into the campo. "You never liked Charles. The two of you were always like oil and water."

"Yes, Latimer rubs me the wrong way and I think that he is an arrogant bastard, but that has nothing to do with this. You are not thinking clearly, Emmy. You don't know what you're walking into. They tried to kill Latimer last night and very nearly succeeded. They also tried to kill you. Is a story worth your life?"

Her eyes narrowed and the gleam within them was deadly. "What right do you have to question my motives?" She was much shorter than he was, but in that moment she could have been a giant.

"I care about you, Emmy. That's the right I have." He tried to pull her into his arms.

She took two steps back. "Care about me? *Care about me*?" Her voice rose an octave.

"Yes," he said quietly.

"Is that why you disappeared the day before our wedding two years ago? Because you *cared* about me so much."

"Emmy, listen, there are reasons why—"

"No." She shook her head and held up a hand to stop any excuses that might roll off his tongue. "There are no reasons. The minute you walked out that door like a thief in the night—Ha, that's good one. Thief in the night. That's exactly what you are, isn't it? Chief Inspector Burnell very kindly regaled me with all your exploits. Do you know that you're quite infamous all over Europe?"

"I'm sure old Oliver had a jolly time doing so. The police cannot prove anything. Nothing. They're just a gaggle of old biddies who have nothing better to do than to sit around coming up with farfetched theories."

"You're a thief and a liar. Charles is my friend and he needs my help. I'm going to help him." She took a step closer to Gregory and poked him in the chest. "You can't stop me. No one can. It's called loyalty. Something you know absolutely nothing about. Now, I'm going to walk across the campo and into my hotel. Go do whatever it is that you do. I'm sure there must be some jewels lying around here somewhere that you can steal."

The salty tears streaming down her cheeks blurred her vision as she entered the hotel lobby. She impatiently wiped them away with the back of her hand and kept her gaze downward as she asked for her key. She took the lift up to the fourth floor. There was no one in the corridor when the doors opened. Her room was just around the corner to the right.

She fumbled with the key in the lock. Why did she allow him to get to her like this? *Why?* She thought she had put it all behind her, that she was stronger. Now, out of the blue, Gregory walked back into her life and everything was topsy-turvy.

"Oh, Gran." She sighed wearily. More than anything, she wished that her grandmother was here at this very moment. Gran always had the right words. She was always so sensible and soothing.

She finally opened the door. "Oh, my God," she gasped.

# CHAPTER 9

## *London*

It was two o'clock by the time Sergeant Finch returned to Scotland Yard. As Chief Inspector Burnell had suspected, Miss Jocelyn Montgomery-Massingbred had nothing to contribute to the investigation. She had met Latimer in October at some posh do and they had been going out on and off since then.

They had a very "relaxed" sort of relationship. No strings. Sometimes she spent the night at his flat and sometimes he stayed with her.

They were planning to go away for a week in April to the South of France. She had a photo shoot and they thought they would combine business with pleasure.

"However," Finch concluded, "she said that he never discussed his work. She did say Latimer seemed to be very tense lately. He had cancelled three of their dates in the last two weeks. She suspected it had something to do with the story he was working on."

Burnell sighed. He leaned back in his chair and closed his eyes. "Well, Finch, that's that. Was our little model very difficult?"

"No, sir. Quite the contrary. She was very helpful. Not your typical model. Quite cultured in fact. She offered me tea and we chatted."

Burnell lifted his head and stared at his sergeant. "I hope that you did not allow a pretty face to lead you down the garden path."

Finch blushed. "No, sir. The fact that she was gorgeous did not distract me from my duty."

Burnell nodded knowingly. "Uh huh."

"Truly, sir."

"Never mind. Let me fill you in on what's been happening, while you had your cozy chat with Miss Jocelyn Montgomery-Massingbred. Latimer called me on my mobile."

"Indeed." Finch's ears pricked up. "What did he have to say?"

"Not a bloody lot, except that someone tried to kill him in Venice and Emmeline Kirby is now somehow involved in this. Oh, and something else. The killer has set his sights on Miss Kirby."

"Nasty bit of business." Finch shook his red head. He, like Burnell, had a soft spot for Emmeline.

"Yes. I called the *Times*. They said Miss Kirby is on assignment in Venice covering the international trade conference. She called in and said that she will be returning tomorrow, a couple of days earlier than planned."

"I'll have a twenty-four-hour watch put on her townhouse in Holland Park."

Burnell put his elbows on the desk and rested his chin on his fists. He fixed an icy gaze on his sergeant. "I've already done that. Finch, she's one person I do not want to find in the morgue. Do you understand me?"

"Yes, sir. The boys and I will not allow anything to happen to Miss Kirby."

"I don't like games, Finch. There's something dark

and sinister about this case. All smoke and shadows and a trail of bodies. No, I don't like it one bit."

ひとつ

The taxi stopped at the top of Kennington Road in Lambeth. The man pulled his cap lower over his face before he slowly opened the door and eased himself out onto the pavement. He felt the beads of sweat forming on his brow from this simple movement. The painkiller was wearing off. He managed to close the door, but it seemed to drain his energy. He was breathing heavily.

"That'll be ten pounds," the driver said. "Sir, are you all right? You look a bit peaked."

"I'm fine," the man replied more brusquely than he had intended.

"Sorry, sir. Didn't mean anything by it."

"It's all right. I'm sorry. It's my stomach. Must have been something I ate at lunch."

"Ah, I see. Same thing happens to me when I eat rich food I'm not used to. My wife always gives me a cup of peppermint tea. Does the trick every time. Try it, sir. You'll be right as rain again."

He handed over the ten pounds. "Peppermint tea. I'll keep it in mind. Thanks."

"You'll feel better in no time. You'll see. Cheerio, then," the driver said as he pulled away from the curb.

The man waited until the taxi was out of sight. He took a quick glance to his right and to his left. Nothing out of the ordinary. He slipped the manila envelope out from the inside pocket of his coat and dropped it into the red pillar box. Then, he slowly started walking down the street toward Number Thirty-Two.

As he got closer, he saw that there was a police car outside Number Thirty-Two. There were two uniformed constables chatting on the steps, while another one went inside. The man pulled his cap so low that he would have to lift his chin to see anything.

"What's going on?" he asked one of the constables.

"Hadn't you heard, sir? A charwoman's been murdered."

"Murder? In a flat? How awful? Such a quiet street. What is the world coming to? You're not safe in your own bed these days."

"Well, sir, nothing for you to worry about. Scotland Yard's got everything well in hand. I suggest you move along, though. The area is still considered a crime scene. We don't want any gawkers. There's nothing for you to see."

"Right. Of course. I see the yellow police tape. Good day, constable."

"Good day, sir." However, the words "daft bugger" floated to his ears as he turned away.

He hesitated for only a moment and then walked to the end of the block. He hailed another taxi.

"Where to, sir?"

"Holland Park," Charles said as he got in. He leaned his head back against the seat and closed his weary eyes. For this reason, he didn't see the blue Opel pull away from the curb and fall in behind them at a safe distance.

# CHAPTER 10

## *Venice*

Gregory had been half a step behind Emmeline and saw over her shoulder that someone had ransacked her room. Her clothes rested haphazardly in a pile on the floor. Her upright was gaping open. The desk and bedside table drawers were pulled out and dumped upside down on the floor. The bed was stripped of its sheets and the mattress was slightly askew. A lamp had been knocked off the bedside table and lay in two halves by the door.

"Stay here." He pushed her back into the hall. Without touching anything, he checked to make sure that whoever had done this was not still lurking about. "It's all right. You can come in now."

Her dark eyes roamed over the mess. "Who could have done this?"

"Thanks to your good chum Latimer, I'd say that your friends from last night dropped by for a visit." He could see the anger that this remark elicited flit across her face. He put up a hand to forestall any defense of Charles. "I think you should call the front desk. Then you should try to determine if anything is missing."

Before she could do either, the telephone rang. The problem was finding it. She followed the wire and unearthed it from under a pillow in the corner. "Hello," she said tentatively.

"Miss Kirby, if you value your life you'll give us the file. Otherwise, they might find your body in a canal or— not at all. Bodies have been known to disappear in Venice," a man's voice hissed into the line.

She sucked in her breath. "Who is this?"

Gregory's head turned sharply at this and he pulled the receiver away from her ear so that he could listen, too. "Let's not play games, Miss Kirby. We know Latimer gave it to you last night because it was not in his hotel room."

"I don't know what you're talking about. Charles didn't give me anything. I have no idea what this is all about."

Gregory smiled down at her profile. He could have told the chap that it was not advisable to be on the wrong end of her short temper. Her fist was clenched at her side and the pulse was throbbing at her temple. There was silence on the other end. For a second, it appeared the chap had hung up.

"Miss Kirby, you're making a mistake. A grave one." There was a soft click and the line went dead.

Gregory took the receiver from her and dialed the front desk. Meanwhile, Emmeline wandered about the room, fuming. She was no longer afraid. "Of all the nerve. Ooh." She kicked a defenseless pillow. "I'm going to find out what this is all about because these people have crossed the line and made me bloody angry. And I won't stop until I find the truth."

"Emmy, darling, be a good girl and check to see if anything is missing," Gregory calmly suggested.

After two rings, the call was answered. He succinctly

explained the situation and was told that someone would be upstairs immediately. Five minutes later, a slender man with thinning gray hair and glasses appeared in the doorway.

"*Madonna mia*," he exclaimed when he saw the state of the room.

"Quite," Gregory said. "Now I think you should call the police."

"Police, signore?" The man stiffened. Clearly, he did not like the sound of this. It would not do the hotel's reputation any good for it to become known a guest's room had been broken into. He had to avoid this at all costs. "Signore, I don't think it is necessary to involve the police. I'm sure this matter can be settled quietly." The man's gaze shifted nervously between Gregory and Emmeline.

"Do you? Is this the kind of hospitality that all your guests can expect?"

"Of course not, signore. You must understand. We are a very respectable hotel. We have never had any trouble. Please, signore."

Emmeline felt sorry for the poor man. It was not his fault. He was probably worried about losing his job because he was on duty at the desk when this happened. She picked up her clothes and a few papers off the floor.

"Gregory, let's drop it. There doesn't seem to be anything missing as far as I can see and my laptop is locked up in the hotel safe. Besides, I'm leaving Venice tomorrow."

Relief flooded the man's face. He looked as if he was on the verge of dropping to the floor and kissing her feet.

"Emmeline, I don't think—"

"I don't care what you think. It's my decision."

"*Grazie*, Signorina Kirby. Naturally, the hotel will take care of your bill." He hurried out of the room and closed the door behind him before she could change her mind.

"Emmy—" The sharp ringing of the telephone cut off whatever it was that Gregory had wanted to say.

Emmeline reached it before he did. "Hello."

"Signorina Kirby?"

"Yes." She had steeled herself for another confrontation, but it was not the man who had called earlier. It was a man's voice, but the accent was different. She thought it was Italian. It was Mediterranean, at any rate, and softer. The other man's English had a harsh Russian tinge.

"Signorina, you must leave Venice. Talamini and the people he deals with, such as Zobrinsky, are very dangerous. They will not hesitate to kill you."

"Who is this?"

"Someone who does not want you to end up like all of Talamini's victims. Dead."

"But—"

"Please, signorina, trust Signor Longdon and no one else."

"*Gregory*?" She stared at him. "What does Gregory have to do with this?" At the sound of his name, Gregory pulled the receiver toward him.

"This is just some advice from a friend. Leave Venice before it is too late."

There was no opportunity to ask any more questions. There had been something familiar about the voice. Gregory had heard it recently. But where?

She turned her dark gaze on him and tapped her foot on the floor. "So who was that and what do you know?"

"It's no good looking at me like that. I assure you, darling, that I have no idea."

"Really?"

"Yes, really. However, I know I've heard that voice before. I just can't place it at the moment."

She sank onto the naked mattress. She rested her elbows on her knees and dropped her head between her hands. "What's going on here?"

She lifted her head and looked across at him as if he had all the answers. He came and sat next to her, putting his arm around her shoulders. "I don't know, but I'm glad you've decided to leave tomorrow." He kissed her hair and pulled her closer into his side.

She started to lean into his embrace and then suddenly pushed him away. She stood up quickly and began pacing around the room, absently straightening things as she went. "What do we know?" she said aloud, more to herself than to him.

"Well, Latimer tumbled onto something having to do with the Foreign Office."

"Yes. He said that it was something explosive. Something about Moscow. Enter our friend Anatol Zobrinsky. Purportedly, he's attached to the Russian trade delegation in London. However, I was talking with Vittorio Franzetti at the conference this morning and he told me that it is widely known in diplomatic circles that Zobrinsky is a spy. He's former KGB and reports directly to Putin."

"Charming. Latimer has dragged you into some international intrigue in which dead bodies are a matter of course."

"If you're not going to be constructive and all you're going to do is sit there criticizing Charles, you can leave right now."

"I stand, or rather, I sit, duly chastened. Please do go on, Miss Kirby. This is highly scintillating," he said sweetly and fluttered his eyelashes at her.

She ignored his facetious tone. "Your friend on the telephone just now said that Zobrinsky is somehow connected to Paolo Talamini. I saw the two of them together outside the conference center as the *vaporetto* was pulling away from San Servolo. They were huddled together with that other chap who attacked Charles last night. What would an Italian industrialist have to discuss with a Russian spy?"

"Darling. Oh, sorry. May one speak?"

"Go on."

"Talamini is a nasty bit of work. Some of his best friends are members of the Mafia, and he's been known to dabble in drugs and gun running."

Emmeline's eyes widened. "I see."

"You have your chum Latimer to thank for introducing you to such lovely blokes."

"I wish you would stop saying 'your chum Latimer' like that."

"But it gives me such a warm glow right here—" Gregory touched his heart. "—when I think about *dear Charles* and the danger he's put you in."

"As if you care what happens to me."

"Whether you believe or not, I do care."

"Let's not argue about that again. We have more important things to think about right now."

Gregory held her gaze for a long moment and then stood up. "Right. Let's get this mess straightened up and then I'll call the airline."

"Why are you going to call the airline?"

"To change my ticket, so that I'm on the same flight as you, fearless warrior," he said as picked the bedclothes off the floor.

"There's no need for that. I can take care of myself."

"It didn't look that way last night. If you haven't noticed, love, your new acquaintances seem to have a shocking propensity for maiming and death." He took a quick glance about the room. "And deplorable taste in interior decorating, if this room is anything to judge by."

She stopped packing her suitcase and looked up at him. "I do not need you. I have gotten on very well without you these past two years. I do not need a bodyguard. And if I did, it certainly would not be you."

"You wound me, Emmy—"

"And stop calling me Emmy. Only Gran does."

"Speaking of your grandmother and my mate, how is the fair Helen lately?"

"Oh, you know Gran. She's always fine. Always the life of the party. She's more like a teenager than a seventy-eight-year-old woman. Nothing ever fazes her. You saw for yourself that she didn't let the heart attack slow her down."

"I'm glad to hear that Helen is as feisty as ever. I look forward to seeing her again."

"When do you plan on seeing her?"

"After we get back to London, I'm going to take you down to Kent and you will spend a few days with your grandmother until things settle down a bit."

"I will not. You cannot order me about. In case it's slipped your mind, I'm working on a story."

He crossed the room and gently, but firmly, forced her to sit down on the bed. "You have been overruled. Ah, ah. That's enough." He held up a finger to stem the flow of angry words that were on the verge of tumbling from her lips. "I will not stand by and see you get yourself killed. End of argument."

He kissed the top of her head. "Now, get packed. I will meet you in the lobby at one-thirty to take you to lunch."

"Plan on dining alone."

He smiled. "Suit yourself. I, for one, do not intend to starve myself. If you are not in the lobby, then I will see you on the plane in the morning."

With that, he walked out of the room. Emmeline

threw a shoe at the door as the latch clicked shut. "Insufferable man."

*e⁄ɔe⁄ɔ*

Somehow it was two o'clock by the time she finished her packing and restored order to her room. She couldn't stay holed up there alone until the next morning, she'd be a sitting duck. No, it was better to go out, to be around people.

There was no sign of Gregory in the lobby, when she got off the lift. Emmeline was relieved and, to her annoyance, disappointed by this fact. She gave her key to the woman at the reception desk and left the hotel to try to enjoy her last afternoon in Venice. Although she hadn't eaten anything since breakfast, she wasn't hungry. It was all the stress of the last twenty-four hours. Gregory was right, though. She should eat something. Perhaps she'd grab a panino and then go to one of the city's many museums. Or she could take the boat to the island of Burano. The rain had stopped and the sun was poking his head from behind the clouds. Yes, that sounded like a nice idea. She would go to Burano. Maybe she could find a lovely lace tablecloth for Gran.

The afternoon went by quickly. By the time she returned from Burano, the sun was a smoldering ball of rose fire. The waters of the Grand Canal were singed a burnished orange as the sun dipped lower and lower, until it finally disappeared in a haze of amethyst mist. At last, the day had retreated into slumber. Emmeline was tired, but it was too early to go to bed. She decided to lose herself in the maze of crooked little streets and alleyways for a couple of hours, doing some window shopping, and then she'd go back to her hotel for some well-needed sleep.

She stopped at a café and treated herself to a gelato. Emmeline sat at a little table in the window and indulged in a bit of people-watching, always a pleasure in Venice and never more so than at Carnival. The streets teemed with color and some of the most fantastic costumes she had ever seen. Emmeline leaned closer to the window and tried to imagine what the people behind the masks were really like. Probably rather dull. Reality was never as exciting as the dream. She sighed and finished her ice cream.

Emmeline pulled up the collar of her coat as she left the café. A chilly wind meandered down the narrow street. She stopped in front of a store to gaze at a display of masks. She laughed when she saw an unusual purple one with a large feather down one side and a velvet tricorn hat that sparkled with gold and silver glitter. It was the perfect thing for Gran. Emmeline hurried into the store to buy it. The transaction was completed in a mere five minutes. The old woman who owned the store carefully wrapped the mask in tissue paper and packed it in a special box, which she tied with a matching velvet ribbon.

Emmeline was so delighted with her purchase as she left the store that, at first, she didn't notice the man following her. He blended in with the other costumed revelers. However, she caught a glimpse of his reflection on the two occasions she stopped. He was wearing a simple *bauta* mask with the tricorn hat and cape. She tried to keep calm. She didn't want him to know that she had spotted him, but she tried to put more distance between them.

There was a little crowd up ahead watching a juggler and a mime. Emmeline squeezed her way toward the front of the small semi-circle. When everyone clapped at a particularly amusing trick, she stole a sideways glance toward the back of the group. She sighed with relief when the masked stranger was no longer there.

She chided herself for being so silly. "He was probably not even following me to begin with." And yet, a nagging voice at the back of her mind told her that she had not been wrong. After another few minutes, the act broke up. Emmeline glanced at her watch. It was nine o'clock. She had enough of spies and conspiracies to last a lifetime. She would return to her hotel for a hot bath and then crawl into bed. Tomorrow she would leave this jewel of a city and head back home to London, where she intended to find the truth. One way or another.

As she neared her hotel, the streets were quieter. The crowds were closer to Piazza San Marco. She stopped on a bridge and listened as the gently lapping waters of the canal whispered Venice's secrets to her, while the moon traced a silvery finger along the dusky surface. She closed her eyes and savored the solitude.

However, the serenity of a moment ago evaporated the instant she opened her eyes. She found fear stalking her once again.

# CHAPTER 11

The man in the mask grabbed her before she had a chance to run. He pulled her close to him and covered her mouth with his hand. "Signorina Kirby, do not scream," he whispered in her ear as she wriggled to free herself from his grip. "I do not want to hurt you. I have some information that I think will interest you." Emmeline continued to fight him. "Please, signorina. Don't you want to find the man who tried to kill Charles Latimer?"

At the sound of Charles's name, she stopped struggling. She let her body go limp in his arms.

"That's better. Now, I'm going to let you go. Promise not to scream or do anything else silly?" She nodded her head. "Good."

She turned to face him. "Who are you and what do you know about Charles?"

"Who I am is of no consequence."

"It bloody well is. I don't like people who play games." This was the second time in two days that she had been confronted by a masked man. Last time, it was Gregory and, so help her, if this was his way of preventing her from pursuing the story he had another think coming to him. Before the man realized what was happening, Emmeline had reached up and pulled his mask off.

Her eyes widened in disbelief. *"Paolo Talamini."*

"Shh," he hissed and pulled her into the shadows of a nearby building. His face was inches from hers and his vice-like grip made her bracelet bite into her skin. "Signorina Kirby, you are a very willful woman. One day your impetuosity will get you killed."

"Is that a threat, Signor Talamini?" she asked defiantly.

"No, it is a warning. If I wanted you dead, believe me, I could have it done just like that." He snapped his fingers. The cold look in those coal black eyes told Emmeline that he spoke the truth.

She finally found her voice again. "All right, Signor Talamini. What can you tell me about Charles? Do you know what's happened to him?"

"If I knew where he was, I would not be here talking to you. Latimer seems to have dropped off the face of the earth."

"Why come to me?"

The Italian tilted his head toward the sky and muttered a string of curses in his own language. Then he said through clenched teeth, "Because, *signorina*, Latimer was coming to meet me the night he was nearly killed. When he didn't turn up, I sent one of my men out to try and find him. He saw the whole attack and he saw *you.*"

Emmeline was stunned. "Then why didn't he help Charles or me? Or are you and your men so used to violence that the prospect of another death doesn't faze you?"

A tense silence settled uncomfortably between them. "You have a dangerous tongue," he whispered menacingly and took a step closer.

She feared he would break her wrist.

"You have no right to judge me. I'm a simple businessman—"

"Ha. You're a thug in a designer suit."

"Signorina Kirby," he hissed. "You may not like my business, but it is still business. Believe it or not, I am a man of honor in my business dealings."

Emmeline wanted to laugh in his face again, but she stopped herself.

"And what I do not like—cannot abide—is being cheated by a lying Russian."

At this, her ears perked up. "Zobrinsky?"

"Ah, I see that what I have heard about you was not a lie. Your reputation precedes you, Signorina Kirby." He inclined his head in a show of respect. "Yes, Zobrinsky."

"So what is this all about? Are you selling arms to the Russians?"

His eyes widened in surprise and he let go of her wrist. She rubbed it where her bracelet had left its mark. "Signorina, before I say any more, I want your assurance that our entire conversation will be off the record. You must understand that, because of the delicate nature of my business, it would not do to be seen talking to the press. That is why I took these precautions to meet you. Do I have your word?"

There was a long pause as Emmeline sized him up. He could be lying to her. On the other hand, what reason would he have to do so? "You have my word. This conversation is off the record."

"*Allora*, last September when I was in London, I was approached by Zobrinsky one night at the theater. Naturally, I knew who he was—officially and unofficially. He said he had a proposition that might interest me and asked if I could meet him for lunch at the Savoy the following day to discuss the matter further. I was intrigued and agreed to meet him. He took his time, though. He talked about all kinds of things through the meal—from politics to art to the merits of the Italian Riviera over the Côte d'Azur. It was not until we were having our coffees that he finally came to the reason for seeking me out.

"He told me—in the strictest confidence, of course—that Russia's once mighty military arms industry had been steadily weakening. Apparently, the country's arms sales declined in 2007 and 2008, after reaching a record $15.5 billion in 2006. Now, the Russians are suddenly plagued by embarrassing quality-control problems. The situation has deteriorated to such an extent that Algeria recently returned a shipment of MIG jets because they had defects. Also, many engineers have emigrated and the ones who are left are nearing retirement. On top of all this, the industry suffered a major economic blow when an increase in revenue from natural resources pushed up the ruble, making exports more expensive on global markets. This has forced the proud—and arrogant—Russians to turn to other countries to buy arms for their military."

His tone indicated that he had no love for the Russians. Business was business, but otherwise he despised them.

"Yes, I remember reading an article in the *New York Times* last year that Moscow was in talks to purchase four amphibious assault ships from France," Emmeline said.

"Yes, that is but one of several transactions they are pursuing."

"And that's where you come in?"

For the first time that evening, Paolo Talamini smiled. A genuine smile. "You know, Signorina Kirby, I take back my original impression of you. I like you. I wish more of the people I deal with were as intelligent and direct as you. It would make my life so much easier."

Emmeline didn't know whether she should feel flattered because such praise was coming from an international arms trader.

"I realize that you cannot return the sentiment and I'm not asking you to. If you can just spare me a few more moments, you will never have to see me again."

"Go on. Tell me about Zobrinsky's offer."

"He said that his government was interested in buying some fighter jets and a shipment of assault rifles. I told him that I might be able to accommodate him, *if* the price was right."

"And was it?"

"No, it was not. He offered me $700 million. I laughed in his face and said that it was an insult. I told him that if his government couldn't come up with at least $1.2 billion and a Caravaggio, then a deal was not possible."

"A Caravaggio?"

"Yes, Signorina Kirby. Didn't you know that I am an art collector? I'm rather partial to Caravaggio. I suppose it is because he is a fellow countryman. A number of old masters stolen by the Nazis were 'liberated' by the Soviets in 1945."

"Fascinating, Signor Talamini. Simply fascinating."

"Zobrinsky said that he would speak to his superiors. He suggested that he might be able to persuade them about the money, but he was certain that a painting was out of the question. I told him that I didn't care if they had to steal a Caravaggio. I was not particular about how the painting was acquired, but there was no deal without one."

"So what happened?"

"Our lunch ended and Zobrinsky said that he would be in touch. The next day I received a call from him, explaining that his country would be willing to pay me $1.4 billion, but no painting. My response was an emphatic, 'No, thank you.' And that was it. About a month later, he called me again with a new offer of $1.5 billion."

"But no painting?"

"No painting. I refused again and didn't hear anything from him until the beginning of December. Zobrinsky contacted me and said that his superiors had finally relented. The money would be wired to my Swiss account by the end of the month and the painting—one that I could not display in public, you understand—would be delivered during Carnival. The painting was delivered this week, but it was *not* a Caravaggio. It was a very clever forgery. I confess I was taken in at first."

"Forgery?" Something about this niggled at the back of Emmeline's mind.

"Yes, I had it tested. If you look closely, there are tell-tale signs. It was almost as if the forger wanted to be discovered."

"Forgers tend to want to show off. It's almost as if the whole thing is a big joke."

"Yes, you are right. I had that sense about the artist when I looked at the painting. But, of course, I remember now. You wrote that series for the *London Sunday Times* last year about famous forgers."

"Yes," Emmeline responded absently. Something bothered her but she couldn't place her finger on what it was. She shook her head to clear her mind of the nagging thought. "So now you want me to expose the whole story?"

"No, Signorina Kirby."

"*No*? But I thought—"

"I told you all this so that you would understand why I was so angry. Signorina, I do not like being made into a laughingstock, as you English would say. If word of this were to leak out, I would be ruined. My business associates would begin to question my judgment. As it is, I cannot go to the police. No, what I want is revenge."

"I don't see how I fit in. As a journalist, I'm in the

business of uncovering the truth. I'm not here to be used as an instrument of revenge."

"Ah, you are wrong there. In this case, you can give me my revenge *and* satisfy your journalistic principles at the same time."

She was skeptical, but waited to hear what he had to say.

"In the late 1970s, at the height of Cold War, there was a promising sixteen-year-old boy enrolled in one of Russia's military academies. He was the top of his class, a brilliant mind. But, above all, he was loyal to the Communist Party. For this reason, he was selected for special training to become a spy. Not just an ordinary spy, but a sleeper. Do you know what that is, Signorina Kirby?"

"Yes, a spy who is planted in another country and could go years without being active. He's trained to act, think, and look like any other citizen in his adopted land. He blends in. However, all the time he's waiting for that call to do his duty for his mother country."

"Yes, that is exactly it. Well, this sleeper grew up and he is now very high up in your Foreign Office. His name is Sergei Konstantin."

Emmeline's jaw dropped. "This is what Charles was after? He said it was something explosive that would rip Whitehall apart, but I never imagined something like this."

"Yes, he wanted the man's name. However, I had the impression he already knew and simply needed confirmation and some sort of proof."

"But why come to you?"

"Because this Sergei Konstantin is working with Zobrinsky, who reports to Putin. And now, I leave it in your capable hands. My revenge is complete."

Emmeline's mind was still reeling as he slipped his mask back on and started to walk away. "Wait."

Talamini turned slowly to face her again. "Yes?"

"You didn't tell me *who* Sergei Konstantin is nowadays."

"Signorina Kirby, you are the journalist and a very talented one at that. I've given you the lead. The rest is up to you." His voice was muffled by the mask. "But be very careful. These people are dangerous. They will not hesitate to kill you. Look at what happened to your friend Latimer. I wouldn't want to read your obituary in the newspaper. No, that would be a great tragedy. Goodbye, *signorina.*"

Emmeline watched him until he disappeared around the corner. She leaned against the wall for a moment. Her knees felt as if they would buckle under her weight. She suddenly had the uncomfortable feeling that she was being watched. It was not safe to linger any longer. Emmeline hurried over the bridge and didn't stop until she was safely in the lobby of her hotel.

ᏋᏗᏋᏗ

There was someone in the nearby shadows who had seen and, more importantly, *heard* their entire conversation. He waited until he was sure Emmeline was inside the hotel. Then he slipped out from his hiding place.

He caught up to Talamini quite soon. He had anticipated the route the Italian would take. He waited for him in the brooding darkness of the narrow alley that led to the Giglio *vaporetto* stop. Talamini's footfalls echoed hollowly.

Not another soul was about. The locals were already tucked up in their apartments and the tourists avoided this way after sunset. The footsteps were getting closer, *closer.* He could see his quarry now. He was only a few yards away. It felt as if the walls of the old buildings were closing in around him. He didn't move, didn't dare to breathe. Talamini didn't hear him until he stepped out of the shadows. By then, it was too late because the knife had been thrust between his ribs straight up into his heart. Talamini's hands scratched furiously at the empty air in front of him and then he slumped backward. He slid slowly down the wall, until he was half-sitting, half-lying down on the cobblestones. He clutched at his chest and his hand came away wet and sticky. He looked down incredulously at his own blood.

"*You?*" It was barely a whisper.

Talamini felt his strength ebbing from his body. The last thing he would ever see in this life was the murderer wiping the blade on his cape before stepping over him and walking away.

ლოლ

Emmeline had tossed and turned all night. Everything she had discovered in the last forty-eight hours kept swimming round and round in her head. Every time she tried to close her eyes, some new idea or detail kept her wide awake. If she got an hour's sleep, she was lucky. Now she sat at her gate in the terminal at Marco Polo International Airport, waiting for the announcement that they could start boarding the plane. Her flight was supposed to leave at two o'clock local time. She hoped that it was on time. As much as she loved Venice, she couldn't wait to get home to London.

She longed for her own bed in her lovely townhouse on the quiet street in Holland Park. The house became hers when her parents died while on assignment all those years ago. She had been only five at the time. How she had wept when Gran had come to take her to live down in Kent. Silly really, since she spent most of her time with

Gran anyway. And yet, Emmeline didn't want to leave
Holland Park. She adored Gran, but it somehow felt as if
she were losing the last link with her parents. She opened
her wallet and pulled out the faded and well-thumbed
photo she always carried with her. She smiled. It was tak-
en on a glorious day in July, two months before her parents died. They had spent an idyllic three weeks in Corn-
wall, just the three of them. It felt like heaven because it
was the first time in months that she and her parents had
spent so long together. Emmeline's parents were journalists like herself, and they were always rushing off at a
moment's notice to some remote corner of the globe to
cover a story. They worked as a team.

Emmeline traced the contours of her mother's beautiful face. She had golden hair that fell to her shoulders in
thick waves. Her hazel eyes were always filled with ten-
derness and her laughter was infectious. Sometimes they
would laugh until the tears rolled down their cheeks.
Emmeline closed her eyes and took a deep breath. In her
mind, she could smell Lily of the Valley, her mother's
favorite scent.

Her gaze now fell on her father's handsome face. He
was dark with curly hair and jet black eyes. Emmeline
got her coloring from him. And yet, her features were
more like her mother's. She smiled because she had the
best of both of them. This thought warmed her as she remembered her father. Tall and slim. For a five-year-old,
he was as tall as a tree. She had to bend her neck way
back just to look up at him. He was always joking and
playing games, and sneaking her a chocolate biscuit when
her mother had said she couldn't have one. It was their
secret.

Oh, how she missed them still. It had been twenty-
five years since their deaths, but sometimes it felt like
yesterday. There were times she wished that she could

ask them for advice or simply give them a hug.

She let out a long, low sigh and took one last look at the photo before slipping it back into her wallet. She impatiently wiped away a tear with back of her hand.

A shadow fell across her lap and she looked up to see what had caused it. She rolled her eyes. "Oh, it's you."

Gregory smiled. "Lovely to see you too, darling. May I sit down?" He didn't wait for her to respond. "I trust you slept well."

She crossed her arms tightly over her chest. "No, I did not, if you must know."

His brow furrowed. "Why? Did something else happen after I left you yesterday?"

She opened her mouth to tell him about her little nocturnal interlude with Paolo Talamini, but decided against it. "No. Nothing at all. I just wish I could find Charles."

"Uh huh. Well, Emmy, I am not forcing you to tell me what happened. But, darling—" Gregory paused and fixed his brown gaze on her. "—like it or not, I'm the only one you can trust in this sordid business. This is not a game. These people are deadly serious and you would do well not to go off on your own like a modern-day Joan of Arc."

She shivered involuntarily when she remembered a similar warning from Talamini. *Be very careful. These people are dangerous. They will not hesitate to kill you. Look at what happened to your friend Latimer. I wouldn't want to read your obituary in the newspaper.*

"Gregory, I—" She stopped because her attention was diverted by a man who sat nearby reading a *Corriere della Sera*. It couldn't be. Could it? She only knew a few Italian phrases, so she clutched at Gregory's sleeve. "What does that headline say?" She discreetly inclined her head in the direction of the man with the newspaper.

Gregory heard the tension in her voice and looked at the newspaper. He leaned forward slightly. His eyebrows lifted in disbelief when he read the headline and the caption beneath the photo. He sat back and spoke so that only Emmeline could hear him. "Paolo Talamini was found dead early this morning in an alley near the Giglio *vaporetto* stop. He was stabbed." He squeezed her hand hard. "That's not far from where your hotel was. Now, tell me again that nothing happened yesterday after I left you."

She closed her eyes for a moment. "Oh, God. This can't be happening. He was right."

"Who was right?"

She opened her eyes. Very quietly and succinctly, she related everything Talamini had told her about Zobrinsky and Sergei Konstantin, the Russian spy in the Foreign Office. She could still hardly believe it.

"Bloody hell." Gregory stood up. "I'll murder Latimer with my bare hands for embroiling you in this. Why didn't you call me? I knew I should never have left you on your own. You and your bloody stubbornness."

"Shh. Sit down. You're making a scene and the last thing we need at the moment is to draw attention to ourselves." She smiled at a woman and her daughter who sat by the window and were looking at Gregory as if he were a lunatic.

He dropped himself heavily in the seat beside her.

"That's better," she said. "Now, I'd better go to the desk and cancel my ticket and then I must find a *carabiniere*."

"Why? You're getting on the flight and going home, even if I have to throw you over my shoulder."

"Don't be melodramatic, Gregory. I can't possibly go home now. I must go to the police and tell them—"

"Tell them what? That Talamini was likely selling arms to the Russians and a Russian spy in the British

Foreign Office decided to kill him. They're never going to believe you. Remember Officer Cavalcante when you reported the attack on Latimer?"

She bit her lip. "You're right."

"Of course, I'm right."

"But I can't just leave."

"Yes, you can. Let the Venice police handle the case. You weren't even there when it happened. Talamini could well have been murdered for another reason entirely. Look at the company he keeps. The Mafia is not known for turning the other cheek when it's been crossed."

"You don't honestly believe that the Mafia killed him. It's too much of a coincidence that he was murdered on the same night he told me about Sergei Konstantin. Plus, as you pointed out earlier, he was found not far from my hotel."

"Emmy, stay out of it. No good will come of you sticking your nose in where it doesn't belong."

"Passengers on British Airways Flight 579 to London Heathrow. Boarding will begin in five minutes. Please have your boarding passes ready," a female voice said over the loudspeaker. "We will be boarding families with small children and those who need extra time first. Please come forward only when your row number is called. Thank you."

Gregory squeezed her hand. "Emmy?"

She was momentarily mesmerized by his brown eyes. "All right. You win."

"Good girl."

"I'm going home, but I'm not giving up the story."

"We'll discuss that later."

"There's nothing to discuss. I'm going to find this Sergei Konstantin—whoever he is—and I'm going to expose him."

"You're playing with fire."
"Yes, but he's the one who is going to get burned."

# CHAPTER 12

The plane was full. Since Gregory made his reservation at the last minute, he and Emmeline did not have seats together. He was several rows behind on the opposite side. However, he had a good view of her. Now that they were finally on board, he felt more relaxed. Another fifteen minutes and they would take off, if all went well.

Emmeline sat staring at the little screen on the seat in front her without really seeing it. A million things were running through her mind. Yet again, she wondered where Charles was. She hadn't heard anything from him since he sent that note to her via the little boy in Piazza San Marco. She fervently hoped that he was still all right and getting medical attention.

"Miss Kirby? Miss Kirby?" Emmeline tore herself away from these disturbing thoughts and looked up into the green-gray eyes of her interrogator, who was dressed in a navy sweater and jeans.

"Ah, yes. It is you. I thought I recognized you."

Emmeline was startled. "Mr. Hayden, forgive me. I was lost in thought."

"That's all right," he said, smiling down at her as he placed his laptop and carry-on bag in the overhead locker and then slipped into the seat next to her. He pushed back an errant lock of dark brown hair that had slipped across his forehead and clicked the seatbelt into place. "We seem to be neighbors on this flight."

"Yes, I didn't expect to see you again until after you got back to London. I thought you said you were returning on Saturday. I'm surprised that you're not traveling in Business Class."

"Ah, you see duty calls and the Foreign Office needs me back for a meeting tomorrow, hence my early departure from beautiful Venice. Apparently, the flight is booked solid and this was the last seat available. Lucky for me, I have such a lovely traveling companion. And you? You're making a bit of a dash yourself."

"Yes, well. It's for a similar reason. A new story has come across my path, while I was here covering the trade conference, and I have to return to London to follow up on several leads."

"I see. Juicy story, is it?" He smiled encouragingly.

She returned his smile. "I'm afraid I can't tell you, Mr. Hayden."

"Giles, please."

"Giles, then. The answer is still the same."

"Ah, well, Emmeline. I may call you Emmeline?" She nodded her head. "That's a pity. I'm the soul of discretion. Besides, if you can't trust a member of Her Majesty's Foreign Office, who can you trust?"

Her eyes flicked briefly toward Gregory, who smiled cheekily back. "Indeed," she murmured. "Who can you trust? That's always a ticklish matter."

❧❧❧

The flight was a little over two hours. They were touching down at Heathrow before Emmeline realized it. The time had passed by quickly. She and Hayden had chatted nonstop about all sorts of things—current events, art, music, old movies. She had thoroughly enjoyed their conversation and found him to be very witty and incisive.

They pulled into the gate and, after a minute, the seatbelt sign turned off. As if on cue, everyone immediately started getting up to retrieve their belongings.

"Well, Emmeline—" Hayden extended his hand. "—thank you for making this flight so delightful. I can't tell you the last time I enjoyed such sparkling conversation with a charming companion."

Emmeline blushed as she shook his hand. "Mr. Hay—"

"Ah, ah, we're not going to start all that again now that we're back on terra firma."

She smiled. "Giles, I enjoyed the flight, too."

"That's better. But don't think you've gotten out of our dinner. Remember you did promise to have dinner with me once we returned home."

"Well, I—" Emmeline caught a glimpse of Gregory as the flight attendants opened the doors and people started to slowly make their way toward the exit. Damn, why should she feel guilty? She hadn't done anything. She turned back to Hayden. "Of course, I didn't forget."

"Good. I'll ring you up tomorrow afternoon, once I have a better idea of what my schedule is like."

"That's fine. Here's my card. My mobile number's there."

He folded it and tucked it into his jacket pocket. "Brilliant."

Finally, it was their turn to squeeze into the aisle. At the door, the flight attendants thanked them for flying with British Airways. Emmeline saw that Gregory was waiting for her in the corridor that led from the plane to the terminal.

"Ah, there you are, darling. I wondered where you'd gotten to."

He took her elbow possessively and propelled her forward. She tried to shake off his hand, but he only tightened his grip.

From beside her, Hayden said, "I say, old chap, that's not the way to treat a lady. I suggest that you remove your hand."

Gregory stopped, his hand still firmly on her elbow. The two men just stared at each other for a long moment without saying a word—Gregory's stony brown gaze level with Hayden's icy green-gray one. Their mutual dislike was palpable and instantaneous. Emmeline took a half-step between them, while the other passengers shoved their way past.

"I don't believe we've been introduced," Gregory said and extended his hand. "I'm Gregory Longdon."

Hayden shook Gregory's hand as if he had leprosy. "Giles Hayden. Old friend of Emmeline's, are you?"

Gregory's smile did not reach his eyes as he put his arm around Emmeline's shoulders and drew her into his side. "Yes, we're *very* old friends. We go way back, don't we, love?"

Both men looked down at her.

"I think we should get out of the way. We seem to be blocking traffic here."

She wriggled free of Gregory's embrace and started walking toward the terminal. The two men followed her.

There was more air and light in the terminal. She had managed to squeeze past a large group of loud and extremely rude Japanese tourists. As she waited for Gregory and Hayden to appear, her mobile started ringing. She scrambled in her purse to dig it out.

"Hello?"

"Emmeline, it's Charles."

She turned away from the door. "Charles? Are you all right? Where are you?"

"Darling, I'm in Holland Park."

"At my house?"

"Yes, I—"

Emmeline saw Gregory and Hayden. "Charles, I can't talk. I'm at Heathrow. I'll see you at the house soon." She pressed the button to end the call just as the two men reached her side. "Giles, thank you for making the flight so pleasant. I'm sure we'll see you in Baggage Claim." She hoped not. If he and Gregory spent any longer around one another, she shuddered to think of the consequences.

Hayden smiled at her. "I didn't check anything. I only have these." He indicated his laptop and carry-on. "I like to travel light."

"Well then, we wouldn't want to keep you. I know you're busy."

"Right, I'll ring you tomorrow about our dinner."

She felt herself blush again. "Yes. I look forward to it." But, she just wished he would go.

He gave Gregory a curt nod and made his way toward the exit.

"Now, what an endearing bloke he is. How do you manage to meet such interesting people?" Gregory said as he watched Hayden's retreating figure.

She swatted his arm. "Shut up."

"Ouch. That hurt." He made a show of rubbing the spot where she had hit him.

"Liar. You are the most incorrigible man I have ever met in my life—"

"Thank you, darling."

"—why you always have to make a nuisance of yourself I will never know," she continued as if he hadn't interrupted. "It's not as if you have any right to do so."

She was warming to her subject and was on the verge of completely losing her temper.

He simply smiled down at her. Insufferable man.

"Shall we go collect our bags?"

"In a minute. Gregory—" She paused and pulled him toward a column.

"Yes, darling? This is not the place for a cozy tête-à-tête. Too many people milling about."

"Stop being so glib and listen for once. Charles just rang me on my mobile."

His mustache seemed to bristle as his lips settled into a grim line. His grip tightened on her arm. "Where is he?"

"He's at my house."

"Why?"

"I don't know why. We couldn't talk because you and Giles were coming. It probably wasn't safe for him to go to his flat."

"I'll strangle Latimer. Come on." He started pulling her toward Baggage Claim.

# CHAPTER 13

Forty-five minutes later, the taxi eased out of the traffic on Kensington High Street and turned onto the quiet streets near Holland Park. In another ten minutes, they would be at Emmeline's townhouse near Stafford Terrace.

The afternoon was rather somber. Angry charcoal clouds had been brooding ominously ever since they had left Heathrow and now they finally unleashed their fury in the form of a cold rain that slashed at an angle against the taxi's windows. The weather seemed to reflect the tension that had settled between them. Gregory hadn't spoken a single word to her since they had gotten into the taxi. From beneath her lashes, Emmeline slid a sidelong glance in his direction. He was staring blankly out the window as his long, elegant fingers tapped on his knee— a sure sign he was in one of his stubborn moods, where he withdrew into himself and shut her out.

Emmeline crossed her arms irritably over her chest and looked out the window as well. What did *he* have to be upset about? She never asked him to get involved in any of this. She was perfectly capable of handling everything on her own.

"Here we are then," the driver said as he pulled up to the curb in front of Emmeline's house, which was on a long street of identical white townhouses with blue front doors.

Gregory paid the driver as she grabbed her upright and dashed up the slick steps. She fumbled with the key in the lock. Leaving the door wide open for him, she dropped her upright unceremoniously in the middle of the hall.

"Charles," she began calling.

She burst into the living room to her right. There was no one there. She went down the corridor to the kitchen. There was a dirty plate on the table and the dregs of some tea leaves in a mug, the only things to indicate that there had been someone in there recently.

Gregory was just closing the door when she came back out into the hall. "He must be upstairs."

"Charles," she called again as she hurried up the stairs.

Everything was very quiet. Perhaps he had gone out. But that didn't make any sense. Why would he go out if he knew she was on her way home? He had seemed so anxious to speak to her.

She went up the half landing to the guest room and knocked tentatively on the door. "Charles."

When there was no reply, she opened the door and went in. The bed was all rumpled and there were some bloody bandages on the floor. A shiver went up her spine. She was suddenly very cold. Something was wrong.

She heard Gregory coming up the stairs. She closed the door quietly behind her and met him in the hall.

"Well, where is the conquering hero?" he asked.

"He doesn't seem to be here."

Gregory laughed, but there was no trace of mirth in his voice. "Brilliant. More games."

"I think—"

They heard the splashing in the same instant. The

door to the bathroom was slightly ajar. He looked down at her for a moment.

"Right. Games *and* he has time for a leisurely bath in the middle of the afternoon. I'll murder him."

But it was too late. Someone had beaten him to it.

Charles was submerged, fully clothed, in the bathtub. The water was slightly pink from a cut on his temple. He couldn't have been dead very long. Gregory recovered his senses when he heard the sharp intake of breath beside him. He quickly pushed Emmeline back into the hall and closed the door.

She didn't scream, but all the color drained from her cheeks. She looked as if she might faint. He gently put his arm around her shoulders. "Why don't we go downstairs, love? There's nothing we can do for him now."

She didn't say anything. She just stared up into his cinnamon eyes, as if she couldn't understand what he was saying.

"Emmy, we have to call the police." This time he firmly guided her toward the staircase.

In the living room, he settled her on the sofa. He went over to the drinks tray and poured her a large brandy. "Here, drink this."

Mutely, she accepted the tumbler he offered. The liquor burned as it traveled down her throat.

"Good girl." He watched her take another sip. "Now, lean back, love." He patted her small hand and brushed a kiss against her dark curls, which were still damp from the rain. "Everything will be all right."

She finished the remainder of the brandy in one big gulp, while he sat at the desk and punched a number into the phone. It rang twice before a male voice barked into the receiver. "Burnell."

Gregory couldn't help smiling when he heard his old adversary. "Oliver, old chap, I'm glad I caught you."

"Who is this?"

"Don't you know? I must say I am hurt."

There was a brief silence. Gregory could hear the chief inspector breathing. "Longdon?"

"Got it in one. I knew you couldn't forget an old chum."

"It's Chief Inspector Burnell to you. What do you want, you scoundrel?"

"Ah, well. There's the rub. We are in need of your professional services. It seems that someone has taken it into his head to murder Charles Latimer."

"What? What are you playing at, Longdon?"

"Oliver, I'm deadly serious. Someone's murdered Latimer in Emmeline Kirby's townhouse. I suggest that you come here at once."

"Miss Kirby's house? Bloody hell." Burnell covered the receiver and yelled, "Finch."

Gregory could still hear the muffled conversation. When his sergeant appeared, the chief inspector briefly explained what had happened and issued instructions for a team to be dispatched and the medical examiner to be called. "What happened to Parker? I thought he was supposed to be watching the house."

"Sorry, sir. We were shorthanded and I had to pull him off to work on the Fitzgerald case."

Burnell grunted. "All right. Shove off now. Wait for me downstairs in the car."

"Right, sir."

Burnell turned his attention back to the phone. "Longdon, I'm on my way. Is Miss Kirby all right?"

"She's fine. I'm rather hurt that you didn't ask about me."

"You can go to the devil for all I care."

"Tsk. Tsk. I say, this is not the welcome I would have expected."

"I'll be there with a team in half an hour. Don't touch anything."

Exactly thirty minutes later, the doorbell rang. "I'll get it," Gregory said.

Emmeline heard a murmur of male voices before Chief Inspector Burnell and Sergeant Finch appeared in the living room. She stood up and extended a hand to greet them. "Chief Inspector Burnell, Sergeant Finch. It's been a long time."

"Yes," Burnell replied. "Unfortunately, we seem to always meet under unpleasant circumstances. I was sorry to hear about—"

She cut him off before he could say any more. "Thank you for the flowers." Her eyes flicked briefly in Gregory's direction and then she turned back to the chief inspector. "It was very thoughtful of you."

Burnell understood that they were not going to speak about some other painful time. So be it. He would respect her wishes. "Yes, well. On to the business at hand." He heard the team in the hallway. "Where's Latimer?"

"Upstairs. In the bathroom," Gregory answered, perplexed by the brief exchange between Emmeline and Burnell.

"Right."

The chief inspector stepped out of the room to issue orders to the constables. The medical examiner would be arriving any moment.

Meanwhile, Finch opened his notebook and quietly motioned toward the sofa. "Won't you please sit down, Miss Kirby?"

"Yes, certainly."

"And me, Sergeant?" Gregory asked, aware of the cheeky smirk on his face. "Shall I sit as well or shall I stand?"

Finch shifted his brown gaze toward him and said through gritted teeth, "If you like, Mr. Longdon."

"Thank you. Then I think I shall."

He settled himself next to Emmeline on the sofa and crossed his arms over his chest.

Finch took the armchair opposite them. "Now, Miss Kirby, can you shed any light on why Mr. Latimer was murdered? When was the last time you saw or spoke with him?"

Emmeline looked at Sergeant Finch. There was a mixture of concern and sympathy upon his face. She swallowed the lump that had suddenly formed in her throat while she fought off tears "The last time I spoke to Charles—" Her voice quavered and she had to stop.

"If you don't feel up to it at the moment, Miss Kirby, we can do this another time?"

She shook her head. "No." It was said more to herself than the sergeant. She cleared her throat and looked him directly in the eye. "No, Sergeant Finch, we'll do this now. I'll tell you everything I know. I want this animal caught."

"Right. Whenever you're ready, Miss Kirby."

"The last time I spoke to Charles was about two hours ago. He rang me on my mobile. I was at Heathrow, just getting off the plane from Venice."

"I see." Finch's pen scratched across the page. "Venice? Mr. Latimer had just returned from Venice as well. Had you seen him there?"

"Yes, I ran into him at a masked ball, which is given at the casino annually to honor Venice's Consular corps."

"Had you planned on meeting him at the ball?"

"No, I'd no idea that he'd be there at the same time. It was the first time that I'd attended the ball. A friend of mine at the Foreign Office secured an invitation for me."

"And this friend's name?"

"Philip Acheson." Finch wrote this down. "Now then, back to Mr. Latimer."

Chief Inspector Burnell returned at this point. "Please go on, Miss Kirby. Don't mind me." He quietly leaned against the drinks table and almost seemed to blend into the background.

Emmeline's gaze flitted toward the ceiling, distracted by the sound of voices and footsteps upstairs. Poor Charles. She would never see him again.

"Miss Kirby?" Sergeant Finch prompted gently.

She dragged herself from these sad thoughts and turned her attention back to him. "Well, as I said, I didn't know that Charles would be at the ball. I hadn't seen him in ages. At the beginning of last year, he was on tour in America to promote his new book on the KGB and, for the last two months, he'd been out of touch. I assumed he was working on a new assignment. I was quite surprised when I saw him. But he knew that I'd be there. He told me that he'd arranged it with Philip to get me the invitation."

"Did he say why he had gone to such trouble? I mean, if he wanted to see you, why not just ring you here in London?"

"He started to tell me he was working on a big story and needed my help. His exact words were that it was something that would 'rip Whitehall apart.'"

"'Rip Whitehall apart'? What did you make of that?"

"As a journalist, naturally my curiosity was aroused. He started telling me about someone he recognized at the Foreign Office about a month ago. However, he never ended up telling me anything. He suddenly seemed nervous and said that it had been a mistake to meet at the ball. It was too dangerous."

"Dangerous? That's not a normal reaction at a party. Had someone threatened him?"

"Not when he was with me. But I did see Dimitri Petrov, the Russian consul, and another man, whom I later learned was named Anatol Zobrinsky, staring at Charles and me. Charles saw them, too. I think that's why he didn't want to talk at the ball. He asked me to meet him at ten-thirty at the church of San Bartolomeo near the Rialto Bridge. He promised to tell me everything then."

"Did you go to meet him?"

"Yes." Emmeline's voice caught in her throat. "That's when they tried to kill him the first time. And now they've succeeded." She could no longer hold back the tears. She impatiently wiped her cheeks with the back of her hand. "I'm sorry, Chief Inspector Burnell and Sergeant Finch. I feel I've let Charles down."

Gregory took her hand in his. "Nonsense, love. I'm sure Charles would not have felt that way. Besides, it was sheer bloody recklessness on his part to put you in such danger. It's one thing if he wants to throw his own life away just to get a story, but quite another to involve you."

"Miss Kirby, I agree with Longdon. Latimer had no right to involve you in this business," Burnell asserted.

"But I understood. He was my friend and I was quite prepared to help him. I still am. I swear I'm going to finish what Charles started. I'm going to get this story out, even if it kills me."

All three men exchanged weary glances at her grim determination.

"Miss Kirby, I don't think that's a wise decision. Naturally, you're upset now."

"No." She put up a hand to stop any more arguments.

"No, I'm sorry, Chief Inspector Burnell. I will not be dissuaded. Please let's continue. There is more to tell."

She went on to detail everything that had happened in Venice from the moment she saw the men attack Charles in Campo San Bartolomeo. She told them about running into Gregory, finding her room ransacked, the threatening phone call, her nocturnal interlude with Paolo Talamini, and his revelations about Sergei Konstantin.

"And then, while we were waiting for the flight to be called this morning, there was a man reading a newspaper next to me. The headlines were all about Talamini's murder. I wanted to remain in Venice to tell the police about my encounter with Talamini last night, but I was persuaded—" She cast a sidelong glance at Gregory. "—that it would be better to return to London."

Burnell's clear blue gaze swept over both of them.

"Oliver," Gregory said.

"Chief Inspector Burnell."

"As you wish. Just because Talamini was found near Emmeline's hotel does not mean that his murder had anything to do with Latimer and this Sergei Konstantin chicanery. It could very well have been a random robbery, as the papers said, or perhaps Talamini rubbed one his Mafia chums the wrong way. In any case, there was no point in further ensnaring Emmeline. She'd already been through enough. Besides, after the incident with Officer Calvalcante, there was no knowing whether the Venice police would even have listened to her."

Burnell stroked his beard in silent contemplation for a moment. "Miss Kirby, much as I hate to admit it, I'm afraid what Longdon says makes sense. Leave it to me. I have a few contacts in Italy. I'll make a few discreet phone calls."

She shrugged her shoulders in mute surrender.

"Now then, my chaps should be finishing up and

we'll soon be out of your hair. However, I was wondering if perhaps you have anyone with whom you can stay? I don't think you should be alone. I'm afraid we'll have to treat your house as a crime scene for a few more days, but we'll try not to be too intrusive."

"Of course, I understand."

"She'll stay with me at my flat tonight," Gregory said. "Then tomorrow I was planning to take her down to her grandmother's house in Kent. She can spend the weekend down there. That should give you plenty of time, Oliver." He finished with a cheeky grin.

"No." She shook off Gregory's hand and stood up. She appealed to Burnell. "Couldn't I stay here tonight and then leave in the morning for my grandmother's? I promise I won't touch anything. I'll keep to my room, the kitchen, and in here. Perhaps, your team could check my room for fingerprints and if it's all right—I'm very tired, Chief Inspector. The past few days have taken more of a toll on me than I had realized and now finding poor Charles dead." She swallowed the lump that constricted her throat. "I'd just like to spend tonight in my own bed. Please." The chief inspector and Sergeant Finch exchanged a look. "Naturally, it's up to you. I can't force you to leave your home, Miss Kirby. I can only offer my professional advice. Now, I'd like to have a word with Dr. Meadows before he leaves."

Finch gave her a weak smile as Burnell left the room. "The chief inspector shouldn't be but a minute."

Emmeline smiled back and they all fell silent.

There was a low murmur of voices in the hall. The chief inspector opened the door again almost immediately. He stood there for a second with his hand on the doorknob, still in conversation with one of the officers. "Right. Fine. Send me the report as soon as Meadows has finished the postmortem."

"Yes, Chief Inspector."

Burnell closed the door again and rubbed his hands together. "It's all right, Miss Kirby. They'll be finished in half an hour. They've dusted the rest of the house and would like to do in here. Once that's done, you'll have your house back. We're going to seal off Latimer's room and—" He looked down at his feet. "—of course, the bathroom. Other than that the house seems to be clean. They've only found your prints and Latimer's. The killer wore gloves. No surprise there. It has all the markings of a professional hit."

"It must be this Sergei Konstantin. Don't you see? It can't be a coincidence. First, the Russians tried to kill Charles in Venice to prevent him from going public with what he had found out and, when that failed, they followed him back to London to silence him permanently."

"Yes, well. I suggest that you leave it to us to sort it all out. Now, if you both would kindly retire to the kitchen, the chaps can dust this room."

She would not be brushed aside so easily. She stood up. "Chief Inspector Burnell, I'm putting you on notice that I'm picking up the story. I will not stop until Sergei Konstantin is exposed and Charles's killer is brought to justice. You have my promise on that."

"Miss Kirby—"

"No, Chief Inspector, I will not be dissuaded by anyone." Her glance swept over all three men, daring them to say something. "Therefore, I hope Scotland Yard will share its findings with the press."

Burnell sighed. "I'll share whatever I can without compromising the case or public safety."

"Naturally, that goes without saying. I'm glad that we understand one another. Thank you, Chief Inspector."

She extended her hand and Burnell shook it. "Always a pleasure, Miss Kirby."

She then smiled and inclined her head toward Finch. "Well, we better get out of your way. Gregory, let's go into the kitchen. I'll put a kettle on. Chief Inspector Burnell, Sergeant Finch, would you like a cup of tea?"

"No, thank you," Burnell answered for both of them.

"If you change your mind, just let me know."

"I will."

Gregory was about to follow Emmeline out, when Burnell grabbed his elbow and pulled him back. "Longdon, I advise you to tread carefully. I don't believe for one moment that you're as innocent as you make out. I'll be watching you. If I find anything—" He took a step closer to Gregory so that they were eye to eye. "— anything at all that ties you to this mess, it will be my pleasure to make sure you rot in prison for the rest of your miserable life."

Gregory smiled benignly and removed the chief inspector's hand from his sleeve. "Oliver, I'm hurt that you show so little faith in your fellow man. But you will learn, to your chagrin I might add, that we are on the same side in this matter. If there's nothing else, it's bad manners to keep a lady waiting."

"Humph." The chief inspector jerked his head in the direction of the door. "Go on."

"Cold as ice," Finch murmured once Gregory was gone. "Sir, do you really think that Longdon is involved?"

Burnell ran a hand through his thinning white hair. "No, Finch, it's not his style. Longdon may be a lot of things, but a murderer is not one of them."

❧❧❧

Night had already wrapped its black cloak tightly around the evening and a fine misting rain was beginning to fall half an hour later. The man in the navy Opel watched from across the square as the last of the constables left Emmeline's house. He pulled out his camera with the long, telephoto lens and shot several pictures in quick succession of the house and the street. He even got a good shot of Emmeline and Gregory talking in front of the bay window, before she pulled the curtain closed. That was about all he was going to get tonight.

The man put the camera down on the seat next to him and punched a number into his mobile. It rang once. "The police are gone. Only Longdon and the girl are in the house and he's going to be leaving soon by the sound of it."

"Did the police find the bug?"

"No. I can hear everything they're saying as if I were in the room with them."

"Good. Whatever you do, keep a watch on the house. You'll be relieved at midnight and someone else will take over at six in the morning. I don't want anyone else slipping through our fingers. Got it?"

"Right. But Longdon said he'll be back in the morning to collect her. He's going to take her down to her grandmother's in the country. They're going to spend the weekend in Kent."

"At last, a break. That will give us all the time in the world to go over the house. Latimer must have hidden it in there somewhere. I don't like this at all. Too many people are involved all of a sudden and everything is starting to unravel. It must end. *Now*."

# CHAPTER 14

Emmeline had been up since five. She hadn't really slept, but she couldn't stay in bed any longer. So she dressed in a pair of comfortable jeans and the cozy rose sweater Gran had given her for Hanukkah. She went downstairs, made herself a cup of coffee, and then went into the living room to do a little research on the Internet.

She was making a few final notes when the doorbell rang at eight o'clock on the dot. A sigh escaped her lips. She put her pen down and went to answer it. There was Gregory, all freshly shaven and smiling mischievously. It didn't look as if anything had disturbed his slumber. He wore jeans and a forest green turtleneck.

"Good morning, Emmy." He bent to give her a kiss, but she averted her face. "Is that a way to greet a chap on such a lovely morning, especially when he's brought warm croissants?" He waved the box under her nose.

"Thank you. If you're going to come in, you might as well do so already, instead of chuntering on like that on the doorstep. I'm nearly ready. I was just doing a little research." She opened the door wider so that he could enter the hall. "Would you like some coffee? There's a fresh pot in the kitchen."

"I'd love a cup." Gregory shrugged out of his leather

jacket and hung it up on a peg in the hall. In doing so, he knocked the mail off the hall table. "Sorry, love." He bent down to pick it up. He handed her several letters—more likely bills—and a larger manila envelope.

"Oh, just leave it. I'll deal with it all on Monday, when I get back from Gran's."

"Very well." He dumped the lot back on the table and followed her down the hall into the kitchen.

Sunlight streamed in through the window practically the whole day, giving the kitchen a warm and cozy feeling even in the winter months.

The ceiling and the walls were a buttery cream color, further enhancing this effect, and the floor was covered in white tiles. The walls were decorated with various tiles. There were little Dutch scenes with windmills and children in wooden clogs, as well as others with flowers and vegetables.

He had always felt at home in this kitchen, Gregory thought as he slid onto a chair at the sturdy table made of polished blond wood. Actually, from the first moment he ever set foot in this house three years ago, he had felt as if he had come home. Funny, since he had never known what a real home was.

He'd been out in the world on his own since the age of seventeen. Alone, restless, and never settling in one place for long. Perhaps—if he was honest with himself—it was the loneliness of living like that for two years that had made him turn to—Ah, but that was a wound he didn't want to reopen. Not now. Not Emmeline's house. The past and all its demons were best left buried. In the darkness. But a little voice inside his head asked, *Is that truly possible?* Didn't the past have a way of rearing its ugly head when one was most vulnerable?

Gregory's eyes followed Emmeline as she bustled about the kitchen getting plates and pouring two mugs of coffee. "I hope so," he whispered under his breath. "I hope so."

"What did you say?" Emmeline asked as she sat down. "Are you all right?"

"Yes. Why?"

"You were looking at me rather oddly just now."

"I'm perfectly all right." He let the past slip into the mists of time and gave her cheeky grin. "I was just admiring your efficiency. You also look extremely fetching in pink."

She rolled her eyes. "Just eat your croissant and let's go. I don't want to run into traffic."

Half an hour later, he tossed her bags into the boot of his blue-gray Jaguar. She stopped as she came down the steps. "New car or did you steal it?"

"Darling, you wound me. Stealing cars is so…so petty. I wouldn't dream of doing such a thing."

She arched one of her eyebrows. "No, I suppose not. You're too sophisticated. I forgot you only steal jewelry," she said as she got into the passenger seat and clicked her belt into place.

Gregory turned the key in the ignition and pulled away from the curb. "You know, Emmy, I shall have to have a talk with Helen. Perhaps she can do something about the language you tend to use and your highly suspicious nature. Stealing, indeed. I don't know where such thoughts come from."

"Humph," she grunted and settled in for the two-hour ride down to her grandmother's house.

The man in the black Audi across the square finished his coffee and watched until the Jaguar had turned the corner at the end of the road. Then, he picked up his mobile.

The line barely rang once. "It's all clear. Longdon and the girl just left."

"Good. Move in. I want every inch of the house searched, but for God's sake don't attract any attention to yourselves. I don't want any of the neighbors getting suspicious and calling the police. Got it?"

"Don't worry. It's all under control. Two of the chaps are already inside. They entered through the garden. The rest of us are going in now."

"Ring me this afternoon." The connection was severed.

‹⁄›‹⁄›

Emmeline must have dozed off shortly after they left London, for when she awoke they were just getting off the M20. They had just passed Barfrestone. It wouldn't be long now. Already she was feeling more relaxed. It was a world away from what she had left behind in London. Her thoughts turned to Charles. She would not let his murder go unpunished. She would strip off Sergei Konstantin's mask and expose him to the world, even if it killed her. But that would have to wait until Monday. At this moment, as the rolling hills slipped past her window and she watched the sun caress the bare limbs of the trees, all she wanted to do was to see Gran, the one person she could always count on.

She sneaked a sidelong glance at Gregory. At one time, she'd thought that she could count on him too. But she had been wrong, oh so very wrong. And yet, he had saved her life in Venice. She couldn't deny that and he had been watching over her ever since. She groaned inwardly. It would be so easy, so very easy to let him back into her life. However, too many things had happened. She was not the same person she was that August night two years ago, when he had disappeared and she found out that he was a thief. And then, two months later—

No, she would not do this. She curled her hand into a ball and hit her thigh. That was the past. That was where it would stay. She would not go through all of that again.

"Nearly there," he said with a smile.

"Yes," she answered distractedly. She spoke more to the window than to him. "I can hardly wait to see Gran."

"Are you all right?"

"Yes, fine."

She turned and looked at him, but Gregory had the impression that she wasn't really seeing him. Her thoughts seemed to be somewhere else entirely. Well, he couldn't really blame her. A great deal had occurred in the past few days. She was probably still in shock from finding Latimer's body.

The rest of their journey continued in silence. At eleven-thirty, they were trundling down the main street of the village of Swaley, a quiet little nook tucked in Kent's southeast corner. She became more animated as they crossed the River Darent over the humpbacked, honey-colored, stone bridge. They turned at the bend in the road and, five minutes later, her grandmother's garden came into view. Smoke was curling upward from the chimney of the Tudor-style house. Emmeline could picture Gran in the kitchen in the midst of preparing a lovely luncheon. Oh, it was good to be home, for that was what this house had been for most of her life. Despite losing her parents, she had had a happy childhood here. Gran saw to it that she had everything she could possibly need or want without spoiling her.

The car had barely stopped in the gravel driveway, when Emmeline flung the door wide and jumped out. The pebbles crunched underfoot as she ran to the front door, which was unlocked. "Gran," she called as she entered the hall. "Gran."

"I'm coming, love. I'm in the kitchen."

Emmeline unzipped her jacket and hung it on the hook. A moment later, her grandmother was bustling toward her. Emmeline flew into her outstretched arms and hugged her tightly. "Oh, Gran, I missed you so much."

"I missed you too, Emmy."

They stood that way for another minute and then her grandmother pulled back. "Let me look at you. Your face is thinner. You've lost weight."

Emmeline laughed and gave her another squeeze, before slipping her arm around her grandmother's plump waist. Gran said that to her every time she saw her. She thought Emmeline didn't eat enough "up there in London."

"No, Gran, I haven't lost weight. It's just in your mind, as usual."

"Hmm." Gran tilted her head to one side and studied Emmeline skeptically. "I don't know about that. I've made a cream of cauliflower soup and a nice shepherd's pie for lunch. And there's apple crumble with lashings of fresh cream for pudding. I'm going to make sure that you eat everything."

Emmeline laughed again. "Ooh, sounds delicious."

They heard the car door slam. "You've brought a friend with you, darling? How delightful. I always enjoy meeting new people. There's plenty of food." That was an understatement. Gran always cooked for a regiment.

"Gran, I'm sorry. Everything was so rushed yesterday, what with the police at the house, that I didn't get a chance to tell you that I was bringing—"

In that instant, a black dervish whizzed past them and out the front door. "MacTavish. MacTavish. What is that devil up to now?" her grandmother asked good-naturedly.

They heard barking and then male laughter floated in to them.

Her grandmother turned and looked down at her. "It couldn't be. That sounds like—"

The next instant, Gregory appeared in the doorway preceded by the impish figure of the black Scottish terrier.

MacTavish stood there wagging his tail furiously. Gregory had given him to Gran on her seventy-fifth birthday and they were all great friends.

He put their bags down and shut the door. "Helen, how wonderful to see you again. Still looking as young as ever I see. Not a trace of gray in your golden curls. Ah, if only you were ten years younger—" He put a hand over his heart in a dramatic gesture. "—I'd sweep you off your feet and we'd run off to elope."

Her grandmother's warm hazel eyes crinkled at the corners and her silvery laughter filled the hall. She went over and gave him a hug.

"Shameless flatterer. As you very well know, this—" She took one of her curls between her fingers. "—has been coming out of a bottle for years. But I will accept the compliment in the spirit that it was intended."

"As well you should. Now, darling." He tucked her arm into the crook of his elbow. "What are those delicious smells tickling my nose? Do I detect shepherd's pie?"

"You do, indeed. There's also a cauliflower soup for starters and apple crumble and cream for pudding."

"Mmm. Ambrosia for the gods. My mouth is watering already."

"Lunch will be ready in half an hour."

"Splendid. How about if I nip these bags upstairs in the meantime?"

"Of course, you know your way around. I'll go up after lunch to make up the guest room. I didn't know you were coming down, too."

"Yes, well. I'm sorry if it's an imposition. Things happened rather quickly and there was no time to—We'll explain everything later."

"Don't be silly. I'm happy to have you here."

"At least two of us are happy."

Both of them looked over at Emmeline, who had been silent throughout this entire exchange.

Helen pushed him in the direction of the stairs. "Go on."

"Right. I won't be a tick."

"Wait," Emmeline said. "I need to get something from my bag."

"Of course." He put the bag down and she unzipped the side pocket. She took out a package. "That's it. You can take it up now," she mumbled.

"Right."

Emmeline waited until he had gone. "Gran, I bought this for you when I was in Venice. I hope you like it."

Helen's eyes lit up and she rubbed her hands together with childlike glee. "Ooh, a present. I'm sure I shall love it because you gave it to me, darling." She gave Emmeline's waist a squeeze. "I must open it now. It would be torture to wait until after lunch. The suspense would kill me."

Emmeline laughed as she watched her grandmother tear at the colorful tissue paper. "Oh, Emmy." She lifted the delicate mask to admire it in the sunlight slanting in through the window. "It's absolutely lovely. I've always wanted a Venetian mask."

"I know and when I saw this one in the shop, I knew it would be perfect for you. I'm so glad you like it."

"I do, darling. Thank you." She kissed the top of Emmeline's head. "Come keep me company in the kitchen, while I get lunch ready."

ℯↃℯↃ

Helen kept them entertained through each course with hilarious tidbits of village gossip. They were all laughing so hard their sides hurt. "Now, my loves, I'll just clear this lot up and get the apple crumble and then you can tell me everything that has been happening lately."

"Let me help you with the dishes, Helen."

"Don't be silly, dear boy. I'm not in my dotage yet. You sit there and chat nicely with Emmy."

Gregory glanced over at Emmeline and she blushed as her grandmother hurried out of the dining room. Her grandmother was not the most subtle of people.

An uncomfortable silence fell between them. They could hear Helen singing—off key, as usual—in the kitchen. Emmeline had been having so much fun that she had nearly forgotten about the events of the past few days.

"I don't hear anyone talking. I hope you're not trying to make me cross by disobeying my orders."

Emmeline smiled. "Heaven forbid, Gran."

"We live in mortal terror of such an event occurring," Gregory added.

"Good. Then why can't I hear the sound of youthful voices?"

"I suppose we were talking too softly."

"There is no excuse for it. You've both eaten a hearty meal and the pudding is just coming, so you must have strength to at least speak in firm, strong voices. I expect to hear details about all of your adventures."

"Yes, Gran."

They looked at one another across the table. "What shall we talk about?"

"The weather is always a safe topic."

Emmeline couldn't help herself, she laughed.

"Or I could tease you, if you'd prefer. However, if I tease you, you'll get all riled up and then your grandmother would have a row on her hands. So perhaps we should stick to the weather."

She stifled a giggle. "Yes, you're right. The weather would be best." She glanced over his shoulder toward the dining room window. "I wonder if we'll have an early spring."

He turned around in his chair and made a pretense of carefully studying the clouds in the sky. "Hmm. If I'm not mistaken those are nimbostratus clouds, which means we'll have an early spring."

"You're wrong. If those were nimbostratus clouds, then it would mean a storm was approaching. They're cirrocumulus clouds."

"Are you sure, darling? They look like nimbostratus clouds to me."

"Then, you need glasses."

He clicked his tongue and wagged a finger at her. "Now, now. Be nice or I shall tell your grandmother and she'll send you to bed without supper."

Emmeline giggled again.

Helen returned with a tray laden with the coffee pot, cups and saucers and the apple crumble and cream. "Did I hear my name being taken in vain?"

Gregory stood and took the tray from her. He gave her a peck on the cheek. "No, you did not, my love. We were having a minor disagreement about the weather and we said that you would know the answer."

"The weather? Is that the only thing you could find to talk about?" Helen shook her head as she set the cups and saucers before them. "I don't know what this world is coming to when the only thing that two healthy and attractive young people can find to discuss is the weather.

Needless to say, I am deeply disappointed in the two of you." But there was a mischievous gleam in her eyes. "Now, who'll have some apple crumble and cream?"

"Ooh, me, please, Gran."

"You know that I cannot resist your cooking, Helen."

"Good. Emmy, you pour the coffee."

"Yes, Gran."

Silence reigned as they savored their dessert. Once their plates were cleaned and they were sipping their coffees, Helen broached the subject they had been avoiding all through the meal. "I think it's about time the two of you told me what's been going on?"

The mood turned serious as her hazel eyes swept from one to the other.

Emmeline sighed and slowly began recounting everything that had happened from the moment she ran into Charles at the masked ball in Venice to when they found him murdered in her bathtub in London yesterday afternoon. Gregory interjected a few times to elaborate on a certain point.

"That's where things stand, Gran."

Helen reached out and gave Emmeline's hand a squeeze. "Thank goodness you're all right, love. I have you to thank for that, dear boy." She turned and kissed his cheek.

Gregory's cinnamon gaze met and held Emmeline's darker ones across the table for a long moment. Then she looked down and started fidgeting with her hands.

"Anyone would have done the same, Helen. I'm not a hero."

"No, you certainly are not. You're a thief," Emmeline murmured under her breath.

"What was that, Emmy?"

"Nothing, Gran."

"You know that I do not like mumbling. From what

the two of you have told me, you were very lucky to have run into Gregory when you did or you would not be here with us now."

"Yes, Gran." She looked up. "I am grateful. Truly. It's just that—"

"Just what?"

"Nothing. It doesn't matter. What's important now is that I find Charles's killer and expose this Sergei Konstantin."

At this point, MacTavish bounded into the room, heedless of the tension that lay so thickly upon the air. He plopped himself at Gregory's feet and barked.

"I think he wants you to take him for a walk," Helen said.

Gregory bent down and scratched the dog behind the ears. "Is that right, old chap? Do you want to go for a walk?" MacTavish barked again and started wagging his tail. "Well, that's it then." Gregory pushed his chair back and stood up. "Helen, it was a superb lunch. I would have offered to wash the dishes, but as you can see this demanding brute wants to go for a walk and he won't take no for an answer."

"Off you go. It's a lovely afternoon for a long ramble."

"Yes." He hesitated, casting a quick glance at Emmeline. "Care to come with us, Emmy?"

"No, I think I'll stay here with Gran. Perhaps I'll go out later. On my own."

Gregory looked at Helen.

"Go on. We'll be fine here." She jerked her head in the direction of the hall.

"Right." He bent down and kissed Helen's cheek. "Come on, MacTavish."

The dog scrambled after him and there was a bit of a commotion as Gregory put on his jacket. They heard the front door open and close, and then there was silence. Helen turned toward her granddaughter. Emmeline was staring downward as she pushed the last remnants of the apple crumble around her plate.

"Don't think I didn't notice that you barely touched your lunch."

Emmeline put her fork down and smiled sheepishly. "I ate the apple crumble."

"Humph. You used to do the same thing when you were a little girl. You call that eating. No wonder you're skin and bones." Helen stood up and started clearing the plates.

"Here let me do that, Gran. Let me wash the dishes."

"Fine. I'm going to put a kettle on and then we're going to sit down and you're going to tell me what's bothering you."

Emmeline opened her mouth to speak, but Helen cut her off. "And don't tell me it's this business of your friend's murder and the Russian chap that's running all over London causing mischief. Because I know that's not it. Now, go." She gave her granddaughter a shove toward the kitchen.

A quarter of an hour later, the dishes had been washed, dried, and stacked neatly back in the cupboard. The kettle was just starting to whistle for attention.

Emmeline set out the cups and saucers and sat down at the kitchen table. She watched as Helen swirled a little of the steaming water around the pot to warm it and then dumped it out in the sink. She measured out two heaping spoonfuls of tea and poured the water over it.

"We'll leave that to brew for a bit," she said as she placed the pot in the center of the table. "Now, then." She reached out, took Emmeline's hands in her larger ones, and rubbed them. "What's troubling you, my dear? Come on, you know you can tell me anything. Haven't we always been best friends?"

"Oh, yes, Gran. The best of friends. Always." Emmeline's heart was full of love for this woman who had raised her and taken care of her all her life.

But Helen could see the turmoil and pain in her granddaughter's dark eyes. "What is it? I won't be shocked. I assure you."

"Oh, Gran—" Emmeline's throat constricted and she almost choked on the words. She felt the tears trailing down her cheeks. "Why did he have to come back? *Why?* I thought I had finally put it all behind me and, suddenly, out of the blue, here's Gregory. It's as if everything is happening all over again." Tears were streaming unbidden. There was nothing she could do to stop the flow. A dam inside her had finally burst.

Helen stood up and came over to the other side of the table. She took her granddaughter in her arms. "My precious, precious girl."

Emmeline threw her arms around Helen's waist and clung tightly, as she used to do as a child. She buried her head against her grandmother's stomach. Sobs wracked her body now.

"Shh. It's all right," Helen murmured as she caressed her granddaughter's dark curls and rocked her back and forth. "Hush, my darling. Everything will be all right."

"Nothing will ever be all right." She lifted red-rimmed eyes to look at her grandmother. "How can it be?"

Helen took Emmeline's face in her hands and smoothed away the tears. "Yes, it will be." She kissed her softly on the forehead. "I promise you it will be."

Emmeline buried her head once more. When she was a little quieter, Helen asked gently, "Have you told him?"

Emmeline's head jerked up. "No. And I'm not going to."

"Don't you think you should, love? After all, he has a right to know."

"Right? *Right?*" Emmeline stood up abruptly, scraping the chair violently against the tile floor. "What right? If you remember, Gregory ran out on me. He has no rights." Her voice grew louder with each word she uttered.

"Darling, I still think you ought to tell him."

"Ought to tell me what?"

They turned to find Gregory leaning casually against the doorframe.

This was too much for Emmeline. "Nothing. You deserve nothing." She pushed past him and ran out of the kitchen.

"Emmy?" Helen called after her. "Emmy, come back here."

The front door rattled on its hinges, as she stormed out of the house.

"I'll go after her," Gregory said.

Helen sighed and put a blue-veined hand on his sleeve. "No, leave her be. She needs to be alone for a bit. Come sit down and we'll have a cup of tea."

He did as he was bid. They were both silent as Helen poured the tea. "Would you like a biscuit with that?"

"Not after that enormous lunch. Thanks."

They both took a sip of the tea. It was scalding and strong. Gregory fixed his eyes upon Helen and waited for her to speak.

Her brow furrowed slightly and she suddenly looked her age. She took another sip of tea. "Emmy is the most precious thing in my life and I love her dearly." She stopped and cleared her throat.

Gregory reached out and took her blue-veined hand

in his own. "I do know that, Helen. It is obvious to any-one with eyes. And Emmy loves you just as much. She's the woman she is today because of the way you raised her. You may not believe this, but I care deeply for your granddaughter, too."

Helen squeezed his hand. "Yes, I think you do, but you hurt her very badly when you ran off. Very badly."

"I'm sorry about—" he murmured softly.

"It's all water under the bridge. We can't turn the clock back, however much we'd like to. And although she denies it, I think deep down she still loves you."

Gregory's eyes widened in surprise, but he said noth-ing. Helen smiled. "A grandmother knows these things. Despite being a rake, I don't believe you're rotten to the core. Perhaps, I'm a sucker for a handsome face, but I rather like you."

"Thank you, Helen. Your opinion means the world to me and the feeling is mutual."

"Having said all that, we are still left with the fact that Emmy was hurt and other things happened after you left that nearly destroyed her." Gregory opened his mouth to say something, but she held up a hand to stop him. "Please let me finish. I am not going to tell you what those things were. That's not my place. Emmy must be the one to tell you. I just want you to understand my granddaughter before you rush off to find her.

"Emmy is one of the most thoughtful and kindest people on this earth. Yes, she has a temper and is impa-tient, but if she cares about someone she is fiercely loyal and would do anything to help him or her. You may think that she has a lot of friends because she's so warm and loving. But no, it always took her a long time to get to know people and, along the way, many took advantage of her good nature. As a result, she is always the one who winds up on the outside. After a while, she kept herself apart before she could get hurt." Helen paused and looked him straight in the eye. "That changed the day she met you. She began to open up more. I think there was a reason Fate brought you back into her life. Please do not hurt her again because I shall not forgive you a second time."

He could see the tears glistening in her eyes. He came over and gently kissed her cheek. "Thank you, Helen. I promise I will not disappoint you."

She shooed him away. "Go on. Go find my granddaughter."

ে৯ে৯

Emmeline had picked up a large stick along her rambles and wielded it as if it were a weapon. She gave the ground a resounding thwack with each step she took. She kept walking and walking until she found herself down by the river. It was not surprising, really. The river had always been her refuge as a child. A confidante and trusted friend. Weariness suddenly settled into all of her bones. Whether it was everything that had happened over the past few days or the turmoil engendered by Gregory's reappearance, she didn't know.

She plopped herself down on a rotting log. How peaceful it was here with the honeyed strands of sunlight dancing on the surface of the water. She took a deep lungful of the crisp country air and closed her eyes. The tension in her shoulders seemed to ease a little as she listened to the soothing babble of the river as it meandered along its merry way. The sound of the water reminded her of the rain the night she first met Gregory. It seemed like ages and ages ago. And yet, she could recall every detail as if it were yesterday. Why was that?

ে৯ে৯

*The rain was relentless. It came down in slanting sheets, driven by a chilly April wind. Emmeline had just finished doing some shopping on Piccadilly and was going to treat herself to dinner. However, the weather changed those plans. She decided to make a dash to the Underground and go home instead, where she'd take a warm shower, have a hot bowl of soup, and curl up with a book.*

*Just as she made these plans, it started raining even harder, if that were possible. She ran for nearest doorway to wait until Mother Nature's wrath quieted down a bit.*

*It appeared she was not the only one with this idea. For a gentleman careened straight into her.*

*She exhaled as the wind was knocked out of her.*
*"Oof,"*

*"I'm terribly sorry, miss. Are you all right?" he asked in concern.*

*She recovered herself after a few seconds. "Yes, I'm fine." She patted herself down. "No broken bones."*

*It was at that moment that she looked up to find herself staring into a pair of eyes that were more like cinnamon than hazel. He was the most handsome man she had ever seen.*

*He smiled down at her. "Well, that's good. Filthy night, isn't it?"*

*For a minute, she didn't say anything. Then, she realized that he had asked her a question. She tore her eyes away from him and looked up at the charcoal sky. "Yes, it's simply awful."*

*"I say, allow me to make amends by taking you to dinner."*

*Emmeline felt herself blush and took half a step backward into the shadow of the doorway. "That's not necessary. I'm fine. Besides, I couldn't possibly go to dinner with a perfect stranger. I'm sorry."*

*"Right. Say no more." He put up his hands. "I quite understand. A pretty young woman like you must be careful these days. You never know who is lurking out there on the streets."*

*"I'm glad you understand."*

*She watched the traffic inching its way along so she wouldn't have to gaze into those mesmerizing eyes again. They both fell silent.*

*After a minute, he said, "By the way, my name's Gregory James Anthony Longdon." He extended a hand toward her.*

*She shook it. "I'm Emmeline Kirby."*

*"I'm very pleased to make your acquaintance, Miss Emmeline Kirby. Now, will you have dinner with me? After all, we can no longer be considered strangers since we know each other by our first names. I'm also famished." His mouth curved into a mischievous smile beneath his mustache as he took a step closer to her.*

*She began to laugh. "No, I don't suppose we can be. All right. I accept your invitation, Mr. Longdon."*

*"My friends call me Gregory."*

*"Then you must call me Emmeline."*

*"Ah, what a lovely name. I'm certain I shall hear it in my dreams as the sirens call to me."*

*She laughed again. She took the arm he proffered and they hailed the first taxi that came along.*

천씨천

That was how it all began. They *had* been happy, blissfully happy. How could something so wonderful have been turned upside down? Emmeline sighed and put her head down on her knees. Suddenly, something wet and cold brushed against her hand. She opened an eye and found herself staring at MacTavish. "How did you get here, oh mighty watchdog?"

MacTavish cocked his head to one side and barked in response. She smiled and scratched him behind his ears. He barked again in contentment.

A shadow blocked out the sun for a moment. "Lucky dog."

She looked up and saw Gregory standing before her. The smile vanished from her face. "I suppose Gran sent you to look for me."

"She was worried about you." He paused and looked out at the river. "And so was I."

"As you can see I'm perfectly fine. So off you go to make your report."

Gregory said nothing. He bent down and picked up a stick. "Go on, MacTavish. Go get it." He hurled it as far as he could. In an instant, the dog was off. "May I sit down?"

"It's a free country. You can do as you like. I was just leaving anyway."

She stood to go, but he pulled her back down beside him. "Oh, no, you don't. You're staying right here until you tell me whatever it is you have to tell me."

"You can't keep me here against my will." Her dark eyes flashed angrily. "Besides, I have nothing to tell you."

"Helen thinks you do."

She folded her arms over her chest and stuck out her chin. "Gran is mistaken."

"I don't think so."

Only the sound of the water rushing past could be heard for a long, uncomfortable moment. "Why do you care all of a sudden? *You* left *me* remember," she said defiantly.

He grabbed her arms roughly and turned her to face

him. "Listen, I do care what happens to you. There was a reason I left the way I did. I—"

"I don't give a bloody damn," she screamed at him. "You can go to the devil for all I care. It doesn't matter anymore." The tears streaming down her face blinded her. They tasted salty. "Nothing matters. No one can bring back the baby." She sucked in her breath sharply. The words had tumbled out before she realized what she was saying. Her hand flew to her mouth. "Oh, no. What have I done?"

He slackened his grip. "*Baby*? What baby?"

The lump in her throat ached and she shook her head from side to side, as if she could wipe away the last few minutes. But, of course, she couldn't. She stared down at her lap, where her hands twisted nervously. Finally, she looked into those brown eyes that she had loved so much once. "Our baby." It was barely more than a whisper.

Gregory was stunned. "What?"

She couldn't say anything else. It all came flooding back and her tongue was suddenly paralyzed.

He pulled her toward him and put his arms around her. "Tell me. *Please.*"

He felt warm, familiar. She nestled closer, her head resting against his chest. She could hear his heart beating. She began slowly. Her voice sounded odd, shaky, to her own ears. "I found out—" She cleared her throat and then, a bit stronger, said, "I found out the day you left. I was so excited. I came from the doctor's office straightaway. I didn't even ring Gran. I wanted to tell you first. It was unexpected, but I was certain you'd be pleased. After all, we were getting married the next day anyway. But when I let myself into your flat, I found Chief Inspector Burnell and Sergeant Finch there already. You were nowhere in sight. I couldn't understand what was happening. Very quietly, the chief inspector sat me down on the sofa and explained that Scotland Yard had long suspected you were a jewel thief. He went on to tell me in great detail of a string burglaries that curiously seemed to have occurred when you had recently been in the vicinity."

"I'll bet he did," Gregory murmured. "The police have nothing. Suspicions do not make a case."

She went on as if he hadn't spoken. "I couldn't comprehend any of it. I told the chief inspector he had the wrong man. I told him that my fiancé couldn't possibly be the man they were looking for. But he was certain. Dead certain. After that, there was nothing left to say. He had Sergeant Finch drive me home.

"Home to an empty house and my shattered dreams of happily ever after with a husband and a baby. It was unreal. I told myself that I'd wake in the morning to find that it had all been a nightmare. But it wasn't. In the cold gray light of morning—I had only managed an hour's fitful sleep, if that—I found that it was all true and I was alone. But I was simply being selfish because I wasn't really alone. I had a baby on the way and she needed me. So I pulled myself out of the morass of self-pity that I had fallen into and promised her that I would do everything humanly possible to make sure her life was happy.

"I called Gran and told her everything. Well, you know Gran. She ordered me to come down to Swaley at once and said that we'd make plans. I was not to worry. Everything would be all right. And it was, for a time. I stayed a few weeks with her and then I had to come back to London. I had an assignment. I couldn't bury myself down in Kent for the duration of my pregnancy. I had to earn a living for the baby. Nothing else mattered. Then, one night—" The words caught in her throat and she couldn't go on for a moment. "And then one night, I was walking home from the Underground and the most terrible cramps seemed to rip through my body. I only managed a few steps before I collapsed onto the pavement. I don't how long I was there. I remember being curled up in a ball because the pain was excruciating. I could feel myself starting to bleed. I must have passed out because when I awoke I was in hospital. The nurse told me that a passer-by had found me and called the ambulance. Apparently, he waited with me until the ambulance arrived. I asked her if the baby was all right, but all she told me was to rest. She said that the doctor would be by in the morning to see me. She must have given me something because no sooner had she left the room than my eyelids felt very heavy. I must have fallen asleep almost immediately.

"In the morning, the first person I saw when I opened my eyes was Gran. They must have called her. I was glad that she was there. The doctor came in shortly afterward. He asked me if I had any pain. I said that I did a little. He assured me it would go away within a few days. He said they would keep me in for observation for another day and then I could go home. 'But what about the baby?' I asked. That's when he told me that he was very sorry, I had miscarried. Just like that. He was very sorry. My precious, precious girl was gone and *he* was sorry. However, he told me not to worry. There was nothing to prevent me from having children in the future.

"*Future*? There was no future. My baby was gone. Nothing would ever bring her back. Nothing."

Gregory could feel her body shuddering. He tightened his arm around her and ventured carefully, "It was a girl?"

She didn't say anything for a moment and then finally, "The baby was only ten weeks when I lost her. It was too early to tell, but in here—" She placed her hand over her heart. "I know the baby was girl. I just know it."

"I see." He gently stroked her hair and kissed the top

of her head. "I would have liked a girl, or a boy for that matter. It wouldn't have made a difference."

She pulled away and looked into his eyes. "Yes. Yes, I think you would have. I know you would have. But we'll never know now, will we? Because the baby's gone."

He had to strain to hear these last words. She settled back against his chest. They were silent for a long time. Only the birds mocked them with their cheery song.

"For months afterward, I cried myself to sleep at night. Often, I woke up in the middle of the night and cried until my throat was sore with tears and my lungs ached from the sobs. At points during the day, I would suddenly find myself weeping uncontrollably. It was as if I was being ripped in two.

"Sometimes I thought I would suffocate from the pain and emptiness. The emptiness was worse. So much worse. There were times when I just wanted to die. Then I wouldn't have to feel anymore. No one could help me back then. Not even Gran. I was in a fog. I was like an automaton.

"I threw myself into my work. I became very good at pretending everything was all right. I had to. It was the only way to get through each day. Otherwise, I would have died. Gradually, though, I started to come out of the sea of pain. I started functioning again. I thought the emptiness would go away too, in time, but it never does. *Never*. It's always there. Oh, Gregory, I miss the baby so much. Not a day goes by that I don't think about her. What am I going to do?"

"Shh. It's all right." He rocked her back and forth and cooed softly into her hair. "We'll get through it to-gether. As it was meant to be."

At this, Emmeline shook herself free of his embrace and stumbled to her feet. "*Together*? There is no together

because there is no *us*. Not anymore. You saw to that
when you left."

"Emmy, please—"

"No, I told you all this because I was tired. Tired of
having to keep the truth all alone. And Gran was right—
as she always is—you had a right to know, but that's it.
There is nothing left between us. There hasn't been for a
very long time. The baby is gone."

Her throat ached from the tears that had lodged there
in a lump. She suddenly felt very cold. A thin wind made
her hug her jacket tightly around her body. The afternoon
sunshine had teased her into thinking that spring would
make an early appearance. But as dusk encroached,
plunging everything into deep shadow, winter reminded
her that it was still only February. Spring's warmth and
renewal seemed like such a long way off, as Emmeline
ran blindly back toward the house.

# CHAPTER 15

The rest of the weekend was largely uneventful. Emmeline took long walks on her own, only coming back to the house for meals. In the evenings, Helen and Gregory would play chess by the fire. Emmeline didn't join in their playful banter as they tried to best one another. She sat with a book in her lap, pretending to read. But the words became a blur on the page. In the end, she simply gave up and went to bed.

Since their talk by the river, Emmeline found that she had little to say to Gregory. It was almost as if he were a stranger. And yet, she was glad she had told him about the baby. The weight upon her heart was a bit lighter now, not gone—it could never go away—but lighter.

He dropped her off at her house at about noon on Monday and disappeared on some mysterious errand. He promised to return later in the evening. She sighed when she reached the top of the stairs and saw the yellow police tape across the bathroom door. An ugly reminder that Charles was gone. As she dropped her overnight bag in her bedroom, she made a mental note to ring Chief Inspector Burnell to find out if he had made any progress in the case and whether he was able to get in touch with his friend in the Venice police about Paolo Talamini's murder. She was certain that both crimes were connected to the elusive Sergei Konstantin. There were too many coincidences for her liking.

With her jaw set in that stubborn line that conveyed steely determination, she went downstairs into the living room and turned on her laptop. She started going through the pile of mail on the corner of the desk. Bill, bill, rubbish, bill.

She stopped. She'd get to the rest of it later. Her mind was too preoccupied with Charles at the moment. She reached over for some notes and decided to start her research by talking to Philip.

She snatched up the phone and dialed his number. It rang twice. Then, the clipped, plumy voice of Pamela, Philip's secretary, came on the line. "Hello, Mr. Acheson's office."

"Hello, Pamela. This is Emmeline Kirby, may I speak to Philip?"

"Oh, hello, Miss Kirby. I'm afraid that Mr. Acheson is in conference just at the moment. May I take a message and he'll ring you back later?"

"Actually, I'd like to come by and see him about a story I'm working on. Is he free at all this afternoon?"

"Let me check his diary. He's been rather busy lately and sometimes he neglects to inform me about meetings he's arranged on his own."

Emmeline could hear the faintly disapproving tone as the secretary spoke these last words and she had to stifle a giggle.

"You're in luck. He's free this afternoon at three-thirty. Would that suit you?"

"Admirably, Pamela. Thanks very much."

"You're welcome, Miss Kirby. I'll let Mr. Acheson know."

Emmeline had arrived at the Foreign Office at precisely three-thirty, but Philip kept her cooling her heels for a half-hour.

"I'm terribly sorry, Miss Kirby. I'm certain Mr. Acheson will be with you presently. He had to take an unexpected call. May I get you a coffee, while you wait?"

"No thank you, Pamela. I'm fine."

"In that case then, I hope you don't mind if I return to my work."

"No, you carry on."

The secretary gave her a weak smile, placed her glasses firmly back on the bridge of her pert little nose, and turned her attention once more to her computer monitor.

Ten minutes later, Philip finally emerged. "Emmeline, I'm so sorry to have kept you waiting."

She stood and he gave her a peck on the cheek. "I was beginning to think that I would never be granted an audience with the great Philip Acheson."

"Please come in." He took her by the elbow and ushered her into his office. Over his shoulder, he said, "Hold all my calls, Pamela, except if it's the PM again."

"Of course, Mr. Acheson."

Once Philip was settled behind his desk, Emmeline had an opportunity to study him little better. She hadn't seen him for about three months. He looked a bit harried today, but overall he was his usual cool, professional self. His blond hair fell diagonally into place across his broad forehead and his bright blue eyes held a look of excitement.

"Maggie and I were just talking about you the other evening. We never seem to see you anymore. The boys miss their Auntie Emmeline terribly. They ask after you all the time. You must ring Maggie and arrange to come over for dinner one evening soon."

"Yes, I promise I will. How are the twins? I do miss

them. They're growing so fast. They must be what? Four by now?"

"The little devils just turned five and they're becoming more mischievous by the day. I blame Maggie, but my mother says that they're mirror images of me as a boy. What a terror I must have been." He rolled his eyes.

She laughed. "You know how much I love chatting about the twins, but I came here for another reason. I'm working on a story. Actually, I'm picking up where Charles left off."

The smile vanished from Philip's face and his brow furrowed. "Yes, I heard about Charles. In fact, a Chief Inspector Burnell wants to interview me tomorrow morning. It's all rather unpleasant. I did warn Charles to back off, but he wouldn't listen. You know how obsessed he could get when he was on a story."

"His tenacity was what made him so good at his job. Knowing the right questions to ask and following the trail until he found the pot of gold."

"But it wasn't a pot of gold this time, was it? He asked the wrong question and paid for it with his life."

"Yes," she mumbled. Everything was still very raw. "That's why I intend to see the story through to the end. Charles told me he came to see you about a month ago. Did he tell you what he was working on?"

Philip didn't answer immediately. Instead, he straightened some papers on his desk that didn't need straightening.

"Yes, he did tell me his theory about this phantom Sergei Konstantin," he said.

"And what did you think?"

"The same as I do now. That he was utterly barmy. A Russian spy *here*? Quite impossible. Everyone is thoroughly vetted."

"It's not that far-fetched a theory, Philip. Don't you

think you're being a little naïve? After all, remember Philby, Burgess, and Maclean."

"That was during the height of the Cold War and they were British. Not Russian sleepers. The Cold War is over, if you hadn't heard."

"I don't think Mr. Putin would agree with you. Plus, look at the group of sleepers he had working in America. No one would have guessed that they were Russians, let alone spies. But getting back to Charles, I trust his instincts. He obviously rattled someone. Besides, he told me that he had seen the spy, quite by chance, when he came here to meet you for dinner. He must have told you *something*."

"Quite frankly, the last time I saw Charles, he was not very coherent. You know how he was when he was in his cups. If he said anything significant, I don't remember. Perhaps, I should have paid more attention."

"But—" She was cut off by the shrill ringing of the telephone.

"Excuse me, but that must be the PM again. I'm afraid I will have to take this call. Lovely to see you, Emmeline. Remember to ring Maggie soon."

"But—Yes, I will." She stood and walked out of the office, dazed by the entire interview and how she had been dismissed so unceremoniously. She was already forgotten. Philip was talking on the phone before she had even closed the door. She said goodbye to Pamela and left. Her thoughts were awhirl as she walked down the corridor. Her heels clicked loudly against the marble floor. What disturbed her the most was that Philip had lied to her. Why? What did he have to hide? Or who was he protecting?

She was mulling over the interview, when she heard someone calling her name. "Emmeline? Emmeline? Wait a moment."

She turned around to find herself face to face with Giles Hayden, resplendent in a well-cut charcoal suit, crisp white shirt, and red silk tie. "Giles, what an unexpected surprise."

He shook her outstretched hand. "Yes, lovely to see you, too. When did you get back from your grandmother's?"

"Oh, just today. Gregory dropped me off at the house at about noon."

"Longdon? I see." He looked up and down the corridor. "Not with you now, is he?"

"No, he had some things he had to take care of."

Hayden's face broke out in a wide grin that touched his cool green-gray eyes. "Splendid, splendid. So what brings you here to the Foreign Office? Dare I hope you came in search of me?"

Emmeline blushed and looked down at the marble floor. "No, I'm afraid not. I came to see Philip Acheson. He and his wife are old friends. Do you know Philip?"

"We have a nodding acquaintance. We're in different departments, though. I'm in UK Trade & Investment. We focus on helping British companies in international markets and help foreign companies to invest in the UK."

"I see." She frowned as she thought of Philip again.

"Forgive me, Emmeline, but you look preoccupied. Is everything all right?"

"Yes. No. Oh, it doesn't matter. It's a story I'm working on and some of the pieces do not seem to fit together."

"Anything I can help you with? I'm a good listener. You can bounce ideas off me."

She chuckled. "Haven't we had this discussion already? No, it's something I'll have to work out on my own. Thanks for the offer." She checked her watch. It was already five-thirty. Gregory would likely be on his way back to the house. "Giles, I'm afraid I must dash."

He put his hand on her arm. "So soon? Look, I can wrap things up in about half an hour. Why don't you join me for dinner? Perhaps, I can cheer you up. Remember, you promised that once we were back in London you'd have dinner with me."

"I did, didn't I? I haven't forgotten. It's just impossible tonight."

"All right. How about tomorrow?"

Emmeline was still reeling from Charles's death and her confession to Gregory about the baby, and she didn't really feel like going out to dinner with this man. However, she couldn't put him off any longer, and he was nice, after all. So, in the end, she acquiesced. "Tomorrow would be fine." Who knew? Perhaps she could wheedle some information out of him about Sergei Konstantin.

"Brilliant. I'll collect you at eight."

"Eight it is, then. Do you have the address?"

"Yes, thanks. Until tomorrow." Hayden watched her walk toward the grand staircase. She turned back once and he gave a little wave.

*ↄↄↄↄ*

While Emmeline was at the Foreign Office, Gregory had been across the river in Lambeth, searching Charles's flat. No one noticed him entering or leaving the building. Unfortunately, he had come away empty-handed. If Latimer *had* hidden anything there, either his killer or the police had it now. Grimly, he thought it was probably the killer. Much as he'd disliked Charles, Gregory admired his journalistic skills and was certain he would not have gone after Sergei Konstantin if he didn't have some sort of evidence. But what was it?

Charles must somehow have managed to get it from

Talamini after he was attacked and went into hiding.

Gregory ran a hand through his wavy hair in frustration. Damn and blast. This was becoming more complicated by the moment and Emmeline was right in the middle of it. She was so blinded by her loyalty to Latimer that she was oblivious to the trap she was walking into. And trap he was certain it was. He didn't like it one bit. It felt like this Sergei Konstantin knew their every move even before they made it. As if they were all puppets on a string and he was just biding his time.

Gregory watched as the wind sent the clouds scudding across the sky, obliterating the sun. Any minute now it would probably start raining. He walked faster toward his car. Just as he turned the key in the Jaguar's ignition, the first raindrops hit the windscreen.

A silver Audi, parked up the block, pulled away from the curb thirty seconds after Gregory did.

The driver punched a number into his mobile as he kept a safe distance behind Gregory. "Longdon's just left Latimer's flat. It doesn't look as if he's found anything."

"Damn," the voice on the other end said. "That means the police have it or the girl does. Who's watching her?"

"Team Two. They should be checking in in about five minutes."

"What about the house?"

"There's a team on it round the clock. It's been quiet all day."

"All right. Stick with Longdon. Don't let him out of your sight and tell me who he meets."

"I'll ring you back once I've spoken to Team Two." He severed the connection, as he followed Gregory across Westminster Bridge and along Victoria Embankment.

Gregory made a left onto Lancaster Place and

crossed the Strand. He parked near the Covent Garden Underground station. He checked the rearview mirror to see if his friend in the silver Audi was still with him. He first caught sight of him when he was on Victoria Embankment. At first, he wasn't sure that he was being followed. Now he was.

"Time to have a little fun, old chum," Gregory said to his reflection.

He got out of the car, locked it, and quickly headed toward the Covent Garden Market. Out of the corner of his eye, he saw that his shadow was following him.

As it was Monday, the majority of the stalls displayed antiques. Gregory jostled with tourists and some London natives as he slowly wended his way through the crowds. In the distance, he could see little a group had gathered in a semi-circle to watch a magician performing in the main square. He stopped at one stall and pretended to be interested in a carved ivory pipe. As he examined it and asked a few desultory questions of the owner, Gregory caught a glimpse of his friend ducking into a doorway. He chuckled to himself.

"Well, sir? That'll be £100," the woman prompted, hoping to make the sale.

"Sorry, love. On second thought, I don't think it is to my uncle's taste, after all," he said with one of his most charming smiles, which generally tended to melt the hearts of even the stoniest of females.

And so it was in this case, too. The woman discreetly patted her graying hair into place and returned his smile. "Perhaps if you tell me what sort of man your uncle is I can suggest something else."

"I'm afraid not. He's a crusty old bird. There's no pleasing him. Thanks again. Must dash." He bestowed another smile upon her and hurried off before she could waylay him any further.

The man was still following him. However, Gregory got a better look at him as he ducked around the corner of the building and allowed the man pass into the square. He was tall—at least a couple of inches taller than Gregory—and lean. His leather jacket was molded to his muscular build and, when he moved a certain way, was just tight enough to reveal that he was carrying a gun. Gregory watched as the man scanned the crowd with a professional's practiced eye. The blond head turned right and left in a slow, deliberate arc.

"Well, well," Gregory murmured. "The plot thickens. And who pray tell do you work for?"

At one point, it looked as if the man was staring directly at him. Gregory flattened himself against the building, but he realized that the man was looking at a spot just past his left shoulder. He stood still and waited. The man received a call on his mobile. It must have been a very heated conversation because even from this distance, Gregory could see the man scowling. After another minute, he snapped his mobile shut and ran a hand angrily through his wavy hair. Presently, a younger man joined him. They spoke briefly. The younger man shook his head. They made a wide loop around the square together. When they came up empty-handed, they abandoned their search and walked toward a dark blue Opel that was parked on a side street near the market.

It started to rain again. The blond man pulled up the collar of his jacket as he leaned on the window and spoke to the driver. The younger man slipped into the passenger seat. The driver nodded and started the engine. The blond man watched as the car pulled away. He made another call on his mobile and then hurriedly walked in the opposite direction. Gregory assumed that he was going back to collect the silver Audi. He waited another minute to make certain that his blond friend was gone.

Suddenly, he felt the cold, hard muzzle of a gun pressed to the base of his head. "Don't turn around, Mr. Longdon," a Russian voice whispered in his ear. "I assure you I will not hesitate to shoot you."

The sound of the safety catch being uncocked reverberated heavily in the space between them.

"You seem to have me at a disadvantage, Comrade Konstantin."

Gregory felt the man's warm breath upon his ear as he laughed harshly. "You're a clever man, Mr. Longdon, but you are mistaken in this case. I am *not* Sergei Konstantin."

"Then who are you and what do you want?"

"Let's just say that I'm a friendly messenger with a warning for you and Miss Kirby to stay out of things that do not concern you."

"Or else?"

"'Or else,' Mr. Longdon?"

"Yes, you know, in the movies whenever someone issues a warning like that it is always punctuated with an 'or else.' Otherwise, you simply cannot take the person seriously."

A sharp blow was administered to his kidney. Gregory fell to his knees as the pain seemed to radiate through his body.

"I hope that will teach you not to be so flippant, Mr. Longdon. Next time, I will not be so nice."

"I'll keep that in mind. I'd hate to see you when you're having a really bad day," Gregory said through clenched teeth. He could barely breathe.

"Still joking, Mr. Longdon? I don't think you will find things so amusing when Miss Kirby is found dead in some alley because she stuck her nose in where it didn't belong."

At this, Gregory tried to scramble to his feet, but he

was in too much pain and the man was too quick. The butt of the gun caught him in the right temple.

Before he passed out, Gregory had a brief glimpse of his assailant hovering above him. Gray curly hair, eyes like two coals burning in the depths of Hell, and a scar over the left eyebrow. Anatol Zobrinsky.

# CHAPTER 16

Chief Inspector Burnell tapped his fingers on his knee. He was fast losing his patience. He and Sergeant Finch had been waiting to speak with Philip for over an hour.

Pamela stopped typing and looked up from her computer monitor. She looped a long chestnut strand of hair behind her ear. "May get you and the sergeant another cup of coffee?"

"No, thank you, Ms. Marsh. I don't suppose you could go and see what is keeping Mr. Acheson. I don't think he realizes that we're here on official business. We're conducting a murder inquiry into the death of the BBC journalist Charles Latimer, a good friend of his, I believe."

Pamela sat up straighter in her chair and drew her shoulders back. "Chief Inspector Burnell, I quite assure you that Mr. Acheson understands the gravity of the situation. His job requires delicacy and diplomacy. When the prime minister calls, Mr. Acheson must attend, no matter the time of day or night. Therefore, the answer to your question is no. I cannot interrupt Mr. Acheson," she said with great superiority.

"Well, that put me in my place," Burnell murmured under his breath.

Sergeant Finch stifled a smile.

"If you'd prefer to leave a message, I'll see that Mr. Acheson gets it," she said. "Otherwise, my only other suggestion is to reschedule your appointment for another day."

"No, we'll stay, even if we have to wait here all day."

"As you wish. That's certainly your prerogative."

"Yes, it is, Miss Bossy Knickers," the chief inspector whispered out of the corner of his mouth, but aloud he said, "Thank you, Ms. Marsh."

She bestowed a frigid smile upon them and turned her attention back to her work. Sergeant Finch had to cough to cover the laughter bubbling in his throat.

After another quarter of an hour had passed, the phone buzzed on Pamela's desk. "Yes, of course, Mr. Acheson." She placed the receiver back in its cradle. "Mr. Acheson will see you now."

"Splendid, Ms. Marsh," Burnell oozed sweetly as he and Finch stood.

Pamela tapped lightly on the door to Philip's office. A muffled "Come in" was heard from the inner sanctum. She opened the door and allowed the two policemen to enter. "Chief Inspector Burnell and Sergeant Finch, Mr. Acheson."

"Thanks, Pamela. Please hold all my calls for the next hour."

"Yes, Mr. Acheson." She softly closed the door behind them.

Philip stood and extended a hand to both of them. He had a strong grip. "Chief Inspector, Sergeant, I'm pleased to meet you. I must apologize for keeping you waiting for so long. I'm afraid there's rather a lot going on just at the moment. Do sit down."

Once they were all settled, Finch took out his note-book and sat back to observe.

"Thank you, Mr. Acheson," Burnell said. "I realize that you're an extremely busy man and I appreciate you seeing us at such short notice. However, you must understand that this is a murder investigation. Naturally, we must look into every lead."

"Quite, quite. What can I do for you?" Philip leaned forward on his elbows and clasped his elegant hands together. He was the very picture of earnest solicitude.

Burnell cleared his throat and hesitated a minute to study him more closely. Not a single blond hair was out of place and his cool blue eyes were devoid of any expression. The chief inspector took an instant dislike to Acheson. Something about the man lacked sincerity. He was certain the man would make a good poker player. One could almost hear the wheels turning inside his head, plotting his next move. Although there was no outward sign, Burnell sensed that Acheson was on the defensive. Now, why was that? Burnell asked himself.

"Mr. Acheson, as I explained to you on the phone yesterday, we are investigating the murder of Charles Latimer. I understand from Miss Kirby that you were friends."

"Yes, that's correct, Chief Inspector. Charles and I had known each other for fifteen years." Acheson glanced over at Finch jotting something in his notebook and then turned his attention back to Burnell. "Shocking business. The last time I saw Charles, I told that him that he most likely had gotten the wrong end of the stick. But you know what journalists are like, always obsessed with getting a scoop."

"I see." Burnell sat back in his chair and crossed one leg over the other. "So you don't think there is any merit in Latimer's theory that a Russian spy named Sergei

Konstantin is running around here—" He waved his hand
in the air. "—in the Foreign Office."

Acheson chuckled, revealing a row of perfectly
straight white teeth. "Good God, no, Chief Inspector. As I
told Emmeline, when I saw Charles he appeared to be
more than a little drunk and not very coherent."

"Did he like to drink?"

"Yes, but I wouldn't want you to think that he was
an alcoholic or anything like that. That was definitely not
the case. He was simply fond of a drink or two, or three."

"Hmm. Funny, Miss Kirby seems to believe that Latimer was on to something."

"Emmeline tends to over exaggerate things. Allows
her friendships to cloud her judgment sometimes."

"Indeed? I'm slightly acquainted with Miss Kirby
and she doesn't strike me as flighty at all. Far from it. She
exhibits an exceptional perspicacity and insight into human nature. I don't think that she would pursue this story
if she didn't have something solid to go on."

"Chief Inspector, I didn't mean to imply—"

"As for Latimer." Burnell cut Acheson off. "I grant
you that he was reckless and arrogant, but he was a damn
fine investigative journalist—just like Miss Kirby, I
might add—and, as such, he was meticulous about getting his facts straight."

Silence fell between them as Burnell's gaze impaled
Acheson's darker one. The tension hovering in the small
space between the two men was palpable.

Acheson smiled. "Yes, of course, you're right, Chief
Inspector. I'm friends with both Emmeline and Charles—
well, was with Charles. However, journalists are a different breed from you and me. They see things differently,
react differently to certain situations. I'm sure Emmeline
cannot be completely objective after having discovered

Charles's body in her home. That would be enough to shake anyone."

It was Burnell's turn to smile. He leaned forward and placed his elbows on the desk. "Yes, it is rather disturbing to find a dead body. But, tell me, Mr. Acheson, how did you know Mr. Latimer was found in Miss Kirby's home? I did not mention it when we spoke on the phone."

"I must have seen it in the papers yesterday."

"We haven't released the story to the press yet. We're trying to conduct our preliminary inquiries as quietly as possible, in view of both Mr. Latimer's and Miss Kirby's prominence."

"I suppose it must have been Emmeline. She came to see me yesterday afternoon to pick my brain about this 'story,'" Acheson said, almost smugly, as he sat back in his chair.

"I see."

"Were there any other questions you had, Chief Inspector Burnell? Only I have a meeting with the prime minister in…" He eased the cuff of his blue shirt from his wrist and glanced at his watch. "…just under half an hour. So if that's all, there are a few things I must attend to before the meeting."

"No, I don't have any other questions—"

"Good. I'll show you both out." Acheson stood and waved an arm toward the door.

"I don't have any other questions—for the moment—Mr. Acheson. But we may return another time, as the case progresses and new evidence comes to light, or if we discover there were inconsistencies with anything you've told us."

Acheson stopped with his hand on the doorknob. He was a couple of inches taller than Burnell and looked down at him. "Of course, Chief Inspector. Anytime. Give Pamela a ring and she'll arrange a meeting." He extended a hand to the two policemen. For the briefest instant, annoyance flashed into Acheson's deep blue eyes and then it was gone as quickly as it had appeared.

"Thank you for your time, Mr. Acheson," Burnell said.

The smile pasted onto Philip's lips vanished the minute the door closed behind the two policemen. He shoved his hands into his pockets and paced back and forth. Soon, he came to a decision. He walked over to the desk and dialed a number.

Philip waited several seconds. "Hello, Richard. It's Philip Acheson. Yes, it has been a long time. I hope Cynthia is well. Good, good. I was wondering if you could join me for lunch today. There was something I want to discuss with you."

"Certainly. I'd be delighted."

"You can. Splendid. Shall we say twelve-thirty at Simpson's?"

"That's fine."

"Good. I look forward to seeing you then."

He returned the receiver to the cradle and leaned back in his chair, steepling his fingers together over his stomach as a grin that would have rivaled the Cheshire Cat stole over his face.

*୧୬୧୬*

Burnell said nothing as they left the elegant Italianate building with its Corinthian columns, niches, and statues designed by architect Sir George Gilbert Scott in the late 1800s. He needed to clear his head. They turned right and walked to the end of King Charles Street. They hurried across Horse Guards Road and into St. James's Park. Sergeant Finch knew the chief inspector well enough not to attempt to speak to him. They stopped on the little bridge and watched as a couple of ducks sent ripples across the surface of the lake as they gracefully skimmed through the water.

"Finch," Burnell said at last.

"Yes, sir?"

"What did you make of all that?"

"As a keen observer of human nature, I'd say that he knows a great deal more than he's letting on."

"Do you, now?" The chief inspector said as he stroked his beard reflectively.

"Yes, sir."

"You're a smart lad, then, because if anyone was lying through his teeth, it was our Mr. Acheson. I don't know what he's hiding, but I intend to find out."

"Where shall we start?"

"I want you to go back to the Yard to do a bit of digging. I want know everything there is to know on Philip Acheson."

"Right. What will you be doing, sir?"

Burnell turned his pale gaze on the sergeant. "I'm going back to the source of this entire mess. I want you to drop me off at Latimer's flat. He must have left some clue as to this Sergei Konstantin's identity."

"But what, sir? We've gone over every inch of that flat. Maybe the killer took whatever it was."

"My instincts tell me that there must be something. Latimer was no fool."

"What about Miss Kirby and Longdon? Perhaps they've discovered something."

"I was planning to speak with Miss Kirby again later on this afternoon. That reminds me, when you get back to the Yard check to see if anything has come in from Venice about Paolo Talamini's murder."

"So you agree with Miss Kirby that it *was* connected?"

"Don't you? She's right. There are too many coincidences. I've got this sinking feeling in the pit of my
stomach that we're wasting precious time. I'm afraid that
if we don't find Sergei Konstantin soon, we're going
have another body on our hands. And I pray it won't be
Emmeline Kirby's. She doesn't know it, but I'm certain
she holds the key."

# CHAPTER 17

Chief Inspector Burnell was already annoyed when he returned to the Yard that afternoon. He had gone over every nook and cranny in Latimer's flat and found nothing. Then John Meadows, the medical examiner, had called to let him know his preliminary findings indicated that Latimer had suffered a sharp blow to the temple first, which likely rendered him unconscious and therefore unable to fight back when he was placed in the bathtub. He was drowned. Bloody help that was. They had already surmised as much. Again, they had hit a dead end. The lift doors opened and the first person Burnell saw was Superintendent Fenton's secretary, Sally Harper.

"The superintendent would like a word, Chief Inspector Burnell."

"What now? I've just got back to the office. I must go over several things with Sergeant Finch. We're working on the Charles Latimer murder. Tell Superintendent Fenton I'll pop over in about an hour."

"I'm afraid that won't do, Chief Inspector. The superintendent said he wanted to see the minute you returned."

Burnell sighed and ran a hand through his thinning hair. "Oh, very well. Lead the way, Sally." He followed her to her desk.

"One moment, please. Let me ring to see if it's all right for you to go through."

"You just said that he wanted to see me *immediately*."

"Please, Chief Inspector, do not take that tone with me." She turned her back on him and reached for the phone.

Burnell gritted his teeth and shoved his fists deep into his pockets. He was afraid he would really lose his temper if he uttered another word to this overbearing woman.

Sally rang off. "Superintendent Fenton will see you now."

"Thank you. I can't tell you what a pleasure it has been seeing you, Sally. It brightened my whole day."

She ignored the sarcasm in his voice and flashed a phony smile at him.

He knocked once and then turned the doorknob.

"Come in" was the response. "Ah, Burnell, there you are. Good of you to drop by."

As if he had a choice. "Yes, sir. Sally said you wanted to see me."

"Indeed, indeed. Do sit down."

Burnell did as he was bid and surveyed his superior across the desk. Fenton, a man in his late fifties with salt-and-pepper hair and light brown eyes, shuffled a few files and cleared his throat.

The chief inspector waited.

"Burnell, what progress have you made on the Latimer case?"

"Well, sir, Sergeant Finch and I are following several leads. We believe Latimer was killed because he found evidence that a Russian spy, a Sergei Konstantin, was working at the Foreign Office in a fairly high capacity."

"Really? What evidence do you have? Sounds like something out of John Le Carré to me." He chuckled. "So who is this…"

"Sergei Konstantin, sir. We don't know yet."

"You don't know? You don't *know*? Then, why are you wasting time and police resources?"

Burnell's knuckles showed white underneath the desk. "I interviewed Emmeline Kirby who, as you know, is a well-respected investigative journalist in her own right and was a close friend of Latimer's. Apparently, he sought her help with the story he was working on when they were in Venice last week."

"Did he tell her who this *supposed* Russian spy is?"

Burnell didn't like the superintendent's dismissive tone. "No, but—"

"No, of course, not. You know why, Burnell? Because there is no spy. It was just two journalists trying for a bit of sensationalism."

"Sir, I don't think—"

"Frankly, in my opinion, Miss Kirby sounds like a very high-strung young woman."

"Sir, I assure you that is far from the truth."

"In any event, it's neither here nor there. You're off the case. Turn over all your files and notes to Inspector Williams at once."

Burnell stood up so quickly that he nearly knocked over his chair. "Superintendent Fenton, respectfully, I think such action is uncalled for."

The superintendent raised a gray eyebrow in challenge. "Are you questioning my judgment, Burnell?"

"No, sir, but—"

"Good. That's it, then. I'm sure you have other cases that require your attention. You may go now. Make sure you close the door on your way out."

They stared at one another for a minute in silence.

Burnell's eyes dripped icy daggers as he impaled his superior's brown gaze. "Yes, sir."

The chief inspector slammed the door and received a little satisfaction when he heard it rattle on its hinges. He was still muttering under his breath when he ran into Finch in the corridor. "Sir?"

"What is it?" Burnell snapped and then more gently said, "Sorry, Finch. Superintendent Richard bloody Fenton has just taken us off the Latimer case. We're to turn over everything to Inspector Williams immediately."

"Why?"

"I don't know, do I? But I think that someone doesn't like the questions we've been asking and has put pressure on our *dear* superintendent. Anyway, what was it that you wanted to see me about?"

"I have that information you wanted on Philip Acheson."

Burnell pulled him aside and took the file from him. "Privileged background. Eton. Read political science at Oxford. Got a double first," he murmured as he skimmed Acheson's background. "Speaks German, French, Italian, Spanish, and Russian fluently. Made a socially adept marriage. Went on to work for the Foreign Office where he specializes in—" He flipped over the page. "Where's the rest of it?"

"That's it, sir. The rest of his file was marked confidential."

Burnell leaned his elbow against the wall. "Confidential? Of course, now everything is starting to become clear."

"I'm not following you, sir."

"It was something Superintendent Fenton said about Emmeline Kirby. He called her 'a very high-strung young woman.' Acheson used almost the same words when we spoke to him this morning."

"You think that he had us taken off the case?"

"I would be willing to bet everything I have that this is Acheson's doing. And, if I'm not mistaken, Acheson's best friend is Peter Rimmington."

"You don't mean—"

"Yes, Superintendent Fenton's son-in-law."

"Chief Inspector Burnell?" Sergeant Marsden called from down the corridor, curtailing any further speculation on Philip Acheson.

Burnell quickly slapped the file shut and shoved it behind his back. "Yes, what is it, Marsden?" he asked wearily.

"Inspector Williams would like to see you about the Latimer case. Please bring him all the files at once."

"Tell him I'm busy at the moment."

Marsden, who was Williams's sergeant, was at his elbow now. "I'm afraid that Inspector Williams is rather inundated and does not have the leisure to wait upon you."

Burnell turned red in the face, but managed to keep his tone level. "That's *sir* to you. Keep in mind that you are speaking to a superior officer and, therefore, you should learn some respect before you find yourself back in uniform walking a beat." He took a step closer to Marsden. It had become deathly quiet in the corridor. Everyone was listening to their exchange. "Do we understand each other?"

The smirk vanished from Marsden's face. His eyes flicked briefly around the corridor, where he did not encounter any sympathetic glances in return. He swallowed hard. "Yes, *sir*."

"Good. Tell Williams that I'll see him at *my* convenience, which does not happen to be at the moment. Finch will get him the files by tomorrow morning."

"Yes, sir." Marsden quickly disappeared.

"Bloody fool," Burnell muttered.

Finch attempted to hide a smile, but failed.

A smile flashed for a second across Burnell's lips. "Now, about this—" He waved the folder in front of him. "See if, through your sources, you can find out what's in the 'confidential' bit of Acheson's file."

"I'll get on it straightaway, sir."

Burnell put a restraining hand on the sergeant's arm. "But quietly, Finch. We're dealing with someone very high up, who likes playing games. I don't like games. Someone always ends up getting hurt."

"Don't worry, sir. I'll watch my step."

"Good lad."

ențeo

Burnell had his hands in his pockets and was still mulling over these new developments when he entered his office. He looked up to find Gregory sitting in his chair with his feet propped up on the desk.

"Who let you in here?"

"Oliver, old chap, it's lovely to see you again, too. I await our every meeting with bated breath. Truly, I do."

"Get out of my chair." The chief inspector slapped Gregory's feet off the desk. "Longdon, I'm in no mood for your antics today. What do you want?"

Unhurriedly, Gregory ceded the chair to Burnell with a wide grin and slight bow. "Please, Oliver, do sit down. You look a bit tired. It must be the stress of the job."

As he took the chair on the other side of the desk, the chief inspector noticed his bruised face. "You look awful. What happened to you? Did a jealous husband corner you in some alley?"

"Funny you should ask me that, Oliver."

"Chief Inspector Burnell."

"If you will insist, Chief Inspector Burnell. Although I must say, there shouldn't be such formalities between old friends."

"Longdon, we are not, nor will we ever be, friends. Now stop wasting my time and tell me what you're doing here."

"As you've already remarked with your professional eye, yesterday my face had a bit of a contretemps with the butt of a gun. Alas, my face was the loser. I was also on the receiving end of some very nasty threats."

"What kind of threats?"

"It was something to the effect that Emmeline and I should keep our noses out of the Latimer affair or we might find ourselves in the same predicament. Oliver, as a gentleman, I'm sure you'll appreciate the fact that it is not very sporting to threaten a lady."

Burnell leaned across the desk. "Who issued these threats?"

Gregory abandoned his glib demeanor. "I had never seen him before, but from the thick Russian accent and Emmeline's description, I'm certain it was none other than our friend Anatol Zobrinsky."

The chief inspector said nothing. He sat back in his chair and pursed his lips. "I was taken off the case today. It came from the top."

"Now that's interesting," Gregory mused. "I think we're getting too close for someone's comfort."

"'We,' Longdon? There is no *we*."

"Who's been assigned to the case?"

"Inspector Williams."

Gregory permitted himself a chuckle. "Of course, they want to ensure that it's never solved."

Burnell despised Gregory, but in this instance he agreed with him. He was still seething about the way Superintendent Fenton had spoken to him.

"Williams will make a hash of the whole thing."

"There's nothing I can do about it. I'm off the case."

"Mmm. I see." Gregory leaned back and laced his fingers behind his head. "Oliver, you cannot stand by idly. Emmeline is determined to find Latimer's killer and to unmask Sergei Konstantin. At the same time, someone is just as determined to see that she doesn't succeed. I don't think either of us wants to wake up one morning and find her dead. Whatever you may think of me, I'm urging you to please continue with this case. For Emmeline's sake. I know she has a great deal of respect for you." They eyed other in silence.

"I am officially off the case." Burnell held up a hand to forestall any argument. "Therefore, I cannot oblige your request, Longdon. However, *unofficially* I already have Sergeant Finch looking into something."

Gregory flashed him a broad smile and, in that second, Burnell understood the power of this man's charm. Gregory extended one of his elegant hands across the desk. "Thank you, Oliver."

"Chief Inspector Burnell," he said, but he took the hand anyway.

"Of course, *Chief Inspector Burnell*. What can I do to assist?"

"Nothing."

"I have a vested interested in this matter."

"I may be breaking the rules by pursuing the case—although you did not hear that from me—but I haven't lost all my senses. I draw the line at consulting with someone who has criminal tendencies. As a result, I must *officially* decline any assistance from you."

Gregory smiled again. They understood each other completely. Never in his wildest dreams had Burnell ever imagined that he would be conspiring with a thief to find a murderer and spy.

# CHAPTER 18

Emmeline had spent the entire morning doing research and making calls to some sources. She also skimmed through Charles's book on the KGB, hoping that it might elicit some clue. The book caused a worldwide stir when it was published last year. Charles must have come across Sergei Konstantin when he was writing the book. But how did Paolo Talamini come into the picture? And Philip's behavior yesterday disturbed her. Why had he lied to her? She didn't have any answers, only more questions.

Although she had tried to put on a brave face, she was becoming frightened. She shuddered at the memory of Charles's dead body and finding Gregory on her doorstep last night after he had been attacked in Covent Garden. He had refused to go to hospital, so she had insisted that he stay the night—in the guest room, of course. She couldn't allow him to wander about the streets, not in his condition.

He could have had a concussion—probably did—although it would take a great deal to crack his thick skull. However, she admitted that, despite the bruising, he looked decidedly like his usual self when he left the house this morning.

She glanced at the clock. It was four-thirty. Where

*was* he? He hadn't called at all. She bit her lip and hoped nothing else had happened to him.

Her eyes hurt from staring at her laptop and her neck was stiff. She got up and stretched. She went into the kitchen and put a kettle on for a cup of tea.

The shrill peal of the telephone made her jump. Emmeline lunged for it. *Oh, please*, she thought, *please let him be all right.* "Hello? *Gregory?*" Her breathing was coming fast now.

There was a pause before a familiar voice on the other end responded. "Emmeline? It's Giles Hayden. Are you all right?"

She slumped back against the counter, chiding herself for panicking. She was just being silly. Gregory was a grown man. Of course, he could take care of himself. Besides, she reminded herself, it was no longer *her* concern what trouble befell him. "Hello, Giles. Yes, I'm fine. I was just expecting another call."

"Oh, good. You sounded a bit odd. That's all."

"As I said, nothing to worry about. Now to what do I owe this call?"

"I just wanted to confirm our dinner plans for this evening. I'll collect you at eight. All right? I know a lovely little Italian restaurant near Leicester Square."

"Great. I'll see you at eight. Bye." She rang off.

The kettle demanded her attention by whistling loudly. She turned off the gas and splashed some hot water into the pot to warm it. Then she spooned two scoops of fragrant tea from a tin and drowned it with the still-bubbling water. She watched the steam rising silently. When she was satisfied that it had brewed sufficiently, she poured some into her cup. She took a careful sip, but managed to burn her tongue anyway. That just capped off a thoroughly unproductive day. She still had a couple of hours. Enough time to do a little more digging, before she had to shower and change. She would also try to wheedle some information out of Giles at dinner.

Emmeline took her tea into the living room. She pulled open the secretary desk to get her address book. She flipped through the Fs until she found Vittorio's name. She punched in his number and waited. Two rings.

"*Pronto. Franzetti. Qui parla?*"

"Hello, Vittorio. It's Emmeline."

"*Ciao, bella.* How are you, *cara?* I heard about Charles."

This surprised her. "How did you hear about Charles? Scotland Yard has kept a news blackout on the story."

"*Allora,* you know how it is in the newspaper business, Emmeline. Everyone knows what everyone else is doing. It is a small world. Nothing is secret."

"Yes," she said distractedly. "You're right. It is a small world. Well, if you know, the police will have to hold some sort of press conference soon. Chief Inspector Burnell will have no choice."

"*Cara,* how are you doing? I know you were close to Charles."

"Oh, Vittorio, it's been horrible." A tear slowly trickled down each cheek and her throat constricted. "I found him. He was—They—" She swallowed hard, trying to regain her composure. "They knocked him unconscious and then drowned him in my bathtub."

"*Dio mio,* Emmeline. I did not realize that Charles was killed in your home."

She nodded at the phone, unable to speak for a minute. "Yes," she finally whispered. "He was like an uncle to me. And he was a superb journalist. He taught me so much. So much."

"I'm truly sorry, *cara.*"

She sat down and swallowed once more. "I'm taking

up the story where Charles left off. I'm going to find out who this Russian spy is. I'm also going to make sure that Charles's killer is brought to justice. So far, I've hit a brick wall. None of my sources have been any help. I'm having dinner tonight with someone from the Foreign Office. Maybe that might lead to something, maybe not. But I have to explore every avenue."

"What can I do?"

"What can you tell me about the investigation into Paolo Talamini's murder?"

"You think that it is somehow connected?"

"Yes. The night he was murdered, Talamini was very angry. He told me that Anatol Zobrinsky and his master—presumably this Sergei Konstantin—had cheated him. Talamini had a deal to provide the Russians with jet fighters and assault rifles, in exchange for $1.5 billion and a Caravaggio painting. Zobrinsky was the go-between."

Vittorio let out a low whistle, but allowed her to continue.

"Apparently, the Russians transferred the money to his Swiss account, but they couldn't meet the other half of the deal. So they decided to hire a forger to supply a Caravaggio. I suppose it was cheaper in the long run. In their arrogance, they supposed that Talamini wouldn't have the painting tested."

"But he did."

"Yes. And for that reason he decided to tell me the story so he could get his revenge." As she related the details to Vittorio, she had a feeling—as she did that night with Talamini—that there was something important she was not remembering. But what *was* it? It was hovering on the edge of her consciousness, just out of reach.

"Well, *cara.*" Vittorio's voice brought her back to the present. "That is a very interesting little tale. I'm afraid you will not like what I have to tell you. The Venice police believe Talamini was killed by some of his Mafia friends. While they say that they will vigorously continue to pursue all leads, it is clear that they are quite content to let it die—forgive the pun—a quiet death."

She slammed her palm on the desk. "They can't do that."

"I'm afraid they can. I believe someone has put pressure—as well a bribe or two into someone's palm—on the police to end the case the sooner the better. Politics is the same everywhere, *cara*. Venice wants to fade from the harsh reality of the limelight to once again become an ethereal world of watery splendor. A lovely dream that leaves a smile on your face. It is the nature of *La Serenissima*."

"No one is smiling, Vittorio."

"No, Emmeline. No one is smiling. I told you that you would not like what I had to say. Let me talk to a few friends. Maybe I can find out something that might be of some help. I'll call you in a day or two."

She smiled for the first time that day. "Thank you, Vittorio. I knew I could count on you, you darling man."

"You make an old man blush, but I will allow you to say it. Also, you must promise to come back to Italy very soon."

She laughed. "I promise. *Ciao*, Vittorio."

"*Ciao, bella*."

అలఅ

At two minutes after eight, the doorbell rang. Emmeline opened the door to find Giles standing on her stoop with a bouquet of cream-colored roses in his hand. He was dressed in a navy pinstripe suit, a pale blue shirt, and a silver tie. He wore no overcoat.

She could smell rain in the air. Goose bumps crept up and down her arms. The burgundy velvet dress she had on did nothing to protect her from the chilly February dampness drifting into the hall.

She smiled and accepted the flowers as she stepped aside. "Won't you come in while I put these in water? You must be freezing without a coat."

Hayden shut the door behind him and followed Emmeline into the living room.

"Please sit down. I won't be a tick," she said over her shoulder once he was settled on the sofa. "Help yourself to a drink, if you like."

She disappeared from the room. He could hear water running from somewhere down the hall. Hayden let his gaze wander about appreciatively. The pastel peach walls gave the room a soft, warm feeling. He stood up to take a better look at some of the oil paintings. A handful of landscapes—no famous artists. Still, they reflected her good taste. Hayden took a tour around the room and stopped to admire the secretary desk. He opened the top and ran his hand along its smooth cherry surface.

She was saying something in the kitchen.

"Sorry, what was that?" he yelled.

The next second, she appeared in the doorway carrying a crystal vase. She looked surprised to see him by the open desk.

He grinned sheepishly. "Forgive me. I was admiring the exquisite craftsmanship. Is it an antique?"

She smiled. "Yes, it is. It belonged to my grandfather."

Hayden closed the lid, his gaze lingering on the desk. "It's lovely. As is everything in this room." He rubbed his hands together. "I don't know about you, but I'm famished. I haven't eaten anything all day."

"Let me turn off my laptop and tidy up my files."

She crossed the room to the table by the window where open folders and a notepad were spread.

"Here let me help you with that." Hayden began straightening some papers.

"Really, Giles, you don't have to."

"Nonsense. I have an ulterior motive."

"Oh, yes?" She arched an eyebrow. "What's that?"

"The faster you finish, the faster we can be on our way. You'll love the restaurant."

She laughed. "I'm sure I shall."

In his haste, he knocked a stack of papers off the table. "Sorry. That was rather clumsy of me."

"Don't worry," she said as she bent down to pick up the pile. "It's only the post. I was distracted earlier this afternoon and didn't finish going through it all." She dumped the envelopes on a corner of the table. "There. Now, we can leave."

"You're sure." He glanced around the room. "Nothing else to do?'

"Nothing."

"In that case—" He proffered his elbow. "Let's go."

❦

The man in the blue Opel a few cars down from Emmeline's house sank lower in his seat behind the wheel when they came out the door. As he watched Hayden hold open the passenger door of his black Peugeot for Emmeline, the man dialed a number into his mobile that he knew by heart. He only had to wait a few seconds.

"Yes?"

"Hayden and the girl just got into his car. Do you want me to follow them?"

"No, we already have a team in place at the restaurant. They'll take it from there. You stay put."

"Right. Any other instructions?"

"Not at the moment. Hold tight. Any sign of Longdon?"

"Not since this morning. Team Two spotted him entering Scotland Yard this afternoon. They never saw him come out."

"Scotland Yard? Damn. I don't like this. Where the devil has he got to? He and the girl could undo everything."

"Perhaps you could do something to ensure they don't. Zobrinsky can pay Longdon another visit."

"It's too dangerous to make a move right now. I don't want to attract any undue attention. I already have Burnell and his sergeant sniffing around asking questions that they shouldn't."

"You're the boss. You know best."

"We're so close. *So close.* We just need a little more time."

"What we *don't* have is the luxury of time. We have to make a move soon."

"Not yet." The connection was severed.

If they did their jobs right, Hayden and Emmeline would be oblivious to the fact that Team Two, posing as an amorous couple out for a romantic evening, was keeping a careful eye on their every move from across the room.

# CHAPTER 19

Emmeline was thoroughly enjoying herself. The restaurant was small and intimate. It seduced with its crimson wallpaper and polished wood floors, creating an atmosphere in which one could relax and exchange confidences.

The waiter and the sommelier seemed to melt into the background, like the Baroque music wafting gently upon the air. The gnocchi Bolognese was superb and the Barolo danced on the palate before slowly gliding down her throat.

For a little while, she was able to forget about everything. They discussed all sorts of things. Giles was charming, knowledgeable, and extremely funny. On several occasions, tears were streaming down her cheeks because she was laughing so hard.

Emmeline stirred a teaspoon of sugar into her espresso. After taking a sip, she rested her chin on her hand and asked, "So what made you join the Foreign Office? Wanderlust? A secret yearning for international intrigue? What?"

He laughed, but didn't answer at first. He drew invisible trenches in the tablecloth with his fork. "I suppose it was a boy's desire for adventure. To meet new people and escape the unbearable loneliness of not having a home and knowing that you were not wanted where you were." There was a boy's sadness in his green-gray eyes when he finally looked up.

"I'm sorry," she said. "Having lost my parents when I was five, I should have realized that it might be a sensitive topic. I was lucky that I had my grandmother, who swooped down and made sure everything was all right. And everything was because she was always there for me. However, I remember you told me on the flight back from Venice that you were shuttled from one aunt and uncle to another."

Hayden reached out and squeezed her hand briefly. "Don't be silly. I'm a grown man. Everything is magnified when you're a child. All your childhood hurts and insecurities. I'm sure everything wasn't as black as I thought it was at the time. To their credit, my aunts and uncles did try. They just weren't very good with children. I vowed to myself that I would do whatever it took to get out of a life that was slowly stifling me. History and languages came easily to me in school. As a result, international relations was a natural step for me. I also added economics to the mix."

Absently, he drank his espresso in one gulp. His mind was still lost somewhere in the past. They both fell silent. After a few minutes, he shook his head as if chasing away unpleasant memories. "Now, it's your turn. What made you become journalist?"

Emmeline smiled. "That's an easy question. It's in my blood. Both my parents were journalists. That's all I ever wanted to be. Actually, shall I confess a secret?"

Hayden leaned closer and nodded his head. "Please do."

"One day—" She lowered her voice conspiratorially and fixed her gaze on him. "I want to become a novelist."

He threw his head back and laughed. "I promise to

keep your secret. Isn't that every journalist's dream?
What kind of books do you want to write?"

"Spy thrillers. What else?"

"I suppose your job would provide a lot of fodder.
Have you tried to write anything?"

"I have a few ideas swirling around in my head, but I
haven't summoned up the courage yet to sit down in front
on my laptop and start writing. One day soon, though, I
think. The itch to write is getting stronger."

"I wish you the best of luck. I'm sure your parents
would have been proud of everything you've accom-
plished and all the accolades you've garnered."

"Thanks. I would like to think so. I just wish they
were here. I still miss them so much." She felt tears prick
her eyelids—as they always did when she thought about
her parents—but she was determined not to succumb.

He reached out for her hand once more. "Yes, that
never goes away. But, as they say, life goes on." He tried
to lighten the mood by changing the subject. "Come on,
eat your dessert. The restaurant is renowned for its profit-
eroles."

The pastries were as light as air and the cream inside
was absolutely delicious. Giles had taken a mouthful of
his dessert, when a thought suddenly struck him. "What a
fool I've been."

"What are you talking about?" she asked, startled.

"Your father was the legendary *Sunday Times* reporter Aaron Kirby. Wasn't he?"

"Yes. Why?"

"And your mother? Your mother was the award-
winning photojournalist Jacqueline Davis Kirby. Right?"

"Yes, but I don't understand. Why is that so important? I thought you knew that already. Many people
do, especially at the Foreign Office. My father spent a lot
of time hounding some of the bigwigs for information.

Some tended to hide when they saw my father coming because they knew Aaron Kirby would get the answers he was looking for one way or another." She smiled with pride as she said this.

"I didn't connect the name until now. If I remember correctly, your parents were killed while on assignment somewhere in the Middle East. Right?"

She looked down at her hands and took another sip of her espresso. "Yes." This was barely audible. Then, her voice gained strength and she met his cool, green-gray gaze. "Yes, they were killed in Lebanon. They were interviewing a group of Israeli soldiers when they came under fire from some Hezbollah fighters. They died instantly."

"I'm sorry. I didn't realize. At least they didn't suffer."

"Yes. That's what Gran said to me at the time. But when you're a child of five, you don't understand these things. All you know is that your parents—who are everything in the world to you—are suddenly, and irrevocably, gone."

"I think they must have been very brave."

"They were just doing their jobs."

"Yes, but as Jews, they must have been frightened to be surrounded by Arabs who hated them."

Emmeline's head snapped up and her back stiffened. "What do you mean? What does being Jewish have to do with anything? They were reporters covering a story. That's it." She could feel the muscle in her jaw tighten and start to twitch as she seethed inwardly.

"Sorry if I offended you. I didn't mean to. I have no prejudice against Jews, I assure you. I just assumed that your parents—and you, obviously—were Jewish. Aaron is a Jewish name, isn't it?

"It means exalted, strong in Hebrew."

"I see. I wasn't sure about the Kirby part, though."

This mollified Emmeline slightly. Her eyes searched his face suspiciously. She was not religious, but she did celebrate Passover and the High Holy days. Emmeline had encountered anti-Semitism before. It always rankled and made her want to lash out at the bigots who spewed such hatred. However, she decided to give him the benefit of the doubt—for the moment. "Well, Kirby isn't Jewish. My great-great grandfather changed his name when he came to England from Russia—well Bessarabia, really, which like many others areas in the region was gobbled up by Russia—in the late nineteenth century. His name was Abraham Haimovic and he was a boy of twelve when his parents sent him away because of the pogroms. They hoped he would find a better life, even if it meant never seeing him again. He had no money. He knew no one. He was utterly alone, but he somehow managed to make it all the way to London. At the beginning, Abraham spoke only Yiddish. But he learned English. He had to, otherwise he wouldn't have survived. He found a job in a tailor's shop and worked very hard. His dream was to one day have a shop of his own. He scrimped and saved, until finally he made his dream a reality.

"First, he bought himself a flat. This was a major accomplishment. Up until then, he had been living in a cramped room in a boardinghouse. When the business starting prospering, Abraham bought himself a house. Now that he had something to offer, it was time to find a wife. And he did. Her name was Rebecca, a petite beauty with long, raven hair and almond-shaped blue eyes, whom he met at the synagogue.

"After six months of courting, they were married. Abraham and Rebecca had six sons. The last of which was my great grandfather who, in turn, had four sons.

The youngest was my grandfather, Simon Kirby, who became a barrister."

Hayden leaned his chin on his hand. "What a fascinating story. Wasn't your grandfather awarded the Order of the British Empire by the queen for his distinguished career?"

Emmeline beamed. "Yes, he was."

"And your mother's family? What about them?"

"They came to England centuries earlier from Portugal to escape the Inquisition."

"Amazing. Coming from such stock, it's no wonder you're so good at your job."

She felt herself blush. "Thank you, Giles. Now I was wondering if perhaps you could help me with something."

"Aha, I see I must steel myself to be grilled."

"You must understand that when you're with a journalist, questions are an occupational hazard."

"Fire away, Miss Kirby. But I must insist that everything I say is off the record. What are you working on?"

"I'm not at liberty to disclose any details or sources."

"Naturally. How about if I make it easier for you? You're working on the Charles Latimer murder, aren't you?"

"How did you know that? Scotland Yard hasn't made it public yet."

"I work at the Foreign Office. There are whispers about everything."

"I see." She didn't know why, but for some reason this piece of information disturbed her.

"Frankly, I don't see how I can help. I didn't know the man."

"I think Charles was killed because of a story he was working on." She lowered her voice. Her eyes flicked to the right and left to make sure that they could not be overheard. "He found out there is a Russian spy—what they call a sleeper—at the Foreign Office. Charles was on the verge of exposing him."

Giles said nothing for a long moment. "That's impossible. Are you quite sure?"

"Yes, Charles told me he had some sort of conclusive evidence. 'Explosive' is the way he termed it."

"What is it?"

"I have absolutely no idea. He was murdered before he could tell me."

"Obviously he trusted you. Perhaps—knowing that he was in danger—he just had time to hide this evidence somewhere in your house, before this supposed spy killed him. Did he give you any indication what it could be?"

"None whatsoever. And there's nothing *supposed* about it."

"I see." Hayden's brow furrowed. He tapped his fingers on the table distractedly. "Still, I find the whole thing very hard to swallow. A spy at the Foreign Office. This is not the Cold War anymore."

"Ooh." She leaned back and crossed her arms over her chest defensively. "You sound just like Philip."

"Acheson?"

"Yes, I spoke to him yesterday and he said exactly the same thing. That it was impossible there is a spy. He thinks Charles was tilting at windmills. Actually, he implied Charles had started drinking heavily and his judgment was impaired. Well, *I* trust Charles's instincts and no one can persuade me otherwise."

"Emmeline, I'm sorry if I upset you in any way. I certainly had no intention of doing so. But if Acheson doesn't believe there was anything in it, he would know."

"What do you mean?"

"We only know each other slightly, but I do know that Acheson is the Defense and Intelligence Directorate's Russia expert. He was stationed at the Moscow embassy for several years."

Emmeline raised her eyebrows in surprise. "I didn't know that."

"Yes, and aside from that, he has the prime minister's ear. As a result, Acheson's influence can be felt in the background in many departments. An *eminence grise*, if you like. Therefore, he would know if anything were going on."

Emmeline digested this piece of information and then shook her head. "No, I don't care what you say. If Charles hadn't been on to something, *why* was he killed?"

And why was everyone trying to dissuade her from pursuing the story? It just made her more determined to find out the truth.

സ്ഥ

Anatol Zobrinsky watched as Hayden walked Emmeline to her door. They spoke for a few seconds. Hayden waited to make sure she was safely inside and patted the outside of the deadbolt lock, doubtless to assure himself she had bolted the door. He went down the steps to his Peugeot.

Zobrinsky ducked down as Hayden looked up and down the street before getting into his car and pulling away.

Zobrinsky flipped open his mobile. "Hayden left. The girl is inside. She turned off the lights downstairs. It looks as if she's going to bed."

"Any sign of Longdon?"

"No. Perhaps, my little chat with him yesterday scared him off."

"I wouldn't bet on it. He's a crafty devil."

"I—"

Zobrinsky's door was suddenly wrenched opened. Before he realized what was going on, a hand snatched the mobile from him and tossed it in the back seat. Another hand with a vise-like grip immediately clamped around his throat.

He looked up to see that the hand was attached to Gregory Longdon's arm. Zobrinsky fumbled for his gun, but it was useless.

Longdon clicked his tongue. "A nine millimeter Beretta. Naughty, naughty, Zobrinsky. Don't you know that guns are dangerous? I'll take that before anyone gets hurt."

Zobrinsky could feel his lungs straining against his rib cage as the oxygen was slowly being cut off. However, he struggled to prevent Longdon from taking his gun.

"My, we are overexcited this evening. I wonder why that is." Longdon punched him in the face. "There, perhaps that might calm you down a bit."

At the same time, the passenger door opened and a large man with thinning white hair and a neatly trimmed beard sat down beside him.

"Good evening, Mr. Zobrinsky. You must forgive Longdon. He's rather impetuous and tends to hold grudges. It was your little contretemps yesterday that set you down in his bad books."

Longdon increased the pressure slightly on Zobrinsky's throat. "Really, Oliver. I have better things to do with my evening than to waste it on rubbish such as this."

"Mr. Zobrinsky, as you can see Longdon is getting impatient. So, perhaps, you can tell us why a Russian official is sitting out here in his car late at night watching Emmeline Kirby's house? If you're ready to talk, Longdon will let go of your throat. Are you ready to talk?" Chief Inspector Burnell asked sweetly.

Zobrinsky's eyes flicked toward Longdon and then

returned to Burnell. His body slackened and he nodded his head.

"Good. I think that is a wise choice. Longdon?"

"Must I, Oliver?"

"Yes."

"Oh, all right." Longdon dropped his hand, but he placed the muzzle of the gun against Zobrinsky's heart. "In case you get any ideas."

For a few seconds, Zobrinsky took big gulps of the damp night air. Through gritted teeth, he said, "Go to hell, Longdon. And you, too, Chief Inspector Burnell of Scotland Yard. I don't have to tell you anything. I have diplomatic immunity."

"Oh, so you know who I am," the chief inspector asked pleasantly. "There you have us at a disadvantage because we don't who your boss is, but rest assured we intend to find out." Burnell smiled, but his eyes held no warmth. He poked his forefinger into Zobrinsky's chest. "Will you give him that message from us? Tell Sergei Konstantin that his days are numbered."

The chief inspector got of the car and then leaned back down. "You know, it's funny that you brought up diplomatic immunity. That makes me think you have something to hide. Oh, and something else, if your boss threatens Miss Kirby again there is no place on Earth he will be able to hide."

"Is that it, Oliver?"

Burnell thought for a moment. "Yes, I think so, unless you have something else to add."

"Just this." Longdon landed a hard blow on Zobrinsky's jaw. "Pleasant dreams." Then, he emptied the fifteen-round magazine from the Beretta and flung it into the square.

Burnell and Longdon crossed the road. Before they disappeared around the corner, Longdon turned around and gave a little salute. Although they were half in shadow, Zobrinsky could see an arrogant grin on his face.

Once he was sure they had gone, Zobrinsky scrambled to find his mobile in the back seat. His hands were shaking with rage as he dialed the number again. It was answered on the first ring.

"What happened?

"Longdon and Burnell were here."

"What did they want?"

"They gave me message for Sergei Konstantin. They said that they won't stop until they find him."

"Damn. The whole thing has spiraled out of control all because of Latimer and his bloody crusade."

"Longdon must be taken care of. *Now.* And the girl, too. I wanted to do it in Venice, but you said no. It would have been neater that way. We wouldn't have had all this trouble. They are like a bomb waiting to explode. Every day they're getting closer."

"I know. I know," snapped the voice at the other end of the line. "Leave it to me."

# CHAPTER 20

The angry lashing of the rain against the window and the distant rumble of thunder awakened Emmeline. It was still dark in her bedroom. She pulled a pillow over her head trying to drown out the noise, but after ten minutes she gave up. There was no way she would get back to sleep now. She unwrapped herself from her downy cocoon and cocked one eye open to look at the clock on her night table. The bright red numbers flashed 6:35. She groaned and rolled over onto her back. There was nothing for it. She flung the bedclothes off and sat up. She flicked the television on BBC 1, as she went across the hall to the bathroom.

She was splashing cold water on her face, when she heard the report. At first, she thought she must still be half asleep. She turned off the faucet and held her breath for a few seconds. Her knuckles showed white as she gripped the edge of the sink harder and harder. She grabbed a towel and hurried back into the bedroom.

She plopped herself on the bed and listened transfixed to the news reader. "…we are just learning this morning that Charles Latimer, the internationally renowned BBC reporter and acclaimed author of *The Secret History of The KGB*, was murdered late last week at the home of a friend here in London." Clips of Charles flashed across the screen. "The news has sent shock-waves around the world. Scotland Yard has made the case a top priority because of Latimer's high profile. Details are still trickling in, but Inspector Malcolm Williams moments ago announced that an arrest has been made." Emmeline inched to the end of the bed and leaned closer to the television. "The alleged killer appears to be well known to the authorities. Although he has never been caught, he is suspected in some of the most notorious jewel thefts across Europe."

Her temples throbbed mercilessly as the blood rushed to her head.

Inspector Williams—a tall, thin man with red-gold hair softened by wings of white—loomed large before her. His deep blue eyes seemed to bore directly into her very soul. The reporter was asking whether he was at liberty to divulge the name of the suspect.

"First, I would like to say that thanks to the skill and dedication of the Metropolitan Police force, we were able to wrap this case up so quickly."

"Yes, Inspector Williams, but who have you arrested?"

"His name is Gregory Longdon."

"What was his connection to Charles Latimer? What was the motive behind this crime?"

"Unfortunately, I cannot discuss that at the present time. You must understand that this is still an open case. Suffice it to say, we have compelling evidence against the suspect. Now, if you'll excuse me ladies and gentlemen." And with that, Inspector Williams turned away from the cameras and went back inside the building.

"You have just heard from Inspector Malcolm Williams. We will be following this evolving story closely and will keep you updated as more information becomes available."

Emmeline aimed the remote control at the television and switched to Sky News and then to Channel 4 and CNN. Charles's murder and Gregory's arrest were the lead story on all the morning news programs. She ran downstairs and opened the front door. Her copy of the *Times* was sitting there on the stoop. She grabbed it and quickly ducked back inside. It was pouring. Sheets of rain were blowing down the street.

She took the paper into the living room and spread it out on the coffee table. The lead story was about Charles. A story that someone else wrote. She sat cross-legged on the floor and devoured every word from beginning to end. Then, she leaned back against the sofa. This was a nightmare.

The police were insane. Absolutely insane. Gregory was many things, but a murderer he was not. What evidence could they possibly have? And what happened to Chief Inspector Burnell? This was his case. She didn't have the answers to any of these questions, but there was someone who was going to answer a few of hers, whether he liked it or not.

She went to the desk and dialed the number of her editor, James Sloane. She drummed her fingers impatiently as she waited. It rang twice, before a rich baritone voice echoed in her ear. "Sloane."

"James, it's Emmeline."

There was a slightly pause. "Good morning, Emmeline. How was the long weekend down in Kent with your grandmother?"

"Gran's fine, but it's not a good morning from where I'm sitting. Let's cut the small talk. Imagine my surprise when I opened the paper this morning to find the front page story about Charles's murder. Not only that, the story was written by Ian Newland. It was *my* story, James."

"Ah."

"*Ah*? Is that all you have to say?"

"We felt you were too close to the story. That you could not be objective because of your friendship with Charles."

"Since when have I not been objective, James? And who is 'we'?"

"We—the publisher and the editorial staff—thought that it might be better if the story was assigned to someone else."

"I see. When was someone going to inform me of this decision?"

"Well, I—"

She slammed her palm on the desk and sat up in her chair. "Do you know what I think, James?" She didn't wait for a response. "I think that you've been got at."

"Emmeline, you have to understand—"

"Oh, I understand perfectly. I'm getting too close to the truth and someone doesn't like it. I never thought that you would cave in to pressure. I thought you, of all people, would always stand up for the freedom of the press. I can see that I was wrong."

"Isn't that a bit rough?"

"Is it, James? From where I'm sitting I don't think so. And now because of your cowardly action and behind-the-scenes political machinations, an innocent man will go to prison for murder."

"I would hardly call Gregory Longdon innocent."

"He is not a murderer."

There was no sound from the other end of the line and, for a moment, she thought that James had hung up on her. Finally, she heard a weary sigh. "Emmeline, I'm sorry. I had no choice in the matter. If it were up to me, I'd let you follow your instincts. Obviously, you were on the right track. But it's not up to me. My hands are tied. That's all I can say in my defense. I would also hate to see our friendship destroyed over something like this."

She relented a bit. "So would I, James, but it doesn't alter the fact that you've taken me off this story."

"What do you want me to do? Ian's covering it now."

"Do you trust me?"

"Do you even have to ask?"

"I want an answer."

"Very well, then. Yes, I trust you."

"And you'll support me no matter what?"

"I don't like the sound of that. What are you up to?"

"You didn't answer my question."

"Yes, I'll support you no matter what."

"Good. That's all I wanted to know. I'll be in touch."

ଔଔଔ

Emmeline squeezed her way through the crush of reporters and camera crews waiting at the Dacre Street entrance of New Scotland Yard. The granite-and-glass building looked grim and forbidding as the rain continued its onslaught.

"Hey, Emmeline."

She turned to find Tony Barstow of Sky News at her elbow. "Oh, hello, Tony."

"I was surprised when I saw Ian's byline on the story in the *Times*. I would have thought that James would have assigned it to you. After all, you're the paper's best investigative reporter."

"There was a minor misunderstanding, but it's all been cleared up. I'm back on the story. Any more news from the police?"

"Nothing since eight o'clock and that was just a brief statement. They're playing this very close to the vest. It's all a bit strange, if you ask me."

"Yes, isn't it?" Emmeline said distractedly as she kept her eye on the door. Just then, Chief Inspector Burnell walked out.

The reporters surged forward and started firing questions at him. Burnell muttered something unintelligible and immediately did an about-face. Emmeline broke from the pack and ducked in behind him. "Chief Inspector?"

"The press is not allowed—" He turned abruptly only to find himself looking down into Emmeline's eyes. "Oh, it's you, Miss Kirby. I'm sorry. I thought you were one of that lot out there." Burnell jerked his head in the direction of the door. "How can I help you?"

"I came to find out why you've arrested Gregory," she said bluntly. "You must realize that you have the wrong man."

The chief inspector looked down at his feet and murmured, "It's not my case anymore, Miss Kirby. You'll have to speak to Inspector Williams, if you want any information."

"Why?"

"Because he's in the charge of the case now."

"No, I meant why were you taken off the case? You know that Gregory could not have done it. We came directly from the airport together. We found Charles together. You know that. You have our statements. I don't understand all of this. Please, Chief Inspector Burnell, can't you speak to Inspector Williams? Can't you make him see sense?" She put a hand on his arm. "Please."

"Come with me to my office, Miss Kirby."

Emmeline's hopes began to rise. It was a mistake, she knew it. Of course, it was a mistake. "Certainly, Chief Inspector."

She followed him to the lift. Two uniformed constables got in with them, so they didn't speak. The chief inspector looked straight ahead. She studied his profile, trying to divine some clue. But it was useless. His jaw was set in a hard line. When they got off on the fourth floor, Burnell stopped by Sergeant Finch's desk and asked him to join them. Finch nodded and briefly bid her good morning.

Burnell ushered them into his office and shut the door. "Please sit down, Miss Kirby."

Emmeline and Sergeant Finch sat down, as he wearily dropped into his chair. "Now then, Miss Kirby, I asked you here because of my great respect for you."

"Thank you, Chief Inspector. I appreciate that. The feeling is mutual."

"However, it does not alter the facts of the case."

"Facts? What facts?"

"Apparently, evidence was found linking Longdon to the murder."

"What evidence? This is preposterous. Can't you see that someone is trying to frame him? It's Sergei Konstantin. We're getting too close and he's trying to silence us. You know all of this. We explained it to you."

"Miss Kirby, the Russian spy theory is mere speculation on your part. You have no proof to back up your claim."

"No, but—"

"As I said, evidence was found—"

"That's impossible. You don't believe it, do you?" She looked from Burnell to Finch, but neither said anything. "You *can't* believe it."

Burnell, his voice full of patience and kindness, said, "Miss Kirby, what I believe or do not believe is irrelevant. Sergeant Finch and I have been taken off the case."

"Why?" she snapped. Suddenly everything was spinning out of control. "Why were you taken off the case?"

"That was Superintendent Fenton's decision."

"Was it because someone put pressure on him?

Someone from the Foreign Office perhaps?"

Burnell and Finch seemed to squirm slightly at this remark. Before either of them could speak, Inspector Williams burst in. "Burnell, I need—Oh, I didn't realize that you had people with you."

Through gritted teeth, Burnell said, "Perhaps if you learned how to knock, you wouldn't be interrupting all the time. What was it you wanted?"

"I need your notes on the Latimer case." Although this was addressed to the chief inspector, Williams kept his eyes on Emmeline. "Aren't you Emmeline Kirby?"

She sat up straighter and cleared her throat. "Yes, Inspector Williams."

"May I ask what you're doing here?"

Burnell responded for her. "That is none of your business, Williams. This is a private conversation. Run along and Finch will get you the notes later."

"It's all right, Chief Inspector Burnell. I'm perfectly willing to answer the question." She turned to Inspector Williams. "I am working on the Charles Latimer murder for the *Times* and I came here today to see if the chief inspector could give me any details."

"I'm in charge of the case now."

"Yes, Chief Inspector Burnell has just apprised me of that fact. Therefore, I will address my questions to you." She calmly opened her purse and took out a pad and pen. "Based on what evidence was Gregory Longdon arrested?"

"I made a statement this morning. I am not releasing anything else at the present time."

"I see. Inspector Williams, perhaps you are not aware that Charles Latimer was investigating a story about a Russian spy in the Foreign Office. He was on the verge identifying this man."

"I've heard some nonsense to that effect, but it's just

rumor and innuendo. There's nothing in it," he replied dismissively.

One of her hands balled into a fist so tight that her knuckles turned white, but her voice was perfectly calm when she spoke. "I see. Don't you think that the police should pursue this line of inquiry to establish its veracity?"

"Listen, Miss Kirby, I don't tell you how to do your job and I don't appreciate you telling me how to do mine. I am also aware that you have a personal connection with Longdon. If you don't want to be charged with interfering with police business, I suggest you leave the premises. Otherwise, I can have you escorted out. It's your choice."

"Steady on, Williams. The last time I looked this was still *my* office. If anyone is going to leave, it's going to be you."

"Shall we see what Superintendent Fenton has to say about all this? I'm certain he'll find it very interesting that you were meeting secretly with the press about a case you are no longer working on."

Emmeline swallowed hard and stood up. "Chief Inspector Burnell, I'll go. I don't want to cause any trouble for you."

Burnell and Finch stood as well. She shook their hands and merely nodded at Williams. She slowly gathered up her coat and her umbrella and walked to the door. With her hand on the knob, she turned back to the little trio.

"Inspector Williams, I want you to know that I will be a thorn in your side until Gregory Longdon is released and the real murderer is behind bars."

Burnell and Finch exchanged a brief smile behind Williams's back.

"As for you, Chief Inspector, I always believed you were a fair man. I'm disappointed to see that you have allowed a personal prejudice against Gregory to cloud your professional judgment. I never thought I would see that day."

She walked out, leaving the three men staring at one another.

# CHAPTER 21

Emmeline was shrugging into her coat, when Sergeant Finch caught up to her by the lift. "Miss Kirby, may I speak to you please?"

She sighed and nodded. He glanced over his shoulder to make certain no one had seen them together. "Let's step in here for a minute." He took her by the elbow and pulled her into an empty interview room.

"What is it, Sergeant Finch? Has Inspector Williams sent you after me with another warning?"

"No, Chief Inspector Burnell just wanted you to know that Longdon is all right. He said that a few nights in jail won't do him any harm."

"But, Gregory's inno—"

"Don't worry, Miss Kirby, please. It will be all right, truly. We're keeping an eye on Longdon. He's fine. The chief inspector also wanted me to tell you that Philip Acheson was in Venice at the same time Latimer was. He thought it was an interesting coincidence. Of course, we couldn't divulge information discovered during an official investigation, *if* we were still on the case. Especially to the press. No, *that* would be a breach of professional etiquette. But as we are no longer on the case—and as Inspector Williams has made it abundantly clear that he is in charge and does not welcome any advice—well, Chief

Inspector Burnell thought he'd mull over some ideas out loud with a friend." Finch smiled as Emmeline's eyes widened in surprise. "Now, I can't be dawdling here all day. I have to get back to work and I believe you have a story to write."

"Yes," she whispered. "Yes, I do."

"Oh, one more thing, Miss Kirby."

"Yes?"

"The chief inspector said to mind your step. Your house is being watched and likely you're being followed. Perhaps even your phone is being tapped. Do not take any unnecessary risks. He and I are available at a moment's notice—day or night—should you run into trouble. Please remember that."

Sergeant Finch saw a range of emotions—from fear to stubbornness—flicker over her face. Then, her eyes narrowed with a steely determination. "Thank you for the warning. It seems I badly misjudged Chief Inspector Burnell and for that I am truly sorry."

A broad smile creased Finch's pleasant features. "I'm sure he wasn't offended. The governor is pretty tough. It takes a lot to rattle him. Just keep yourself out of harm's way. Off you go." He gave her a little nudge toward the door. "I'll wait here five minutes. It's best if we leave separately. It wouldn't do for old Williams to think we were conspiring against him, now would it?"

She returned his smile and shook his hand. "No, it wouldn't do at all. Thank you again."

かつ

It was still raining when Emmeline left Scotland Yard. Her mind was reeling as she walked up Dacre Street. Philip was in Venice. Could Philip have attacked Charles and then followed him back to London when he realized that he was still alive? He knew what Charles was working on. Could Philip be the mysterious Sergei Konstantin? Did he feel threatened? He had certainly done his best to put her off the other day.

At the time, she was sure that he had been lying about something. Was he trying desperately to cover his tracks? She couldn't believe it—didn't want to believe it. Not Maggie's husband and the twins' father. And yet, it made sense.

What was it Giles had said last night at dinner? "Acheson is the Defense and Intelligence Directorate's Russia expert. He was stationed at the Moscow embassy for several years—Acheson's influence can be felt in the background in many departments. An *eminence grise*, if you like. Therefore, he would know if anything were going on."

Emmeline's head felt as if it was going to explode. She needed help, but who could she turn to? Gregory was in jail. She couldn't go to Chief Inspector Burnell and Sergeant Finch. They had already taken a big risk by telling her about Philip. No, she needed someone with influence and connections on the international stage. Someone discreet and whom she could trust. Then it came to her and she smiled. Of course, she should have thought of him at once. She pulled out her mobile and quickly dialed a number.

"Media Relations, Duncan Redmond speaking." With his clipped tones and precise diction, one would swear that he was an English aristocrat—and one would be completely wrong. It always amused the Torontonian that he could deceive people in this manner.

"Hi, Duncan. It's Emmeline."

"Little Emmy." She could hear the smile in his voice. "What a wonderful surprise. To what do I owe this pleasure?"

"I stopped being 'little Emmy' a long time ago, Duncan."

"Forgive me. I can still picture you as a curly-headed little girl with curious dark eyes who liked to follow your father and me around when we were on assignment. You were always asking questions about everything. I forget that you're a young woman now and an excellent journalist in your own right. Your parents would have been very proud of you. However, to me you will always be that little imp."

She laughed for the first time today. It was good to speak to Duncan, who had been one of her father's oldest friends.

They had met at Oxford and had remained close until her parents died. When Emmeline was young, Duncan was always coming over to her parents' house. He would tell her all kinds of stories but, above all, he would make her laugh and laugh until she cried.

When she was five, she had developed a crush on the dashing Canadian.

"Oh, Duncan, I have missed you. I'm sorry I haven't called. It's been a bit crazy lately."

He became serious. "Yes, I heard about Charles."

They had been good friends, too. Her father, Duncan, and Charles were the three Musketeers in their younger days.

Now Duncan worked in the Media Relations department at the Canadian embassy.

"Apparently, the police have made an arrest. A Gregory Longdon. Isn't that the young man you were involved with for a time?"

"Yes, it is. But, Duncan, it is all a big mistake. He's being framed. Gregory couldn't have done it."

"Oh?"

"He was with me. We went directly from the airport

to my house. We were together the entire time. We found Charles *together*."

"Your house? Charles was murdered in *your* house?"

"Yes. Chief Inspector Burnell didn't disclose that information to the press to protect my privacy. But now an Inspector Williams is conducting the investigation. If you can call it an investigation. He's arrogant and knows absolutely nothing. All he's interested in is making a name for himself with a quick arrest in such a high-profile murder."

"Chief Inspector Oliver Burnell? I met him once a couple of years ago. He seemed very competent and intelligent."

"He is—too sharp for someone's liking. Duncan, I think someone from the Foreign Office put pressure on Superintendent Fenton to remove Burnell from the case because we were asking too many questions. They decided to take care of two birds with one stone. Gregory was arrested and Chief Inspector Burnell was shunted to the side where they could keep an eye on him."

"I don't understand, Emmy. What is all this about?"

"Oh, Duncan, it's become so complicated. I'm sorry, but I didn't know who else to turn to. I need your help."

"Anything. You know that. Where are you? Come to my office and you can explain everything to me. I will do whatever I can to help."

"No, I don't think it's a good idea if I come to the embassy. Chief Inspector Burnell said my house was being watched and I might be followed. Let's meet in a public place. No one would dare try anything out in the open."

"I don't like the sound of any of this, but I will bow to your wishes."

"Thank you. I hate to take you away from your work."

"Nonsense. For you, I'd do anything. Look." He paused. "I'm tied up until two o'clock, but the rest of my afternoon is free. How about if we meet by Round Pond next to Kensington Palace at three? It's only a stone's throw from your house."

"That would be perfect. I can't tell you how much I appreciate it. Thank you."

"Just be careful."

"I will. I promise."

She snapped shut her mobile. She had an hour and a half. Plenty of time to make one stop and it wouldn't be out of her way. There was no need to worry Duncan. She didn't think he would approve, but he didn't know everything that had transpired in the last week.

She smiled at the thought of what she was about to do. "Let's shake things up a bit and see what comes loose," she murmured to herself as she hurried up Broadway toward the St. James's Park Underground station.

Suddenly the hairs on the back of her neck began to prickle. She had the eerie sensation that she was being watched. She threw a glance over her shoulder as she quickened her pace. In that fraction of a second, she glimpsed a well-dressed man in a dark trench coat.

Twenty minutes later, Emmeline was climbing up the stairs out of the High Street Kensington Underground station. The rain had finally stopped and watery sunshine was struggling to part the clouds. She walked along the High Street until she reached Kensington Palace Gardens. She was stopped at the checkpoint by two Diplomatic Protection Group officers. They each held a Heckler & Koch semi-automatic carbine. The officers checked her credentials before allowing her to pass. She followed the road until she came to the embassy of the Russian Federation.

She shivered involuntarily. It would no good to lose her nerve now, she chided herself. She took a deep breath. "Into the lion's den we go."

She walked sedately up the path. The door opened onto a rather dark entrance hall, where she was greeted by a tall, grim-faced guard with sandy blond hair and clear gray eyes. "Good morning. How can I help you, madam?"

The way in which he asked the question left no doubt in her mind that she was unwelcome here.

She swallowed hard. "Good morning. My name is Emmeline Kirby. I'm a reporter with the *London Times* and I would like to see Anatol Zobrinsky."

He checked a clipboard. "I do not see your name on today's list. Do you have appointment, Miss Kirby?"

"No, but I'm sure he would agree to see me."

"I cannot allow you to see Mr. Zobrinsky without appointment."

"Tell him I'm working on the Charles Latimer murder and would like to ask him a few questions."

"I cannot allow you to see him without appointment."

"Then I'll wait here until he's finished with his business. I'm not in a rush." She plopped herself down onto a wing chair and smiled up at the guard.

"I cannot permit that."

"Oh, why not?"

"You are an unauthorized foreign journalist. If you persist, I will have to arrest you."

"You can't arrest me. I haven't done anything."

"You are on Russian soil. The laws of England do not apply here."

She stood up and, though he dwarfed her, she met the guard's steely gaze without flinching. "Then if you don't want an international incident on your hands, I suggest that you allow me to see Mr. Zobrinsky."

"Since you do not have appointment, that is impossible."

She was trembling inside, but she stood her ground. "I want to speak to someone in charge. Call whoever you like, but I'm not leaving this building until I have some answers."

The guard sighed with resignation. *Let her be someone else's headache.* He picked up the telephone and punched in an extension. He waited a few seconds and then spoke in rapid Russian.

He glanced in her direction once and shook his head. He hung up a moment later.

"Well?" Emmeline prompted.

"Vladimir Rudenko, chief of security, is on his way."

"The chief of security. I feel honored." She resumed her seat and crossed her legs with an air of nonchalance. However, she gripped the armrests very tightly to keep her hands from shaking.

After ten minutes, a bald man of medium height emerged from the end of the corridor. He was slim and she guessed he must be in his early sixties. He walked directly over to the guard who towered over her. They spoke in Russian before the newcomer turned his attention to her and extended his hand.

Emmeline stood up.

"Miss Kirby, I am Vladimir Rudenko. How may I help you?"

"I'm doing a story on the BBC journalist Charles Latimer's murder and I would like to ask Mr. Zobrinsky several questions."

"Mr. Zobrinsky is a very busy man. He does not do interviews. He is not involved in this matter. You must direct your questions to the press office."

"I don't think Mr. Zobrinsky would like me to do that."

"If you will not submit your questions to the press office, I will have to ask you to leave the premises. You cannot harass embassy staff." He nodded to the guard, who took her by the elbow and led her forcibly toward the door.

She yelled over her shoulder. "You're all covering up for him. What does Zobrinsky know about the murders of Charles Latimer and Paolo Talamini? Tell him Sergei Konstantin cannot hide in the shadows for much longer. I'm going to find him."

Zobrinsky watched the whole scene on the television screen in the security control room.

A minute after Rudenko disappeared from the screen, he opened the door. "What the hell was that all about, Zobrinsky?"

"I don't know."

"Why does she think you have anything to do with Charles Latimer and Paolo Talamini? Are you working on something that I should know about?"

"No."

Zobrinsky pushed past the security chief and slammed the door behind him. He went directly to his office, grabbed his coat, and left the building without speaking to anyone. He quickly walked up tree-lined Kensington Palace Gardens to Bayswater Road and hailed a cab.

He told the driver to take him to Trafalgar Square and then he made a call on his mobile. The conversation was very brief.

"We have trouble."

"What's happened?"

"The girl came to the embassy. I think I'm blown."

"Bloody hell."

"Exactly. I'll be at the usual place in an hour. Don't be late."

# CHAPTER 22

Duncan had arrived before her and was skipping pebbles across the slightly ruffled waters of Round Pond in Kensington Palace Gardens. There were a few people about, strolling and chatting. He hadn't seen her yet. She studied his profile from a distance. He was still handsome at fifty-six and Emmeline thought he looked extremely dashing in his Burberry raincoat.

As she got closer, she could see that his thick wavy hair, which had once been jet black, was now steel gray. But this only seemed to enhance his good looks.

He turned around just then. His whole face was lit up and his deep blue eyes danced with delight. "Emmy."

He opened his arms wide and she flew into them. All of a sudden, it felt as if she was five years old again—a time when things were much less complicated. She closed her eyes and tried to hold onto the memories for a moment longer.

Duncan pulled away first and held her at arm's length. "Let me look at you." He tilted his head to one side. "You're as lovely as ever."

Her cheeks flushed bright pink. "Oh, Duncan, always the charmer. No wonder I fell in love with you when I was five."

He laughed and tucked her arm through his. "Now tell me what this is all about."

She flinched and had to extricate herself. She rubbed her arm. Beneath the layers of clothing, she could feel bruises forming where the Russian guard's fingers had bit into her arm. "Ouch."

"I'm sorry, my dear."

"It's not you. I just had a little encounter with a guard at the Russian embassy and my arm was the loser."

They stopped walking and Duncan turned her so that she was facing him. She tried to avert her gaze from those piercing eyes that seemed to be able to read everything she was thinking.

"Russian embassy? I didn't like the way you sounded on the phone earlier—not that you told me anything—but I'm liking this less and less. Now, young lady, I insist that you tell about this imbroglio you have gotten yourself mixed up in."

They stared at each other without saying anything. Then, she carefully threaded her arm through his and said, "Let's walk. It's safer that way. You never know who is watching."

So they walked and, with each step, she unraveled another strand in her deadly tale, concluding with her unceremonious ejection from the Russian embassy.

"Hmm. I predict that you won't be receiving any invitations from the Russian embassy in the near future. What possessed you to walk in there like that?"

"I was looking for answers."

"There are better—more discreet—ways to go about doing so."

"I was desperate, Duncan. The police have actually arrested Gregory for murder. It's ludicrous. Someone has fabricated some evidence against him *and* has used his influence to have Chief Inspector Burnell taken off the case."

"He? Do you have anyone particular in mind?"

"That's where you come in." A sheepish grin crossed her lips. "I know you have contacts with, let's just say, people who like to keep a low profile and their real identities a secret. I was wondering whether, perhaps, you can ask them a few questions about Philip Acheson."

"*Philip Acheson*? You think that *he* is this Sergei Konstantin? I can't believe it."

"I didn't want to at first, but little things keep piling up against him."

"Such as?"

Emmeline enumerated the points on her fingers. "Fact one, Philip speaks Russian fluently. Fact two, he was stationed at the Moscow embassy for several years. Fact three, he was in Venice at the same time as Charles and Anatol Zobrinsky. Fact four, when I saw him the other day, he did everything in his power to get me to drop this story."

"Emmy, that's all circumstantial."

"That's why I need your secret friends to ask a few questions. I can't ask Chief Inspector Burnell. He's already risked a great deal to give me the information about Philip being in Venice."

Duncan shook his head. "This is sheer insanity. You're playing with fire."

She could see that he was wavering. She stood on her tiptoes and threw her arms around his neck to give him a kiss on the cheek. "But you'll help me because you are the most darling man in the world and you adore me."

"Manhandling me will not persuade me to engage in this folly of yours."

"Are you sure? It used to work when I was a little girl."

She gave him another quick peck and fluttered her eyelashes.

"You know what you are?"

"No, what?"

He smiled down at her. "One of those sirens who tried to lure Odysseus to his doom."

Emmeline had won, just as she had known she would. "Thank you, Duncan. I can never repay you for this." She gave him a hug.

"There is one condition, though." Something in the tone of his voice told her that she was not going to like what he was about to say. "You must let me handle this from here on out. You are to halt your investigation, until we are certain that this Sergei Konstantin can't hurt you."

She thrust out her jaw and squared her shoulders, a warrior girding herself for battle. "You know I can't do that."

He started laughing. "You reminded me of your father just then. Aaron didn't listen to sage advice either."

She softened. She realized he was not going to press her on this point. "What can I tell you? I come from good stock."

He laughed again and glanced at his watch. "More like a dog with a bone. All right, my little Amazon warrior, it's time for me to get back to the embassy. I'll let you know if I discover anything. In the meantime—" He wagged his forefinger at her. "—you must promise me to be careful. If you run into any trouble, call me. I'll be at your side immediately. Do you understand, Emmy? I'm serious."

She nodded her head and gave him another hug. "Thank you. I owe you one."

He dismissed this with a wave of hands. "If I had a pound for every time you've said that to me since you were a girl, I'd be a very rich man by now."

"But you would have missed out on a lot of excitement along the way."

"That's true, my dear. It's never dull when you're about. Now, I really must go."

"Go. Go." She gave him a gentle shove. "I'll make my way home on my own."

"You're sure?" His brow furrowed with worry. "I could have an embassy car take you home."

"Don't be silly. It's a short walk and the weather has cleared up. No one would try anything in broad daylight."

She could tell he was not convinced, but in the end he surrendered.

Once Duncan had vanished from sight, she flopped down onto a bench by the pond and paused. Why did she feel like she was being watched again? She swiveled her neck around, but couldn't pick out anyone that looked suspicious. She shrugged her shoulders. The stress must be getting to her. Then, she started digging in her handbag.

"Hello?" she answered the insistent ringing of her mobile.

"Now I know why you made me swear to support you 'no matter what.'"

"James, is that you? How nice to speak with you again so soon. I don't know many editors who are as concerned about their reporters' well-being."

"Drop it, Emmeline. Guess who I've been chatting on phone with for the last forty-five minutes."

"I can't imagine. Was it someone interesting? If so, did you get any good quotes for tomorrow's edition?"

He ignored her question. "The Russian ambassador has been on to me about one of my reporters, who nearly caused an international incident this morning."

"Really? How fascinating."

"Have you lost your mind? What possessed you to

go to the embassy and start hurling accusations about?"

"Let's just say that I was rattling the cupboards a bit to see what I could shake loose."

"Well, you succeeded. It took all my powers of persuasion not to have *Times* reporters barred from Russian embassies worldwide."

"I congratulate you, James. You're a true diplomat."

"You're just lucky that the ambassador didn't call the publisher. Otherwise, we both would have been out without so much as a by-your-leave. As it is, I had to promise that you would never set foot in the embassy ever again."

Emmeline stiffened. "You didn't?"

"I most certainly did."

"That's blackmail."

"Call it what you will. I had this paper to consider. That's where things stand, whether you like it or not. Don't ever test my loyalty and friendship like that again."

"I'm sorry, James. Truly I am. I never imagined you would be placed in such a position. I was just trying to get to the truth."

"Are you going to tell me what you've found out and the leads you're following? After all, I'm only your editor."

"Yes, of course. I should have told you everything earlier, but I was upset that you had allowed Ian do the story on Gregory's arrest."

For the second time in less than an hour, Emmeline went over the entire story.

James was silent for several seconds once she had finished. "I don't like it, Emmeline. You're a damned fine reporter—if somewhat reckless—but this is getting dangerous. What am I saying? It already is dangerous. Charles is dead and you're in the killer's crosshairs."

"That's exactly why I must press on. Don't you see?

I'm getting close. I can almost taste it and that has some-one worried."

"I still don't like it."

"James, I'm begging you. Please don't take me off this. This is the most important story of my career."

He didn't say anything. Emmeline was afraid that he had hung up. "James?"

"This goes against my better judgment, but I agree that you're on to something. I just hope it doesn't get you killed."

"Have no fears. I'm like a cat. I have nine lives."

"See that you don't use them all up. Keep me in-formed about what you're doing and stay away from the Russian embassy."

"Yes, boss. Thank you for trusting me. It means a lot."

"Oh, go on. Ring me tomorrow morning to give me an update on your progress. And be careful."

"Why does everyone keep saying that to me?"

"Maybe it's because we know you."

"I'll be careful. Don't worry."

# CHAPTER 23

There were only a handful of people in Room 38 at the National Gallery. A hush enveloped the room as they studied the Canaletto and Guardi paintings, as well as ones by Bernardo Belloto and Giovanni Panini. Anatol Zobrinsky sat on a black leather-covered bench admiring Canaletto's view of the Doge's Palace and the Riva degli Schiavoni. The red damask walls only seemed to enhance the elegance of the painting.

When the taxi had dropped him off in Trafalgar Square, he took two circuitous tours around it then down Pall Mall, past Buckingham Palace, and into Green Park, before heading back to the gallery. Once he was satisfied that he didn't have a shadow, he entered the imposing building and slowly climbed the marble staircase in the Central Hall to Level Two.

Zobrinsky had been waiting for ten minutes, when he heard the crisp footsteps echoing across the highly polished parquet floor.

They stopped just behind him. He didn't have to turn around. He knew who it was.

Without taking his eyes off the Canaletto, Zobrinsky said, "Ah, Venice. Her beauty never ceases to amaze me. And yet, she has a dark side, too. So many intrigues and assassinations have been plotted there over the centuries.

It is still the same today. Nothing changes and everything changes. Isn't that true, Mr. Acheson?" He looked up at Philip, not really expecting an answer. He patted the bench next to him. "Please sit down. Let's talk about our little dilemma."

Philip shot a furtive glance around the room before taking the seat indicated. "Were you followed?"

"No, but it may be just a matter of time. I have to disappear. *Now.* You have to help me."

They kept their voices low and kept their eyes forward.

"It's too risky. I can't attract any more attention. Chief Inspector Burnell is still sniffing around."

"I thought you made sure that he was taken off the case."

"He was, but he's like a vulture circling around its prey."

Zobrinsky let out a soft chuckle. "The fat man is smarter than he looks. You should have listened to me in Venice. It would have been so much easier to take care of everything then. But no, you had to wait until we got back to London. Things have gotten very, very messy. The girl is a bigger problem than Longdon. It won't be long before she fits all the pieces together."

"Damn it. Don't you think I know that?"

Zobrinsky laughed again, knowing it would infuriate Philip even further. "Losing your temper will not solve anything, Mr. Acheson. Cool heads must prevail in this situation. For better or worse, we're partners. Neither of us likes the other—nor trusts the other, for that matter—but our fates are inextricably tied together. We've come too far and we both have too much to lose."

"You're right, of course."

"That's better. You're an intelligent man. I knew you would see reason."

"I have a plan."

"That's always a good start. I'm all ears."

ↄↄↄↄ

Gregory was lying on his back with his hands tucked behind his head. He was contemplating the crack in the ceiling when Sergeant Finch appeared with a constable. Keys jangled as the constable fumbled to open the cell door.

"Sergeant Finch, what a pleasure. If you've come for afternoon tea, I'm afraid I can't offer you any. The service and accommodations in this place leave a lot to be desired. Perhaps you can take up the matter with the proprietor."

"On your feet, Longdon."

Gregory swung his legs onto the floor. "Are we going somewhere? What fun."

"Stop chuntering on and get moving. We don't have all day." Finch handcuffed him and gave him a shove toward the door. "That will be all, constable. I'll take it from here."

"Certainly, Sergeant. Only I'd better check with Inspector Williams."

"There's no need for that. The inspector sent me to get Longdon."

The constable hesitated then shrugged to acknowledge that it wasn't any of his business. "That's all right, then. Afternoon, Sergeant."

"Good afternoon." Finch waited until the constable had gone. He pulled Gregory's arm. "Come on, Longdon." Then he lowered his voice and whispered, "Chief Inspector Burnell said that you had better not cause any trouble, otherwise he'll make sure you rot in prison for the rest of your life. Understand?"

"I must say that it is heartwarming to see how much Oliver cares. Lead on, Sergeant, by all means. Can we stop at Savile Row on the way? I must have a new suit made. As you can see—" He gestured to his prison uniform. "—this is last year's style and I wouldn't be caught dead in it."

"If you're dead, what does it matter?"

"I must say that is a rather cynical point of view. One always tries to look one's best."

"Oh, shut up. We're stopping to get your clothes. All right?"

"Splendid, old chap. Why didn't you say so from the beginning?"

Finch groaned and rolled his eyes.

෴

As Emmeline approached her house, Giles was coming down the stairs. "Well, hello." He met her at the bottom of the steps. "I'm in luck after all. On a whim, I thought I'd pop over. I was about to leave—disappointed I might add—but here you are."

"Why didn't you just ring me? I was out on assignment."

He took her by the elbow and pulled her closer. "I thought it best not to trust the phone. It was about something we discussed last night at dinner." He took a quick glance up the street, then mouthed, "About the Russian spy."

He had piqued her curiosity. She nodded. "Come inside. I'll put a kettle on and you can tell me what you discovered."

He followed her up the steps. She fumbled in her purse for her keys and unlocked the front door. "Let me take your coat."

She hung it on the peg and then shrugged out of her own. They walked down the hall to the kitchen. She filled the kettle with water and placed it on the stove.

"What can I do to help?" he asked.

"The cups and saucers are in that cupboard over there," she said with an incline of her head.

"Right, you are."

She watched as he set out the cups and saucers. She tapped her fingers on the polished wood table, wishing he would hurry up. Finally, he sat down.

She smiled. "Now, what is it that you wanted to tell me?"

"I've been thinking a lot about our conversation and your Russian spy theory."

"It's not a theory."

"That's why I'm here. I think you're right."

Her right eyebrow lifted in surprise. "You mean you believe me?"

"Yes, I do."

"You didn't last night. What changed your mind?"

"I can't put my finger on anything in particular. It was a lot of little things that didn't make sense at the time, but now—in hindsight—seem to be glaringly obvious."

The kettle screamed. She got up and turned off the stove. "It needs to brew for a few minutes. Please go on with what you were saying. What was obvious?"

"Well—This is strictly off the record. I don't want my name mentioned at all, not even as an 'informed source.' Do I have your word on that, Emmeline?"

"Yes, of course."

His shoulders relaxed and the anxious look in his eyes was replaced by relief. "Thanks. As I said, it wasn't anything in particular. But then this morning, I happened to pass Acheson in the corridor—"

"Philip? What about him?"

"He got a call on his mobile. He was speaking very softly, but I could tell that he didn't like what was being said at the other end."

"I don't see what that has to do with—"

"When he noticed me, he switched to Russian. I don't speak the language so I couldn't understand, but I recognize the cadence. With whom would a Foreign Office official speak Russian? I distinctly heard him say Emmeline and Longdon in the same breath. Then he rushed past me out the building and hasn't been seen since. Before I left, I went to his office on the pretense that I wanted to ask him a question. His secretary told me that Acheson had told her to clear his calendar for the rest of the afternoon and left no word where he could be reached. I found it all very odd."

"Very odd, indeed," she murmured as she poured the tea and took a small sip.

"I wouldn't have given the incident a second thought, if I hadn't heard him mention your name. I'm not saying that Acheson *is* the spy. Naturally, I don't have any evidence to support such a claim and wouldn't want to accuse him of anything. It just made me think."

"Yes, it provides a lot of food for thought, doesn't it? Thank you for telling me. I promise to keep your name out of it."

They finished up their tea in silence.

"I hate to dash," he said as he checked his watch. "But, I'm afraid I must be getting back to the office. Plus, I'm sure you have a lot of work to do as well. Thank you for the tea. It was lovely." He stood to go.

"I'll walk you out."

The phone in the living room rang as he was putting his coat on. "Excuse me for a moment."

Emmeline gasped when she opened the door. "Oh,

my God." Her files were tossed all over the floor and the desk drawers had been riffled. Even the contents of her grandfather's secretary desk had been pillaged. Why lately did everyone find it necessary to toss her things about?

"What's wrong?" She could feel Giles's breath brush the back of her neck. "Oh, Emmeline. You must call the police immediately."

When he said that, it brought her attention back to the phone that was still ringing. She dug under a few papers and finally found it. "Hello."

"Miss Kirby, you are in more danger than you know. It is not safe for you in the house. You are being watched. Please get out. *Now.*"

Her hand started to tremble and her voice was shaky. "Who is this?"

"A friend." The voice was familiar. She had heard it somewhere very recently.

"Did you do this? Are you the one who killed Charles? If you're trying to frighten me, it won't work. I'll find you." *But it was,* she said inwardly. *It was working very well, indeed.*

"No, Miss Kirby. Please you must listen. It was Sergei Konstantin. He's very near and he wants you dead." She heard a soft click and the dial tone buzzed in her ear.

"Emmeline, you don't look well. Who was that?"

"He said he was a friend."

"A friend? I wouldn't want a friend who terrorized me like that. What did he say?"

She stared at Giles without uttering a word. *He said that Sergei Konstantin wanted to kill me.* She looked down, surprised to find the receiver still in her hand. She replaced it in the cradle as her eyes roamed over the mess. "Nothing. He said nothing. I have to call the police and you have to get back to the office."

"I can't leave you like this. What if the chap comes

back? I'll wait with you until the police get here."

"No," she snapped and then said more gently, "No, it's all right."

"It's not safe."

"I'll be fine. Really." She attempted a weak smile and pushed him toward the door.

It was clear he was not convinced, but he acquiesced. "I'll ring you later to see if you're all right." He gave her a peck on the cheek.

She looked at the jumble of papers again. Hopefully, she would be around later to take his call.

# CHAPTER 24

After they retrieved his clothes from Property and he changed, the handcuffs went back on and Gregory was remanded into Sergeant Finch's custody. He told the constables on duty that Chief Inspector Burnell wanted to question Longdon at headquarters. This did not arouse any suspicions because these constables were not aware that Inspector Williams was now in charge of the case.

Gregory docilely followed Finch's lead and said nothing during this entire exchange. Once they were outside in the car park, he asked, "What does Oliver have up his sleeve?"

The sergeant opened the passenger door. "Just get inside. It's best not to linger here too long."

Gregory shrugged his shoulders and slipped into the seat. Finch came around the car and got into the driver's seat. He clicked his belt into place. But before he started the engine, he leaned over and unlocked the handcuffs.

"What's this, Sergeant? You're not afraid to be alone in the car with a dangerous murderer?"

Finch sighed. "Longdon, I'm going to be honest. I don't like you. You're arrogant and conceited and far too suave for my tastes. You're many things, but—"

"Your compliments are making my head swim."

"—but I don't think you are a killer and neither does Chief Inspector Burnell."

"That's good of old Oliver. However, the two of you seem to be in the minority."

"Don't forget Miss Kirby. She's your biggest champion—God knows why. She's running around London trying to tell anyone who will listen that you are innocent. That's going a bit far in my book. You're not a murderer, but you're far from being an innocent lamb."

"What can I say? She has good taste. How is she, by the way?" Gregory asked.

"She's fine. She's too good for you, though, but that's a different story. That's for the two of you to sort out on your own. Right now, Chief Inspector Burnell wants to have a chat with you somewhere far from the prying eyes at the station. He has a few theories about Sergei Konstantin and Latimer's murder." Finch turned the key in the ignition and they pulled out of the car park. "It's perfectly obvious to all and sundry that we were removed from the case because someone rather high up put pressure on Superintendent Fenton."

Gregory raised one eyebrow. "Anyone particular in mind?"

"As I said, the chief inspector has a theory. What we lack is proof."

"I don't understand. Where do I come in?"

"You'll see. The chief inspector will explain it to you."

Twenty minutes later, they were following the sweeping curve of Park Crescent in St. Marylebone. "Regent's Park, Sergeant Finch? Oliver asked you to drive me home. How thoughtful."

Finch pulled into an empty space and turned off the engine. "Not quite. Come on, get out. The chief inspector will be waiting for us."

They crossed the road and followed the path over the footbridge until they reached the Inner Circle, in the heart of which nestled Queen Mary's Rose Garden.

In June and July, the air here was laced with the heady, delicate scent of full-blown blossoms and the garden was a riot of color. Now, however, there were no velvety petals and it looked a bit forlorn in the watery February sunshine seeping from the cleft between two thick gray clouds.

They could see Burnell pacing back forth. He glanced at his watch once.

"Sir," Sergeant Finch called, when they were about one hundred feet away.

"Ah, there you are." The chief inspector stopped pacing. "I was beginning to think you had some trouble getting Longdon out."

"No, sir. None whatsoever."

Gregory extended a hand. "Oliver."

Burnell hesitated for the briefest instant before shaking it. "I'm sorry for all this cloak-and-dagger business, Longdon, but I needed to see you."

Gregory grinned mischievously. "I'm flattered, Oliver. I missed you, too."

"Stop being flippant. The only reason you're here is because Williams is a damned fool without an original thought in his head. He'd arrest his own mother, if Superintendent Fenton told him to do it."

"I can't argue with you. We both agree that Inspector Williams has the wrong end of the stick, but I don't see how we're going to solve this little problem here in the middle of Regent's Park."

"We have reason to suspect that Philip Acheson is up to his neck in this whole mess. He seems to be pulling the strings behind the scenes."

"Acheson?" Gregory quirked an eyebrow upward.

"That's very interesting. How did you come to this conclusion?"

"A number of things have come to our attention. First of all, we are certain that he rang Fenton to have us removed from the case. Acheson's best friend, the businessman Peter Rimmington, is Fenton's son-in-law. Second, Acheson was stationed at the Moscow embassy for six years. He speaks Russian, among several other languages, like a native. Finally, we received confirmation early this morning that Acheson was in Venice at the same time as Latimer. So he could have attacked him."

"That's very interesting," Gregory said as he took a turn around the bare rose bushes. "Why would he have gone to all that trouble? Surely, you don't believe he is Sergei Konstantin, do you?"

"Actually, everything seems to be pointing in that direction."

"I never liked Acheson—a bit too full of himself for my taste—but I think you're wrong, Oliver."

"Chief Inspector Burnell."

"Oh, Oliver, you're always so formal. This is *not* a formal occasion, if you haven't noticed. I do think a little relaxation of the rules may be permitted."

They glared at each other for a moment—warm brown eyes dueling with cool blue ones.

Burnell relented, but he wagged his forefinger at Gregory. "All right, but only for the moment, mind you. Now, back to Acheson. Everything seems to point to him."

"So why don't you bring him in for questioning?"

"Ah, that's the tricky bit. He has friends in high places, the prime minister being one of them. We have no proof, just strong suspicions. That's where I was hoping you would be able to play a role."

"Me? Oliver, I'd like to help—especially if it would

keep this murderous Russian spy away from Emmeline and clear my name at the same time—but I don't see what I can do."

"Ah, well, you see...you have certain skills and we thought...perhaps, you could—"

Suddenly, everything became clear to Gregory. "Oliver, surely you're not suggesting that I should *break into* Acheson's office, are you?"

Burnell shuffled his feet and kept his eyes on the ground. He was silent for a minute. Finally, he looked up. "Oh, all right. Yes, we want you to break into his office."

Gregory looked at the chief inspector in mock horror. "I'm shocked that you could even suggest such a thing, Oliver. I'm a law-abiding citizen."

A snort escaped Finch's lips at the latter remark. His momentary burst of mirth disappeared quickly, though, as Burnell shot him a sideways glance.

"Are you going to do it or not?"

"Rather. I wouldn't want to miss out on all the fun. Mind you, I still think that you're wrong."

The knot between Burnell's shoulder blades eased.

Gregory lowered his voice conspiratorially as he asked, "When do you want me to carry out this 'job,' boss?"

Burnell winced at this term. "Tonight."

"Tonight? That's rather short notice. Ah, but when duty calls, one must attend." Gregory gave a little salute.

"It has to be tonight because Finch found out that Acheson will not be working late as usual. He has to go to some embassy do."

"That's convenient. When's zero hour?"

"Nine o'clock."

Gregory gave a small salute as he clicked his heels together. "At your service, *mon général*."

"All right. All right. That's enough of that. Sergeant

Finch will stay with you at your flat, until you have to leave tonight."

Gregory put his arm around the chief inspector's shoulders. "Oliver, we're partners in this little endeavor. I'm hurt to see that you don't trust me."

"No, I don't. That's why I'm leaving Finch behind. However, tonight you're on your own. We can't risk being seen anywhere near the Foreign Office. Now, get off." He shrugged himself free of Gregory's arm.

"I suppose we'll just have to make the best of the situation, won't we, Sergeant?"

Finch did not look too happy at the prospect of spending the rest of the afternoon with Gregory.

"Sir, how will you explain Longdon's absence from the jail?"

"I had to pull a few strings, but the judge finally agreed to grant bail. However—" He pointed a finger at Gregory. "I've had to vouch for you. So see to it that you don't get caught."

Gregory flashed a charming smile. "Oliver, you should know by now that I never get caught. Never."

"Humph," the chief inspector grunted. "I—" Whatever he was about to say was forgotten as his mobile started to ring. He pulled it out of his pocket and flipped it open. "Hello. Oh, Miss Kirby, it's you. How are you?" He listened closely. His blue eyes narrowed and deep ridges appeared on his forehead.

Gregory, whose ears had pricked up at the sound of Emmeline's name, did not like the dark look upon Burnell's face. "What is it?" he mouthed.

The chief inspector held up his index finger. "Right. Don't touch anything. We're on our way. Lock the doors and don't open them for anybody but us, do you understand?" He nodded his head as he listened for a few more seconds. "Don't worry. Everything will be fine." Burnell turned to the other two men. "Someone's broken into Miss Kirby's house and gone through all her files. She also received a threatening phone call about Sergei Konstantin. She's not hurt, though. She wasn't home at the time the break-in occurred."

Gregory and Finch looked at one another. Concern was clearly written on each man's face. The muscle in Gregory's jaw twitched. "Let's go, Oliver."

"Longdon, you can't come. It's not a good idea for you to be seen gallivanting about town at the moment."

"I'm coming," was all he said and started making his way out of the garden.

⋐⋑⋐⋑

Emmeline had been watching from the window in the living room and saw when the car pulled into a space two doors down. She flung open the front door before they even had a chance to ring the bell.

"Thank you for coming so quickly, Chief Inspector Burnell. I'm sorry to bother you. I know that you're not on the case anymore, but I didn't feel comfortable calling Inspector Williams."

"It's quite all right, Miss Kirby."

She opened the door wide so that they could step inside. "Gregory, what are you doing here? How did you get out of jail?" Her eyes narrowed as a thought struck her. "You didn't escape, did you?" she asked anxiously.

Despite his worry, Gregory laughed. "No, darling, I didn't 'escape' as you put it. I'm at liberty thanks to dear old Oliver here." Once again, he slipped an arm around Burnell's shoulders and gave a rough squeeze.

"Keep this up, Longdon, and you'll find yourself back in jail."

"Oh, don't dash my hopes like that, Oliver."

"All right. Enough of this. Miss Kirby, can you show us the room and tell us precisely what the caller said?"

"Yes, of course. It's the living room."

As Burnell and Finch took a careful look at the upheaval that had been wrought, Emmeline told them everything she did from the minute she left Scotland Yard to her little foray at the Russian embassy. She also mentioned her talk with Duncan. She ended with the phone call warning her about Sergei Konstantin.

"You went to the Russian embassy? Are you out of your mind?" Gregory snapped. "What possessed you to do such a foolish thing?"

Her nerves had been pulled so taut in the last week that she snapped back, "I am not foolish."

"No, you're right. Reckless would be a better word from where I'm standing."

"Ooh!" Her fists clenched into tight balls at her sides and she impaled him with her eyes. "We weren't getting anywhere, so I thought I would push things a bit to see what would happen. You know what? You have no right to speak to me this way." Her breathing was coming fast as she seethed.

"Oh, no?"

"No."

Burnell stepped in at this point, before the argument could escalate any further. "This will not get us anywhere."

They both turned and faced him. They had forgotten that they were not alone.

Emmeline's cheeks flushed in embarrassment. "I'm sorry, Chief Inspector. You're quite right." She slid a sideways glance in Gregory's direction. The expression in her eyes told him that they would finish their argument later.

The doorbell rang. "Finch, go see who that is?"

"Yes, sir."

Burnell must have seen the look that flickered across Emmeline's features. "Even if he is watching, he wouldn't try anything with us here."

She exhaled slowly. She hadn't realized that she had been holding her breath. "Of course, you're right. I'm just being silly."

They heard Finch and another man speaking in the hall. "I'm an old family friend of Emmeline's. Has anything happened to her?"

It was Duncan. She could hear the concern in his voice. She went to the door and popped her head out into the hall. "It's all right, Sergeant Finch. This is Duncan Redmond. He's an old friend of my father's. He's also the director of the Media Relations Department at the Canadian embassy."

"Sorry, Mr. Redmond." Finch allowed him to pass. "Please go right in."

Duncan walked into the living room and held out his hands to Emmeline. "What's happened, my dear? Are you all right?"

She smiled up at him. "I'm fine. Don't worry. Someone has broken into the house and riffled my files. I called Chief Inspector Burnell immediately."

Duncan looked around and extended his hand to Burnell. "Forgive me, Chief Inspector, I was so worried about Emmeline. It's nice to see you again."

Burnell shook his hand. "Yes, and you too, Mr. Redmond. I'm just sorry it has to be like this."

"Yes, we always seem to meet under stressful circumstances, don't we?"

"Unfortunately, it seems so."

Then Duncan's blue eyes settled on Gregory. He turned back to Emmeline, his eyebrow quirking upward in a question.

"You remember Gregory, don't you, Duncan?"

There was an awkward silence. Duncan knew how badly Emmeline had been hurt when Gregory had disappeared two years earlier. However, he saw the imperceptible nod that she gave him and squeezed her arm reassuringly. "Yes, of course. I remember you quite well. It's been a long time," he said graciously.

"A pleasure to see you again, Duncan."

Emmeline sighed with relief as the two men shook hands. They both had decided to play nice for her sake.

Chief Inspector Burnell and Sergeant Finch missed none of this little drama, but they had more important matters to deal with at the moment. "Mr. Redmond, what brings you here this afternoon?"

"Emmeline and I met earlier today. She told me about Charles Latimer's theory about the Russian spy at the Foreign Office and she asked for my help because she didn't want to cause you anymore trouble, Chief Inspector. She also was determined to prove that Scotland Yard had arrested the wrong man for Charles's murder." Duncan's eyes briefly drifted toward Gregory.

Emmeline broke in at this stage. "Everything seems to be pointing to Philip as Sergei Konstantin. A little bird told me he was in Venice at the same time as Charles and I were." She smiled and nodded at Burnell, but continued, "I don't want to believe that it's Philip. His wife Maggie is my best friend. We went to university together. They have lovely twin boys. If Philip is the spy, I didn't want to arouse his suspicions by asking questions around the Foreign Office. So I called Duncan. I needed someone who has international connections and who could look into this matter quietly for me. He has friends who, let's say, prefer to work in the shadows."

"I see. It takes a spy to catch a spy," Burnell murmured.

Duncan smiled at him. "Something like that."

"Were you able to learn anything from your 'friends,' Mr. Redmond?"

"Yes." He unbuttoned his Burberry coat and pulled out a piece of paper that he had tucked in an inside pocket. "They e-mailed me this photo about an hour ago. It was taken in Venice as you can see."

Emmeline leaned forward to get a better look at the printout in Burnell's hand. There was Philip standing near the Rialto Bridge huddled deep in conversation with—Anatol Zobrinsky.

A knot formed in the pit of her stomach and her knees felt like jelly all of a sudden. She grabbed a chair for support.

"Then, it's true. I didn't want to believe it. Even when Giles told me that he had overheard Philip talking about me and Gregory, I didn't want to believe it."

"What's this about Hayden?" Gregory asked.

"He was here when I discovered all this." She waved her hand in the direction of the desk.

"Why was he here?" Gregory pressed.

She rolled her eyes and explained about coming home to find Giles just arriving. "So I invited him inside for tea. That's when he told me about Philip's heated telephone conversation in Russian. He doesn't speak Russian, but he distinctly heard Philip say my name and yours. Apparently, Philip unexpectedly cancelled all his meetings this afternoon and dashed out of the building. He hasn't been seen since."

"That's a bit of interesting news. Acheson would have had ample time to break into your house, Miss Kirby."

Two deep frown lines appeared between Gregory's eyebrows, but he kept his own counsel.

"But what was he looking for, Chief Inspector?"

"Obviously, Acheson thinks you have something that identifies him as Sergei Konstantin."

"I don't. Until Duncan brought this photo that clearly ties Philip to Zobrinsky, I hadn't been able to discover anything. It's as if I have been deliberately sent in the wrong direction."

"Well, now we know why Acheson's been having you followed."

"That still doesn't explain why he would break into my house."

"Think, Miss Kirby, did Latimer leave a file, a disk, a note, *anything*?"

"No, Chief Inspector Burnell, I didn't find anything in his room or in here."

Burnell crossed one arm over his chest and stroked his chin with his other hand. "There's got to be something. Otherwise, Acheson would not have risked coming here in broad daylight. Perhaps Latimer hid it—whatever 'it' is."

"I'll check the house from top to bottom, Chief Inspector."

'I'll help you," Gregory stepped forward and offered.

Burnell gave him a pointed look. "No, you have other things to deal with, Longdon. Don't forget that you still have a murder charge hanging over your head."

Gregory smiled. "Ah, yes, of course, Oliver. It nearly slipped my mind."

Emmeline's eyes narrowed as she watched this exchange. There seemed to be a double meaning in what they had said to one another. Something was going on. They seemed very cozy all of a sudden, which was highly unusual—and suspicious.

"It's all right. I can do it on my own, Gregory. I wouldn't want to prejudice your case. Chief Inspector, it was very good of you to use your influence to at least get him out on bail. I'm terribly sorry for all those things I said to you in your office this morning. I should have known better."

"Don't be silly, Miss Kirby. What else could you have thought under the circumstances?"

"That's very kind of you, Chief Inspector. Thank you."

"Well, I—" Burnell stammered and then tried to change the subject. "I could get the boys down here to dust the house for fingerprints, but I very much doubt that we'll find any."

"No, it's all right. The only room that was touched was the living room and only my desk at that."

"I'll stay with you, Emmeline," Duncan said.

She touched his arm lightly and shook her head. "No, Duncan, you've been away from the embassy too long as it is. Go back to work. Please. You've been a great help." She gave him a little shove toward the door.

Concern was clearly evident in his blue eyes. "Aaron would never forgive me if I let something happen to you."

"Nothing is going to happen to me," she said. Even to her own ears this sounded forced. "Daddy would understand. He would not have dropped the story and I'm certainly not going to either."

All the men in the room looked at one another. In the end, Burnell shrugged his shoulders. "It goes against my better judgment to leave you here on your own, Miss Kirby. I don't like it one bit. But if you're adamant about it, the only thing I can do is to have a couple of chaps watch the house."

Emmeline laughed. "Terrific. Then you'll be watching me and Sergei Konstantin will be watching me. I'll be looking over my shoulder all the time and I won't know who is who."

"It's better than winding up dead," Gregory said bluntly.

"You don't need to remind me that there is an element of risk involved."

"Oh, no? You seem to have forgotten. And since when has murder been described as merely an 'element of risk'? Emmy, you're not thinking straight. This bloody story has clouded your judgment. You've become obsessed."

She threw her hands up in exasperation. "Just go. All of you. Thank you for coming so quickly. I appreciate it, but I will be fine. I'm going to look for this evidence Charles has hidden and, the minute I find it, I promise to give all of you a call. Is that all right?"

"It will have to do, Miss Kirby. Please be careful," Burnell urged as he shook her hand.

Duncan bent down and gave Emmeline a kiss on the cheek. "Listen to Chief Inspector Burnell, my Amazon warrior." He wagged a finger at her. "Promise me, no more little excursions to the Russian embassy."

She smiled sheepishly and gave him a hug. "I promise. Besides, the guards probably have orders to shoot me on sight."

"That's not amusing, Emmy."

"No, sorry. I was just being flippant."

"Make me happy and be careful instead. No story is worth your life."

She thought of her parents as he said this. "Yes, you're quite right," she whispered as she gave him a kiss.

She walked the men to the door. Dusk's charcoal shadows mingled with the smoky curtain of fog that was descending heavily from the sky. The square had nearly vanished and soon the street would be swallowed up as well.

Gregory lingered in the doorway for a moment. He

didn't say anything. He just looked down at her and traced a finger lightly along one cheek.

"Longdon, are you coming?" Chief Inspector Burnell's disembodied voice drifted up to their ears from the bottom of the steps.

"Yes, I'm coming." Gregory gave her a quick kiss and then turned his back to follow the others.

ღოღ

The man in the blue Opel next door to Emmeline's house watched as Burnell, Finch, and Gregory climbed into a car and drove away. He ducked down in his seat and pulled his coat collar up as Duncan passed his car on his way back to the embassy. He waited a few minutes and then made a call on his mobile.

It only rang once. "What's happened?"

"The police and Longdon just pulled away and the other chap left on foot. The girl is all alone."

"Did they find the bugs?"

"No, they're still in place and in perfect working order. I can hear everything being said as if I'm in the room. She still doesn't know who the spy is."

"A bit of good news, at last. If the girl leaves, follow her. Stick to her like glue. Whatever you do, don't let her slip through your fingers. Keep in contact with the other teams. I want a report every hour. Do you understand?"

"Yes, boss."

"Good. I must ring off. There's a damned do at the French embassy tonight and if we're late my wife will murder me. I'm on my way home to change."

"Don't worry, boss. We'll handle everything."

"With any luck," Philip said, "the secret of Sergei Konstantin will be buried tonight. One way or the other."

# CHAPTER 25

Exuding confidence and carrying a sheath of papers under his arm, Gregory passed between the Corinthian columns of the Foreign Office's main entrance. He calmly showed the guards the badge that Chief Inspector Burnell had somehow procured for him. They allowed him to pass without a second glance. His footsteps echoed loudly as he crossed the elegant hall with its high, vaulted ceiling, gilded walls, and red-veined marble columns. When he reached the Grand Staircase, he fought the urge to take the steps two at a time. He didn't want to attract any undue attention to himself. He wanted to get in and out of the building as quickly, and as quietly, as possible. He risked one glance over his shoulder as his feet slowly carried him up the red-carpeted staircase to the gallery. He had no need to worry. The guards had returned to their conversation and took no notice of him.

At the top of the landing, he turned left, recalling the rough map that Burnell had drawn in the car. Gregory didn't pass anyone as he followed the corridor until he came to the office at the far end. Although it was already eight o'clock, he knocked on the door to determine whether Philip's secretary was working late. There was no response. He tried the doorknob, but it didn't budge. That would have been too easy. So, with a practiced hand, he inserted a special file into the keyhole and fiddled with it for a few seconds until he heard a soft click. The doorknob gave way to his touch.

He slipped into the outer office and closed the heavy oak door behind him. Miss Marsh's desk was spotless. Not a speck of dust anywhere. The desk was devoid of any photos or personal items. He wondered whether this was one of Philip's dictates or simply a matter of choice on her part. There were no files either. She must lock away whatever she was working on at the end of each day. He gave the room another cursory glance and then focused on his real objective. Philip's office. This was unlocked.

He carefully surveyed the room, which was more like a gentleman's study than an office. The plush red wall-to-wall carpeting covering the floor muffled his footsteps. An elegant mahogany desk dominated the center of the office. In the corner to the right of the door, a Chesterfield sofa and two armchairs in the same claret leather were clustered around a highly polished oval cherry-wood coffee table. This little area sat next to a large window that overlooked King Charles Street. On the opposite side of the room near the desk were two mahogany bookcases with glass doors, through which he spied leather-bound tomes.

Gregory decided to begin his search here. After ten minutes, he came to the conclusion that this was fruitless and turned his attention to the desk. He sat in Philip's chair and tried the middle drawer. It was locked. Once again, he pulled out his little file. Soon, the drawer was open and ready to yield up its secrets, if any, to him.

A few minutes later, he closed the drawer with a frustrated sigh and reached for the top right-hand drawer. Methodically, he went through each drawer, careful to put the contents back exactly as he had found them. This was repeated two more times. However, he could find nothing. His last hope was that the drawers on the other side would contain irrefutable evidence tying Philip to the murders of Paolo Talamini and Charles Latimer, as well as proving he was the elusive Russian spy Sergei Konstantin. Gregory had to find *something*, for Emmeline's sake. She was taking too many risks that he did not like.

He was about to give up when a manila envelope tucked at the very bottom of the third drawer caught his eye. He pulled it out and set it upon the desk. It was addressed to Emmeline and had a London stamp. He looked at the date. It was mailed a couple of days before they returned from Venice. The fact that Philip had it in his possession—not to mention that he had hidden it in his desk—seemed to indicate that he was the one who broke into Emmeline's house this afternoon.

The envelope had been neatly slit open, so Gregory dumped its contents on the desk. There was a photo and a scrawled note from Charles.

> *Emmeline,*
> *This is Sergei Konstantin. He tried to kill me in Venice. He may be after you now. Please be careful.*
> *Charles*

Gregory cursed Latimer under his breath. He snatched up the photo angrily. It appeared to be a class at a military academy. He scanned the three rows of teenage boys—all stiff and unsmiling in their uniforms—looking for that one familiar face. He squinted and pulled the photo closer to the lamp. Then, he slumped back in the chair, trying to collect his thoughts. He looked at the photo one more time just to be certain. Yes, it was true.

He reached for the telephone and quickly dialed

Chief Inspector Burnell on his mobile. After only half a ring, the detective's voice hissed in his ear. "What the devil have you been up to?"

"Oliver, these delicate matters take time. If you are unsatisfied with my performance, then I suggest that next time you hire a common criminal to break into other people's offices. Or better yet, send Sergeant Finch to do your dirty work."

"Oh, get on with it, Longdon. Did you find anything?"

Gregory became serious. "Yes, I've found something."

"Good. Finch and I are around the corner. Meet us on Pall Mall in ten minutes."

"We have a slight problem."

"More than you can ever imagine."

Gregory's head snapped up and he found himself staring into Philip's cool blue eyes, which glinted with the hardness of steel. He hadn't heard him come in.

"Put the phone down, Longdon. *Now.*"

Gregory hesitated for only a second, but he chose not to argue since Philip was pointing a gun at his chest.

Burnell was frantically yelling in his ear. "Longdon? Longdon, are you still there? What's going on? Longdon?"

Gregory ignored the chief inspector's questions and focused his attention on Philip. "Acheson, old man, what a pleasant surprise."

Philip walked over to the desk and took the receiver from him. A soft click was heard as he quietly replaced it in the cradle. "Get up. Slowly." He jerked the gun impatiently. "I will not hesitate to use this, so I suggest that you do as you're told."

"How could I refuse such a friendly invitation?"

"Shut up and move."

சுல்சு

Burnell slammed his hand against the dashboard. "Bloody hell."

"Sir, what's happened?"

"Acheson walked in on Longdon."

Ever calm in a crisis, Finch digested this unwelcome piece of information and asked, "Shall I call for reinforcements?"

"No time. We'll go in alone." Burnell was already halfway out of the car. He checked the magazine clip on his gun to make sure it was fully loaded. The sharp snap echoed eerily upon the foggy night air as he slipped it back into place.

They ran up Horse Guards Road to King Charles Street. When they got inside the Foreign Office, they showed their identity cards to the guards on duty and explained that they'd had a tip about a possible threat against Philip Acheson. The guards said that they had not received any such notification and would not allow them to go any farther until Scotland Yard verified their identity.

"Damn it. A man's life is at stake and you're standing here quibbling with me about verification."

"I'm sorry, sir, but we have certain procedures that we must follow."

"You're a bloody imbecile." Burnell pushed past the guard with Finch hard on his heels. They took the steps two at a time as they dashed up the Grand Staircase.

The gallery was empty and each footfall reverberated wildly off the marble floor as they ran toward Philip's office. The guards were not far behind them, guns drawn. They were yelling for Burnell and Finch to stop, but they didn't.

They burst into the outer office and flung the door

open to Acheson's, where they found Gregory seated on the Chesterfield sofa.

Acheson, who was dressed in a tuxedo, was in one of the armchairs opposite holding a gun in his hand. Without looking up, he said, "Ah, Chief Inspector Burnell, we've been waiting for you."

A guard, breathing heavily, came in at this point. "It's all right, Denis. The situation is under control. You can return to your post."

The guard hesitated. "Well, if you're sure, Mr. Acheson."

Acheson turned and smiled at the guard. "Quite sure. No need to trouble yourselves anymore tonight. Thank you." He waited until the guards had gone and turned to the two policemen. "Gentlemen, if you would kindly give me your guns and please join Longdon over there on the sofa where I can see you."

"Acheson, you won't get away with this. We're officers of the law. Our deaths will not be so easy to explain away as Charles Latimer's and Paolo Talamini's were. We're not the only ones who know that you're Sergei Konstantin," Burnell said, as he and Finch handed over their weapons.

A serene smile crept across Acheson's handsome features. "Ah, yes, you're referring to the lovely—and nosy—Emmeline. Once she gets here, our little group will be complete."

Gregory stood up abruptly, overturning the coffee table in the process. "Acheson, I will personally rip you limb from limb, if a single hair on her head is harmed because of your little games."

"Sit down, Longdon. Your bravado is very touching, but it does not impress me. I don't take orders from a thief." He waved the gun impatiently at Gregory when he did not move. "I said *sit down*."

Burnell reached up and tugged on Gregory's sleeve. "Easy, Longdon. This won't solve anything."

"But you're wrong, Oliver." His voice was soft and dripped ice. "It would make me feel a thousand times better, if I knocked that smug smile off Acheson's bloody face."

A deep-throated chuckle escaped Acheson's lips, as Gregory resumed his seat. "I never realized that you could be quite so entertaining, Longdon. Now, gentlemen, sit back and relax. As it is ever the case, we must wait until the lady arrives so that the party can begin in earnest."

���

Emmeline had restored order to her files and her desk. As far as she could tell, nothing had been taken but she couldn't be certain. She had carefully searched every nook and cupboard in every room. After two hours, though, she was no closer to finding anything that proved beyond a shadow of a doubt that Philip was Sergei Konstantin. If Charles had hidden something in house, she couldn't find it.

"Where is it, Charles?" she asked aloud as she plopped down onto the sofa in the living room. She rested her elbows on her knees and ran her hands through her dark curls in frustration. "Where is it?"

She leaned back and closed her eyes, replaying in her mind everything that had been said and that had happened from the moment she met Charles at the ball in Venice. It was all a muddle. The pieces of the puzzle were not falling into place. Something was missing. There was something that she was not seeing. Something important. Suddenly, her eyes flew open and she sat bolt upright. "He wasn't coming. He was *leaving*. And how did he know that Charles was killed here in the house? Oh, what a fool I've been."

She ran to the phone and dialed Chief Inspector Burnell's mobile. No answer. She tried Scotland Yard, but was told that the chief inspector was out and had left no word about where he could be reached. "Can you please tell him to ring Emmeline Kirby as soon as possible? It's of the utmost urgency."

"Miss Kirby, perhaps someone else can assist you? May I ask what this in reference to?"

"It is of a rather sensitive nature and I'd rather not say over the phone. Chief Inspector Burnell is familiar with the matter. Please tell him to call me." She hung up before the secretary could ask any more questions.

Emmeline tapped her fingers restlessly on the desk. She picked up the phone and tried Gregory's mobile. It rang and rang and then went to the answer phone. She replaced the receiver once more and paced back and forth. She simply couldn't sit here and wait. And she wouldn't.

She grabbed her purse and ran into the hall to get her jacket. The front door rattled on its hinges as she flung it open. She jumped back startled, but not because of the noise. A knot had formed in the pit of her stomach. For there, standing in the doorway was Anatol Zobrinsky—a gun in one hand and a malevolent grin playing about his ugly face.

# CHAPTER 26

She tried to slam the door in his face, but he deftly put his foot between the door and the jamb. His vice-like grip clamped itself around her upper arm. "Ah, Miss Kirby, how kind of you to save me the bother of breaking down your door."

She struggled to free her arm, but couldn't. "You're hurting me."

He ignored this complaint and dragged her outside onto the steps. "You've caused quite enough trouble already. Let's go." He pulled the door shut behind them.

"I'm not going anywhere with you." She spat these words at him.

The fog had thickened since Gregory and the others had left earlier. The steps were wet and slick. Zobrinsky was not that much taller than she was, she judged, perhaps three inches. If she could catch him off guard with one good shove, maybe she had a chance.

"Come on." He pulled her down the top step and she continued to resist. Then, he turned his head to the left for just an instant and she pushed him hard against the railing. He teetered backward and nearly lost his footing, but he quickly recovered himself.

His hand tightened around her arm, which was still sore from the guard's manhandling this afternoon. "That was a silly thing to do, Miss Kirby. You're starting to annoy me," he grunted through gritted teeth. "Now, *come on.*"

❧❧❧

The telephone on Acheson's desk screeched to life, startling all of them.

He was across the room in two strides. "Uh, uh," he said, motioning for Gregory to sit down. "Longdon, I needn't remind you that this is fully loaded and at this range I can't possibly miss."

He picked up the receiver and listened. "Good work. Hold your positions for the moment. Report to me in an hour."

Acheson turned back to find three pairs of eyes intently following his every move. "Well, gentlemen, it shouldn't be long now. Zobrinsky is on his way with Emmeline."

Chief Inspector Burnell stroked his beard and inched himself to the edge of the sofa. He raised an eyebrow in Sergeant Finch's direction. Finch, in turn, gave a slight shrug of his shoulders in helpless appeal. Meanwhile, Gregory was outwardly calm. Only the muscle twitching in his jaw betrayed his trepidation. His eyes never left Acheson's face.

❧❧❧

Emmeline's throat constricted as she tried to swallow down the panic that was rising within her. Zobrinsky held her close to him with one hand. She could feel the hard muzzle of gun pressing through her jacket and into her ribs. They could barely see a few feet in front of them. The houses, the square, the parked cars all seemed to

have disappeared as if they had entered some nether-
world.

The hairs on the back of her neck stood on end and
she shivered involuntarily. The deadly stillness was un-
nerving. No one else seemed to be about. And then she
heard the footsteps. They were a little distance behind
them. Tap, tap, tap. Slow, precise, but coming closer.
Hope surged through her body. She began to breathe
again. She hadn't even realized that she had been holding
breath all this time. But halfway down the block, the tap-
ping suddenly came to a halt and so did they. Zobrinsky
pulled her closer toward him as a murky silhouette
emerged from the vaporous swirl in front of them. The
fog must have been playing tricks on her mind. Obviously, the footsteps hadn't been behind them at all.

As her eyes adjusted to the smoky darkness, she
sucked in her breath. "Giles." This was barely above a
whisper. She felt Zobrinsky's fingers digging deeper into
her poor, defenseless arm.

"Emmeline, what a surprise to find you out on such a
filthy night."

She didn't say anything. She slid a sideways glance
toward Zobrinsky and saw him stiffen slightly. Then he
said something in Russian and Giles responded.

She took half a step backward. "You're Sergei Konstantin, aren't you? It's not Philip. It's you. You killed
Charles and Paolo Talamini."

Giles laughed and bowed theatrically. "I stand before
you in the flesh. One must bask in the glow of one's ac-
complishments. Don't you think? For a while, it was
amusing to watch Latimer scurrying about, but then he
found the photo, so he had to die. He left me no choice in
the matter. You do understand that. I couldn't let him de-
stroy my work here. It's too important."

She simply gaped at this man who was so calmly

standing before her and describing how he had murdered her friend. She was too paralyzed with fear to say anything.

"But things didn't die—ha, no pun intended—with Latimer because he had hidden that bloody photo somewhere in your house."

She suddenly found her voice. "You broke into my house today. You weren't arriving when I got home. You were *leaving*."

"It was a close thing. I must admit. Just as I walked out the door, I saw you coming down the street. Luckily, you hadn't seen me."

"How? How did you know Charles was at the house? I didn't even know he was there."

Hayden smiled and for the first time she saw a ruthlessness in those green-gray eyes that she had missed before. "I have to thank you for that, my dear."

"Me?"

"If you'll remember when the flight from Venice arrived at Heathrow, you managed to squeeze past the throng in the passageway and were waiting at the door in the terminal. Latimer rang you on your mobile and I overheard your half of the conversation. You told him to wait at your house. Then it was a matter of pure luck. You and Longdon were delayed at baggage claim, giving me just enough time to dispatch Latimer. It's funny, if you think about it. I managed to leave only minutes before you and Longdon arrived. I saw your taxi pull up as I got into my car across the road."

Emmeline couldn't believe her ears. If they'd gotten home five minutes earlier, maybe Charles would be here today. "You're a monster. You won't get away with any of this." She took another step backward and tried to run, but Zobrinsky was still holding onto her and Hayden caught her other arm.

"Well, that's enough of that. You can spare me your moral superiority. After all, when all is said and done, underneath that polished British exterior you're still only a Jew. And I will not tolerate being lectured by a stinking Jew."

She felt the color drain from her cheeks. She looked from Giles to Zobrinsky and felt her knees turn to water. She couldn't control the trembling traveling up her body, which now felt like lead. "What—" She tried to lick her lips, but her mouth was bone dry. "What are you going to do to me?"

Giles laughed again. "Ever the inquisitive journalist. You're a smart girl. What do you think is going to happen?"

He said something over her head in Russian to Zobrinsky, who nodded.

She wanted to scream, but she could not will her vocal chords to obey her mind. She was going to be murdered tonight and there was nothing and no one around to stop it. *Sh'ma Yisrael, Adonai, Elohaynu, Adonai Echad.* At least her soul would be prepared.

# CHAPTER 27

The phone rang again half an hour later. Philip didn't like it. It was too soon before the next report. Why weren't Zobrinsky and Emmeline here yet?

"Acheson," Philip said as he snatched the receiver.

"We have trouble."

Philip turned his back on the three men and lowered his voice. "What kind of trouble?"

"Our friend showed up just as Zobrinsky was leaving with the girl. They all got into his car and drove off."

"Hayden? Hayden's with them. Blast." Gregory was suddenly at Philip's side.

Philip gripped the desk so hard that his knuckles turned white.

"I didn't want him to get suspicious, so I didn't follow. Team Two picked them up on Kensington High Street, but they lost them in this bloody fog."

Philip ran a hand through his hair. "Damn and blast. Damn and blast. So we have no idea where Hayden's taken them?"

There was a slight pause. "No."

"How did he find out? *How*?"

"I don't know. Obviously we weren't as careful as we had thought we'd been. Should I put out an alert? You know that he's going to kill the girl. She knows too much."

"You don't have to tell me that," Philip snapped.

"Sorry, boss. I forgot that she was a friend of yours."

"Is. *Is* a friend of mine."

"Yes, of course. About the alert?"

"Put one out. What does it matter anymore? The whole nasty business is out in the open. The most important thing now is to find Emmeline and Zobrinsky." Philip slammed the phone down.

Gregory seized him by the lapels and threw him down on the desk. "Who the bloody hell are you? What gives you the right to play around with Emmeline's life?" His red, contorted face was only inches from Philip's.

Chief Inspector Burnell and Sergeant Finch were immediately on their feet and struggled to pull him off Philip. "Steady on, Longdon," Burnell said calmly. "This is not helping anyone. Besides, he's not worth it."

No one moved for several seconds. Gregory's seething cinnamon gaze held Philip's icy blue eyes. Then, in disgust, Gregory suddenly released his hold. He went to sit down on the sofa again, his elbows resting on his knees and his throbbing head in his hands.

"That's a good chap," the chief inspector said as he patted Gregory's shoulder. "Now, Mr. Acheson, I think you have a little explaining to do. And you'd better make it fast by the sound of things."

Philip drew himself upright and sat on a corner of his desk, his left leg dangling over the edge. He stared at each of them in turn, trying to size them up. Finally, he shook his head and sighed in resignation. "What is said in this room tonight, gentlemen, stays in this room. You'll each be asked to sign the Official Secrets Act. I say *ask*, but you have no choice in the matter."

"Acheson, cut the official mumbo-jumbo," Gregory

said. "We sit here making polite conversation, as precious time is lost. Emmeline is in danger from Giles Hayden, or should I say Sergei Konstantin?"

One of Philip's eyebrows shot up. "Of course, you've seen the photo."

"Yes, I've seen the photo. Now, get on with it. What are you? MI5? MI6? Special Branch?"

Philip looked directly at Chief Inspector Burnell, when he spoke again. "Officially, I work for the Foreign Office in the Defense and Intelligence Directorate. My purview is Russia. However, only a select few—which now includes you three—know that I am MI5. Not even my wife knows and I would like to keep it that way.

"About eighteen months ago, one of our highly placed assets informed us that certain Defense documents were falling into Moscow's hands. It caused a minor ripple. But since the files were relatively harmless, the director-general put it down to a half-hearted attempt on the Russians' part to infiltrate the FO. He ordered us to keep our eyes open, but to take no action for the moment.

"About seven months ago, our agent was alarmed when a file on some secret negotiations Number 10 was having with another country suddenly appeared across Putin's desk. Then one of our undercover operatives was killed in Munich. By that time, it was obvious we had a mole in our midst. We scrambled to do damage control, but we had no idea who the spy was. He could be anyone. A disgruntled staff member, lured to the other side with the promise of cash or women, or both. Or he could be a sleeper, someone planted long ago and who was watching and waiting for his orders. I suspected the latter and quietly launched an investigation with the help of our double agent."

"Who's the agent?" Burnell asked.

Philip smiled. "That is on a need-to-know basis. He's

already walking a very fine line. Because of Latimer's, and now Emmeline's, interference his cover is most likely blown."

"Zobrinsky?" Three pair of eyes turned toward Gregory. "Isn't it?" he insisted.

Philip dropped his head and exhaled slowly from his pursed lips. His voice was very low when he looked up again. "Yes. I'm his control officer."

"Ah, now things are beginning to fall into place," Burnell murmured more to himself than anyone in particular.

"We had been planning to take care of the entire situation away from home, in Venice. But then Latimer appeared on the scene determined to unmask the Russian spy and everything suddenly became a shambles. A perfect example of the 'best laid plans of mice and men gang a-gley.'"

"How did Paolo Talamini become a part of this fiasco?" Gregory asked.

Philip smiled, a genuine smile this time. "Ah, that was the beauty of the plan. His arrogance and his underworld connections made him the ideal pawn. Talamini was a known arms dealer and Zobrinsky was trying to use him to lure Hayden into betraying himself."

"By trying to pass off a forged Caravaggio as the real thing?" Finch prompted.

"Very good, Sergeant. We knew that little ploy would make Talamini so angry he would lash out."

"Wait a minute. You didn't want to expose Hayden. That would have been a major embarrassment for the Foreign Office," Burnell said, getting to his feet. "My God, you wanted Talamini to do your dirty work for you. You wanted him to kill Hayden. That would have solved all your problems, wouldn't it? All neat and tidy, no loose ends."

"I don't have to justify our actions to you, Chief Inspector. Hayden is a spy and a threat to Britain's security. Therefore, I would have done anything, *anything* to see that this problem went away."

"Does that include jeopardizing the life of an innocent woman? Your supposed friend. Or does the Foreign Office believe that human life is a mere commodity?" Gregory's voice was calm, but his right hand trembled slightly.

Philip looked him in the eye. "I did my best to warn her off—to try to convince her that Charles was chasing a dead end. But when Emmeline gets an idea in her head, there's no stopping her. She's like a bulldog."

"Your half-hearted efforts have failed miserably and now Emmeline is Heaven knows where with an unpredictable and dangerous Russian spy, who likely suspects that she knows more than she does. Meanwhile, you're sitting here trying to assuage your conscience." Gregory stood up abruptly and made his way to the door. He turned back with his hand on the handle. "Well, I for one don't intend to let her die."

Philip shut the door and blocked his path. "Unfortunately, I cannot allow you to leave this office at the moment. First of all, you—" He waved a hand, taking in all three men with the gesture. "—know too much. And secondly, where would you go? I've had surveillance teams watching Hayden's movements for months. As soon as Emmeline returned from Venice, I put two crack teams on her house around the clock. We even searched the house and planted bugs while you were down in Kent at her grandmother's. We knew her every move."

"But your *crack* teams have her lost in the fog. That does not inspire much confidence. How do you mean to find her again *alive*?" Gregory took a step closer and poked him in the chest with his forefinger. "Eh, Philip, old man? No answers?"

"Sir, what about the CCTV footage? One of the cameras is bound to have caught them somewhere." Sergeant Finch's voice came to their ears as if from a far distance.

"Of course, Finch, I should have thought of that earlier. At least one of us is still thinking." Burnell slapped him on the shoulder. He stood and quickly flipped open his mobile. He punched in a number and waited a few seconds. "Right, this is Chief Inspector Burnell, get me Inspector Williams."

"But, sir—"

Burnell cupped his hand over the phone. "Beggars can't be choosers, Finch. This is an emergency and we need all the help we can get—Williams, good. Look, we have a bit of a crisis on our hands here. A very hush-hush matter. I don't have time to argue with you. Just listen. Time is of the essence. According to new information that has come into my possession, MI5 has concluded that Giles Hayden is the Russian spy that Charles Latimer had been chasing. Hayden killed Latimer. Yes, they have indisputable proof. The problem is that Hayden has flown the coop and he has kidnapped Emmeline Kirby. The MI5 surveillance team watching him has lost them. They were last seen in Holland Park a block from Miss Kirby's house. I need you to put out an alert and check all the CCTV cameras across the city, but urge caution. Consider Hayden armed. Also, there may be a Russian embassy official, name of Anatol Zobrinsky, with them. He is not to be harmed. I repeat Zobrinsky is not to be harmed." He waited for several seconds, nodding his head. "Good. Ring me on my mobile as soon as you have any news." Burnell turned to the others. "Well, that's that. Now comes the hard part."

"What's that?" Gregory asked.
"Waiting."

# CHAPTER 28

The wind's gelid breath had dissipated the heavy, cloying fog, but its chilly dampness had already seeped into Emmeline's bones. She tried to keep her teeth from chattering.

She could hear the angry splashing of the Thames below them. They were standing on the south side of the river along the pedestrian promenade. Giles had parked his car near the Victoria Embankment and they had walked across Westminster Bridge to Lambeth.

The moon had emerged from the clouds, suffusing everything in creamy gold light. As she gazed across at the Palace of Westminster, better known as the Houses of Parliament, her mind was racing. Was there a way out of this nightmare?

Despite the wind, the night was almost romantic— almost, but not quite. If she weren't here with two Russian spies clearly intent on killing her, things would be much better, especially if she did not have a gun jabbed into her ribs. They had dragged her to Charles's flat because they assumed she would know of any little secret nooks where something could be concealed. Hayden was certain that she knew where some photograph was. Since he hadn't found it in her house, the only conclusion he could draw was that it must still be in Charles's flat. Only

Emmeline had absolutely no idea what photograph he was talking about and she didn't know for how much longer she could bluff.

Hayden and Zobrinsky were arguing in Russian. They were inches from one another. Giles's eyes flashed with green fire. He poked Zobrinsky in the chest. Zobrinsky took a step backward, placing himself between Emmeline and Hayden. Perhaps she could break free and make a dash for the steps leading up to Westminster Bridge. She could flag down a car and call the police. Her glance flicked toward the steps, assessing her chances of success. She quickly realized that she would be dead before she was five feet away.

"*Nyet,* Zobrinsky. *Nyet.*" Hayden's words were snatched away by the wind. He pulled out a gun and calmly twisted a suppressor into place. Then he shoved Zobrinsky aside and leveled the gun at her heart.

Emmeline's mouth went dry. Unconsciously, she fingered the gold bracelet Gregory had given her. She was about to die. All she could do was imagine poor Gran's face, when they broke the news to her. A single tear rolled off her eyelashes and trickled down her cheek.

In English, Hayden said, "Emmeline, there's one thing I hate more than Jews. Do you know what that is?"

Fear had paralyzed her tongue and she shook her head dumbly.

He smiled. "I'll tell you."

He turned suddenly and fired off two rounds. Zobrinsky crumpled to his knees, knocking her to the ground as he did so. She gasped and her eyes widened in horror as she looked at the dead man beside her. His jet-black eyes stared at her, shock frozen on his face. She felt bile rising in her throat.

"Traitors. That's what I hate more than Jews. Traitors," Giles continued as if nothing had happened.

She glared at him. Still sitting on the ground, she began inching her way backward on the cold concrete of the promenade. "You're—you're a savage animal." She tried to scramble to her feet, but one of his strong arms went round her waist and he pulled her toward the parapet. There was no one around. No one who could help her.

"I wouldn't try something silly like that again."

She could feel his warm breath as he hissed in her ear.

"Do you understand? You've already made me very angry with this little goose chase tonight. I'm going to give you one more chance to redeem yourself. Where is the photo? You can cooperate or I will simply shoot you now and toss your body into the Thames. It's your choice."

She swallowed hard. "Choice. What choice? You're going to kill me regardless. I never said the photo was in Charles's flat. You *assumed* that, so don't blame me for wasting your precious time."

She could feel him smile against her hair.

"I always said you were very smart—perhaps too smart for your own good. That will be your undoing in the end." His grip tightened and the gun dug deeper into her side.

Her mind was whirling. "All right, I'll tell you."

"That's better. It will make things easier for you in the end. Less painful."

She shuddered, but she had to play for time. "Gregory has it. I gave it to him."

"Longdon has it?"

"Yes. I found it just after we got back from Kent and gave it to Gregory. After Charles's murder, I didn't think it would be safe in my house."

"So Longdon's had it all this time? Damn. I should have guessed. Interfering bastard. This complicates matters slightly, but there's nothing for it. Where's Longdon now?"

"I—I don't know. We had another row and he stormed out. I haven't seen him since this afternoon. He could be anywhere. He tends to go off to sulk in private. Frankly, I could care less where he is," she finished with more bravado than she felt.

He spun her around to face him. His fingers were biting into her shoulders. "Well, you had better start caring, because he is the only thing that stands between you and death." He slipped his hand into his pocket and pulled out his mobile. He tossed it to her. "Call him. *Now*."

She stared at the phone for a second and, with trembling fingers, punched in Gregory's number. She silently prayed that his mobile wasn't turned off.

∂∞∂

They all jumped when Gregory's phone began to ring in his pocket. He quickly took it out. "Hello."

Three pairs of eyes were fixed upon him.

"Longdon, I have someone here who is anxious to talk to you. I suggest that you pay attention."

"You're a dead man, Hayden. That's a promise," Gregory hissed.

"Keep him talking," Burnell mouthed.

Gregory nodded, while the chief inspector went into the outer office to call Scotland Yard. Vaguely he heard Burnell give his mobile number and ask for an immediate trace.

"Emmy, are you all right? Has he hurt you?" Gregory asked as he walked back into Acheson's office.

"Yes, I'm all right." Her voice cracked with suppressed tears, but he could hear relief in her tone. "He killed Zobrinsky. We were wrong about Philip—about everything. I—I'm scared. He says he'll kill me, too, unless we give him the photo. I told him you had it. I'm sorry."

He could tell she had started to cry in earnest.

"It's all right, love. Try to stay calm. I'm here with Acheson, Oliver, and Sergeant Finch. We have the photo. Where are you? Can you tell me?"

"Yes, we're—" Her words were cut off.

"Emmy? Emmy?"

"That's enough, Longdon. I want the photo in exchange for Emmeline's life and safe passage out of Britain. I'll also need some money. One million pounds sounds like a nice round figure."

"I can get you the photo, but I have no authority over the rest."

Giles laughed. "Don't treat me like a fool, Longdon. I'm sure you can arrange something with Acheson and Burnell. I bet they're with you right now, hanging on your every word. Listen carefully. I. Want. The. Photo."

"I have it. I'll come to you. But what guarantee have I you'll keep your end?"

"None. I'll ring you back in half an hour. That should give you ample time to make sure all my demands are met. And I do mean *all*. Mind you come on your own, or else Emmeline will be a fleeting memory on this earth." The line went dead.

"Damn it, man. What did he say?" Acheson asked impatiently.

Gregory cleared his throat. His voice was low and steady when he repeated Hayden's demands. "He will ring back in half an hour."

"Blast." Acheson punched his right hand against his left palm. The sharp crack only seemed to increase the tension fomenting in every corner of the room. "I've got to call the PM."

He reached for the telephone on his desk.

Gregory grabbed his arm. "We don't have time for that, Acheson. Emmeline's life is at stake."

"She wouldn't have been in this predicament, if she had simply taken my advice and dropped the story."

"It's too late for recriminations. Give him what he wants."

"I can't do that. Only the prime minster can. Now, if you'll kindly let go of my arm, I will call the PM. We'll only lose more time, if you go on like this. *Time that Emmeline does not have.*"

℮ↄℰↄ

Hayden had forced Emmeline to help him drag Zobrinsky's body toward the pool of shadow next to the steps. This corner was not visible from the bridge. Only if someone came down the steps would he stumble upon the body. Zobrinsky was unlikely to be found until the morning. She looked around, desperately hoping someone—anyone—would come along. To her right, in the distance, she saw the lights of the London Eye, the huge Ferris wheel that loomed over the Thames. But there was no one around at this end of the promenade.

No one except her and a cold, ruthless spy.

"That's good enough. Come on." Giles pulled her roughly by the arm up the steps.

"Where are we going?"

"This is not one of your interviews. I don't have to answer your questions. If you want to stay alive, you'll do as I say and keep quiet. I don't think I need remind you that it would be ill advised to upset me. There would be severe consequences. Remember our late lamented friend." He pointed down at the shapeless lump that had been Zobrinsky. "He chose to betray his country and paid

for it with his life. As I said, there are always consequences to our actions. Now, *move*." He shoved the gun
in his pocket as they slowly climbed the steps. "And
don't forget that this gun is pointed at you all the time."

"How could I *possibly* forget?"

"Guard your tongue, old girl."

They reached the top of steps and were on the bridge.
He looped her arm through his elbow and drew her close
to him. To any of the cars crossing Westminster Bridge,
they looked like lovers out for a late-night stroll. Emmeline could feel the hardness of the gun through her
jacket.

જીજીજી

The prime minister had made it abundantly clear to
Philip that under no circumstances was Hayden to be allowed to slip out of the country. He had already caused
too much damage.

The Foreign Office was still scrambling to unravel
everything that Hayden had done. If possible, he was to
be taken alive. If not, Philip was to ensure that it was
done quietly. Whatever the outcome, the PM wanted this
nightmare to end tonight. "Is that clear, Philip?"

"Yes, Prime Minister. Crystal clear."

Philip picked up the receiver again before any of the
others could ask him anything. He made a call to MI5
headquarters to update his superiors on the situation.
Then he rang Special Branch to advise them to have a
unit on stand-by to arrest a suspected Russian spy. He
said he would provide more details soon. He replaced the
receiver and sat on the corner of his desk. "Well, gentleman, the PM wants Hayden taken tonight, preferably
alive. If that's not possible, he is to be eliminated to
staunch the flow of secrets being fed to the Russians."

"Acheson, that's all very nice." Gregory paced the office like a caged lion. "But Hayden still has Emmeline. How do you intend to keep her from getting hurt? Or don't you?"

"Don't be silly, Longdon. Of course, Emmeline's safety is of the utmost concern. But our priority at the moment is to neutralize Hayden."

"Even if it means sacrificing the life of an innocent young woman in the process?"

"All right, that's enough," Burnell said as he stood up. "Sniping at one another is not going to help Miss Kirby. Whether we like one another or not is of no account. We have to work together."

"You're right, Burnell. I do apologize. We can't make any plans until we know where Hayden wants to meet Longdon. Any suggestions?" Philip asked.

"Actually, I—" Burnell was interrupted by his mobile. "Excuse me. Hello. What have you got, Williams? How long ago?" He pulled his cuff back and looked at his watch. "I see. And he was sure? Good. No, he did well. We want him to feel safe." The chief inspector listened for a few more seconds. "Right, have them follow at a discreet distance. This man can detect a shadow from a mile away. No heroics. Is that understood? He's dangerous. Finch and I are coordinating with MI5 and Special Branch. Ring me if there are any new developments. Great job, Williams. I'll see that Superintendent Fenton hears about this." He ended the call and rubbed his hands together. "Gentleman, for the first time tonight, Fate is on our side. Hayden and Miss Kirby were spotted walking across Westminster Bridge not more than ten minutes ago."

Gregory stopped his pacing. "He's certain it was them?"

"Yes. He recognized her from this morning."

"Did she look all right?"

"Miss Kirby appeared to be unharmed, but she looked tense and ill at ease."

"What about Zobrinsky? What did he say about him?" Philip asked

"He only saw Hayden and Miss Kirby."

"Damn. Zobrinsky was afraid that his cover had been blown. Damn. He was a good man."

"I don't mean to sound callous, Mr. Acheson, but we have to get Miss Kirby away from Hayden. Williams has an unmarked unit waiting along the Victoria Embankment and two others have been dispatched. Their orders are to follow, but not to approach. At last, we're in with a chance."

"I certainly hope so, Burnell. For all of our sakes."

ᘓᕼᘓ

They hadn't uttered a word to one another as they crossed the bridge. Emmeline couldn't banish from her mind the image of Zobrinsky's lifeless eyes staring back at her. She squeezed her eyes shut, but this didn't help. Giles was guiding her down Bridge Street now. They made a left at Parliament Square and continued down Abingdon Street until it became Millbank. They turned into Victoria Tower Gardens and walked past the Burghers of Calais, the bronze replica of Rodin's famous statue. He led her to a bench overlooking the Thames that was plunged in a pool of shadow.

She shivered and the hairs on the back of her neck prickled. A thin, curling wind stirred the bare branches of the nearby trees. They were being watched. She felt it in her bones. She twisted her head to the right and left, half expecting to see millions of pairs of glowing eyes ogling her. She could have sworn that she heard the rustle of footsteps behind them. But when she looked over her shoulder, there was no one about. It was simply nervous tension—the not knowing how all this would end or, rather, knowing that, in the end, she was going to die.

She swallowed hard. "Giles?" Her voice sounded strange to her own ears. "I can't call you that anymore, can I? But it seems so odd to call you Sergei."

Only half his face was visible. "What do you want?" he asked wearily.

"Why?"

"Why what?"

"What drives someone to become a spy and a killer?" She thought she could reason with him, but she had miscalculated. She felt, rather than saw, his body stiffen in the shadows beside her.

He continued to look straight ahead at some spot across the river. "Because of people like you—stinking Jews, who lie and cheat their way into positions of power." He turned to her then, his voice dropping to a harsh whisper. "If I could, I would kill all of you. You're nothing but scum. However, at the academy they taught us that it was better to hit your enemy where it inflicts the most damage and embarrassment. So I steal your secrets. I'm damned good at it. You don't know the tremendous pleasure and satisfaction it gives me to know that, with each assignment, I'm doing something to hurt you and your Zionist-loving friends in the West. Another chink in the armor."

She sucked in her breath. Russians were known to be notoriously anti-Semitic, but she shuddered at the vehemence of his words. "You're nothing more than an arrogant bigot. I hope MI5 and Scotland Yard find you and crush you."

He threw back his head and released a deep-throated chuckle. He had lowered the gun in the process and she tried to reach for it in the dark. But he recovered his composure. "Ah, ah. That's not part of the game. Like I said, you can never trust a Jew to play by the rules."

"You can go straight to hell."

She tried to break for it, but he snatched her wrist. He squeezed it so hard she thought it would snap in two.

"Listen, my little Jewess. You've disrupted too many of my plans already. The only reason that I haven't killed you is because you're going to be my ticket out of this country."

"What happens if they don't meet your demands?

He leaned very close to her. His warm breath grazed her cheek. "It's very simple. You die. You and Longdon—the other thorn in my side. But enough talk. It's time we called your boyfriend. Let's see how much you really mean to him, shall we?"

സ്ക

Inspector Williams had been in close communication with Chief Inspector Burnell. His men had followed Giles and Emmeline to Victoria Tower Gardens. Officers were in place in Smith Square and Great College Street, ready to move in and take Hayden down. Special Branch was also helping to coordinate these efforts and had dispatched a team to the scene to arrest Giles. They were all waiting for him to make his move. Would he remain where he was or make contact somewhere else?

The tension in Acheson's office was stifling. The room was not big enough to contain the four men. Gregory, hands shoved deep in his trouser pockets, paced back and forth the length of the office. He stopped from time to time to listen to the animated conversations between Burnell and Sergeant Finch. Meanwhile, Acheson sat at his desk and absently toyed with his letter opener. He hadn't uttered a word since his call to Special Branch.

Gregory thought he would go crazy from all the waiting. He was not used to sitting around. He hated this feeling of helplessness. He was a man of action. He thrived on the thrill and adventure of planning a theft— selecting the jewel, staking out its location, and then basking in the warm afterglow of a successful job. But this?

This was torture and what compounded the feeling was the fact that Emmeline's life was at risk. God, what a fool he'd been. He had developed an instant dislike toward Hayden and yet he hadn't listened to his own instincts. He had allowed her to get close to Hayden/Konstantin and now she would pay for his mistakes with her life.

"Fool. Bloody idiot," he cursed himself under his breath.

"What was that, Longdon?"

Gregory's eyes traveled to Burnell's face. "Nothing, Oliver. Nothing."

A second later his mobile start to scream in his pocket. Gregory snatched at it. "Hello. Hello."

"My, don't we sound eager tonight, Longdon. Have you and your friends complied with my demands?"

"Yes, Hayden, I have the bloody photograph. How's Emmeline?"

"She's fine. Frankly, between you and me, you could have done better than a Jewess."

Gregory bit back a caustic retort. "Put her on the phone. Let me talk to her."

"No, I told you already she's fine. You'll talk to her when you bring me the photograph."

Gregory clenched and unclenched his fist at his side. It was imperative that he keep a cool head. "Tell me where you want to make the exchange."

"Tell Acheson to call off Special Branch and tell the fat man to get rid of the Scotland Yard men. And don't lie to me by telling me they have no one watching us. I spotted half a dozen men already. Very amateurish. Their clumsiness surprises me." Hayden clicked his tongue. "If they do not disappear in the next ten minutes, I shoot dear Miss Kirby. Do you understand?"

"Don't be a fool, Hayden. You'll never get what you want if you kill Emmeline. Special Branch and Scotland Yard would pursue you to the ends of the Earth."

"Let me remind you I hold all the cards. You are in no position to bargain. I'll ring you back in ten minutes. If the watchers are not gone by then, Emmeline's death will be on your head." There was a soft click and silence.

A second later both Burnell's and Acheson's phones began ringing. Their conversations were short. Hayden was on the move. Special Branch and Williams's men wanted permission to go in, *now*. Gregory shook his head as Acheson's icy blue eyes searched his face. Acheson sighed. "Hold your positions. I repeat hold your positions—for the moment."

The chief inspector issued identical instructions.

ഏഏ

Emmeline struggled to keep her eyes open. It was nearly midnight. Her eyelids felt so heavy. Her mind was numb. Every part of her body was exhausted—nervous tension, revulsion at seeing a man murdered before her eyes, and fear had combined to sap her of her energy. For the last hour and a half, Giles had dragged all over London trying to shake anyone tailing them. And yet it was almost as if he was trying to kill time as well. After he made the first call to Gregory, they doubled back to the Westminster Bridge Underground station. They purchased tickets and took the train one stop to Embankment and changed to the Northern Line. They got off the train at Charing Cross, where they hailed a taxi to Regent Street. Along the way, Giles made two calls to Gregory. He took immense pleasure in goading Gregory. At Regent Street, they got out, walked a couple of blocks, and caught another taxi that took them to Marble Arch. From there, they plunged into the shadows on Bayswater Road. All was quiet here. Their footsteps echoed against the rain-slicked pavement. There were few cars about at this hour. The hotels and apartment buildings along the way dozed peacefully. They jumped into another taxi outside the Notting Hill Gate Underground station. Hayden told the driver to take them back to Piccadilly Circus. After he had paid the fare and the taxi pulled away from the curb, they turned onto Haymarket Street. They followed the street south until they reached Pall Mall. Then they wended their way to Admiralty Arch and the Mall along St. James's Park.

Not for a second did he let down his guard or the gun. His eyes were constantly scanning the shadows. He tightened his grip on her arm and glanced over his shoulder twice. At one point, she thought she heard footsteps again somewhere behind them. However, she was so tired that it could very well have been wishful thinking on her part. She was certain that if they stopped now, she would fall asleep standing up. But she couldn't allow that—wouldn't allow it. She had to keep her wits about her. She shook her head, opened her eyes wide, and squared her shoulders. She had to get away from him. At the moment though, he was dragging her past the Queen Victoria Memorial and Buckingham Palace. Finally, his pace slackened as they turned onto Birdcage Walk and followed a footpath into the park.

Big Ben was striking midnight, just as they stopped

by Duck Island. They were quite alone. The fog made its reappearance. It silently slithered through the naked trees and along the path, until it had folded them into its smoky embrace. Giles pulled out his mobile once more. He waited a few seconds. "Longdon, old chap, glad to see you're still there."

"You're becoming tiresome, Hayden. Do you want this photo or not?"

"Actually, the photo is rather useless to me now. My cover is blown. What I want to know is whether you've taken care of those other arrangements? You've had ample time. Trafalgar Square. Heathrow. Private jet. Money on the plane."

Gregory finally lost his patience. "Damn it, man. We've done everything that you've asked. There's a car waiting in Trafalgar Square to take you to Heathrow and there's a private jet on stand-by with instructions to take you anywhere you want. The money's on the plane. Now, let Emmeline go."

"What about Special Branch? How do I know they won't grab me once I set foot on the plane? No, I think Emmeline will keep me company a little while longer. Just until the plane is ready to take off." He smiled down at her.

She tried to scratch his face, but he easily swatted her hand away.

"That was not part of the bargain."

"What can I say, Longdon? I lied."

"Bastard."

"Such language will get you nowhere."

"Take me instead. Let Emmeline go and take me instead."

Hayden laughed. "My word, I thought such heroic gestures were only confined to the movies. What would I do with you, Longdon? No one cares about you, old chap.

Emmeline, on the other hand, would be sorely missed. Look at the stir tonight's little adventure has caused already. She's my insurance. Therefore, she comes with me. If you want to see her alive again, tell Acheson to make sure we're unmolested as we make our way to the car. I'll be in touch—once I'm safely on the plane."

"Like hell you will," Emmeline said as she rammed her shoulder into his ribcage with all her might. He was knocked off balance and fell to the ground. He gasped for air. The gun slid into the water with a soft, gurgling plop. His mobile arced into the air and came to rest at her feet. She snatched it and began to run, holding it to her ear as she ran. "Gregory. Help me."

"Emmy? Where are you?" He snapped his fingers for silence. Acheson, Chief Inspector Burnell, and Sergeant Finch crowded around the desk.

"We're in St. James's Park. By Duck Island. Ahh—" she screamed and the line went dead.

"Emmy? Emmy? Bloody hell." Gregory got up and ran toward the door. Over his shoulder, he said, "They're in St. James's. Duck Island. She managed to get away, but something's happened." And then he was gone.

Acheson called after him, "Longdon, don't be a fool." But all he heard in response was Gregory's dying footsteps echoing in the corridor.

# CHAPTER 29

Emmeline clawed and thrashed at the damp ground as she fought to get away from Giles. He had lunged for her as she was talking to Gregory. The mobile went flying in the opposite direction and was now lost in the fog. He was stronger than she was, but she kept up a continuous barrage with her fists. She pummeled at his face, his head, his shoulders, any exposed part of his body that she could find. She scrambled to her knees and managed to run a few feet.

But Hayden reached out with one long arm and grabbed her ankle. She lost her balance and fell forward, groaning, as she landed hard on her stomach. For a moment, she couldn't move. Could she have broken a rib? He was pulling her toward him by the ankle. She kicked out viciously and was satisfied when she heard a crunch as her foot made contact with his nose.

He cried out and immediately released her leg. She got up and started running, blindly. The fog was so thick she became disoriented. She just ran—as fast and as far as she could in the opposite direction from where she had left him. Her heart was pounding in her chest. Her lungs were on fire and her breathing was coming in ragged rasps. Tears were streaming from the corners of her eyes. She angrily swatted at them with the back of her hand.

She collided with something in the murky darkness. She kept on screaming when she realized it was a man. His hands reached out and grabbed her by the shoulders. Giles had found her and now she was going to die. *Oh, God, help me. Please*, she pleaded silently.

"Emmy, calm down. It's me. You're all right. Hush, Emmy. You're safe now."

She stopped screaming when the familiar voice penetrated her ears. It wasn't Giles, after all. "Duncan?" Her body trembled with relief and her lungs filled with the damp night air. "Is it really you?"

He pulled out a torch from his coat pocket and flicked on the switch. "In the flesh."

She threw her arms around him and squeezed as if she were holding on for dear life, which she was. Her tears fell on his neck. She was saying something, but her words were muffled.

"I'm sorry, Emmy. I didn't understand." He loosened her grip and held her away from him.

"I've never been so happy to see anyone in my entire life."

"I'm glad I was here. Suppose you tell me why you're running through St. James's Park in the dead of night."

Once she started, Emmeline couldn't stop the story from tumbling out. She told him about Zobrinsky coming for her, their encounter with Giles, the trip to Lambeth, Zobrinsky's murder and, finally, how she came to be standing here. "I thought he was going to kill me and then I ran into you. Thank God." She hugged him again and then she pulled away. "We have to get away from here. He's still out there in the fog somewhere. We have to get to Philip and Chief Inspector Burnell."

She slipped her hand into his larger one and started to pull him. But he wouldn't budge. "Duncan, you're

shining that torch right in my face and I can't see anything." She raised her hand to shield her eyes.

"Sorry, Emmy. I didn't realize. Is that better?" He
shifted the beam to the right over her shoulder.

She smiled and dropped her hand. "Yes, that's much
better. Now, I can see."

"So can I."

She froze when she heard Hayden's voice. She
swung round abruptly and saw that he was only five feet
from her. Blood was streaming from his nose. "Did you
really think you could get away from us?"

"*Us?*"

Giles laughed and looked over her shoulder. "She
doesn't know. The little Jewish bitch still doesn't know,
does she?" He addressed this question to Duncan.

Emmeline looked from one to the other. "Duncan?"
She took a step backward, but he grabbed her arm. "What
is he saying?"

She stared up into the deep blue eyes of her father's
old friend and, with sickening dread, realized that she already knew the answer. "It was *you*. It was you all along.
You're Sergei Konstantin, aren't you?" This was barely
more than a whisper.

Duncan flashed her that smile she had known since
childhood. "I always said that you were a very smart girl.
Very smart, but extremely reckless. Just like Aaron. And
sadly it has been your undoing."

She squeezed her eyes shut. Perhaps, it was all a bad
dream. It couldn't be true. Not Duncan. Not Daddy's
friend. She opened her eyes, and saw the two men and the
nightmare she had walked into. A tense silence hovered
in the fog between them.

"I don't understand. Why?"

"I got into the game so long ago the reasons hardly
matter anymore."

"How could you do it? You killed Charles. I was stupid. Giles couldn't have gotten to the house before us. His story didn't make sense. There wasn't enough time. He rang *you*. He overheard my conversation with Charles at Heathrow and he rang you. You went to the house. Of course, Charles didn't put up a fight. Why would he? You were an old friend. He trusted you and you murdered him. You managed to slip away before Gregory and I arrived. I'm right, aren't I?" She didn't wait for a response. "You must have been laughing when I came to you for help this afternoon."

"I must admit it was amusing. All I had to do was sit there. You walked right into the center of the web. You made it so easy for us. I must also thank you for outing Zobrinsky. That scene you caused at the Russian embassy was a brilliant move. Brilliant. I couldn't have orchestrated it better myself. For months, we've suspected him of being a double agent, but we didn't have proof."

She felt the sharp sting of betrayal like a slap across the face. Her shoulders sagged. She stared at the ground and shook her head. Her throat was sore with unshed tears. Finally, she looked up at Duncan. "What happens now?"

"I think you know the answer to that question. But there is one little loose end that must be dealt with before I take care of you."

"And what would that be?"

The first bullet hit Giles's shoulder and spun him around. By the time the second bullet tore through his heart, he was dead. Emmeline stood there with her mouth gaping open. Then the trembling started. Her hands and feet felt like ice. She wanted to run, but she couldn't move. A scream bubbled in her throat, but died before it reached her lips. She looked up at Duncan.

Outwardly, he appeared to be the same as ever.

However, there was a stillness and coldness about him that she had never noticed—like a panther stalking his prey. His deep blue eyes bored into hers and she realized that she had never known this man at all. She wondered if anyone had.

He took a step toward her. Instinctively, she recoiled and backed away. He was saying something, but she heard him as if from a long way off. "Come now, Emmy. We can't stay here. We have to be going."

She found her voice at last. "I—I'm not going anywhere with you. Don't come near me you vile, evil monster." She wished she could stop her limbs from shaking.

He came a little closer, gun outstretched in front of him. "I promise I'll make it quick and painless. I owe at least that much to Aaron."

"Don't you dare defile my father's memory by bringing him up on this sordid, filthy night. *Don't you dare*. If Daddy were still alive, he would be heartbroken to see that the man that he called friend—a man he thought of as a brother—was really a liar, a traitor, and an assassin."

"Spare me the boring sentimentality. It's time to go. It wouldn't do to have too many bodies littered across the park. What would Scotland Yard say? We must find a quiet, secluded place to kill you."

He grabbed her arm. She tried to yank it away, but his grip was too strong. He slowly pulled her toward him. She kicked his shin and he howled in pain, but he didn't let go. It only made him angrier.

"That was a big mistake, my girl, and you'll pay for it."

His features were twisted into an ugly grimace. He raised the gun in the air. She threw up her arms to shield her head from the coming blow.

"I wouldn't do that if I were you, Redmond."

Emmeline's eyes flew open when she heard Gregory's voice. Duncan's hand dropped to his side. Gregory was emerging from the fog like a fairy-tale knight. But unlike a fairy tale, he had a gun instead of a suit of armor—much more practical.

"Because you'll be dead in the next second. If I don't get you at this range, then Special Branch and Scotland Yard certainly will."

Duncan guffawed. "How cliché, Longdon. That line only works in the movies."

"I'm not joking, Redmond." There was a soft click as Gregory eased off the safety. "Personally, I'd love you to make a move." He waved the gun in Duncan's direction. "Then, we could get it over with right now." He took a step closer. "Right here."

Emmeline saw Duncan's mouth curve into a feline smile. His eyes glinted in the torchlight. She could almost hear his brain contemplating his chances of escape. No one moved for an interminable moment.

Without taking his eyes off Duncan, Gregory asked out of the corner of his mouth, "Emmy, are you all right?"

She nodded, not trusting her voice.

"That's one point in your favor, Redmond. Let her go. *Now*." Gregory raised his gun and leveled it at Duncan's head. He was focusing on a spot just between the eyes.

"Why would I do that? One more body really doesn't make a difference to me." Duncan looked down at her. "It's nothing personal. You do see that, don't you, Emmy? There comes a time when everybody must die. Yours just came sooner than expected."

Gregory was fingering the trigger. "Don't say I didn't warn you."

"Longdon, stop."

Chief Inspector Burnell, Sergeant Finch, and Ache-

son came running up to them, flashing their torches on
the trio. The two policemen were panting.

The chief inspector said, "Don't do it. You'd be no
better than he is."

"Go away, Oliver. Turn your back and pretend that
you arrived five minutes too late. Come on, Oliver. Bend
the rules just this once. No one here will say a word. In
fact, we'll all thank you."

Burnell looked at Duncan, but he appealed to Gregory. "Think of Miss Kirby. Hasn't she been through
enough for one evening?"

Gregory's cinnamon gaze flicked toward Emmeline.
Their eyes locked for a second. "Emmy—"

There wasn't time for anything else. While everyone
was focused on Burnell and Gregory, Finch had inched
his way behind Duncan and knocked his feet out from
under him. They rolled around on the damp ground. The
sergeant tried to wrest the gun from Duncan's hand. The
older man was bigger and broader than the sergeant. He
was gaining the upper hand. With one swift motion, he
raised the butt of the gun and brought down hard against
Finch's temple. The sergeant immediately went limp and
lost consciousness.

"Watch out," Gregory yelled, as he tackled Chief Inspector Burnell to the footpath. A bullet whizzed over
their heads, grazing Acheson's arm. He quickly clamped
his hand over the wound and hit the ground. In the tu-
mult, Gregory's gun tumbled from his hand and landed
near Redmond.

Emmeline dove for it, but Duncan reached it before
she could.

She was on her knees, so close to him that his breath
ruffled her hair. She didn't dare to move or breathe. Her
heart hammered in her chest. Surely, everyone could hear
it. Wave upon wave of blood crashed in her ears and

throbbed against her temples. Beads of perspiration sprang up on her forehead. Her mouth had gone dry. She licked her lips. They felt rough and cracked. Out of the corner of her eye, she could see Gregory and Burnell slowly rising to their feet. They were helping Acheson up.

"Easy, Redmond. Don't do anything rash," Acheson coaxed.

Duncan laughed and released the gun's safety hammer. "Oh, Acheson, I have never been prone to rash gestures. Everything is calculated to the smallest detail. It's the only way to survive in this game. You should know that. Now, I'm going to stand up and you're going to tell all those friends of yours lurking in the shadows to let me pass without any interference. Otherwise, Emmeline will die right here. I will shed no tears over it, believe me. It's your choice, gentlemen. However, if I were in your shoes I wouldn't want to have the blood of a pretty young woman on my conscience."

Redmond pocketed Gregory's gun. He grabbed Emmeline by the nape of her neck and dragged her toward him, placing his gun against her temple. "Take a good look at her. It may be the last time, depending on the choice you make in the next ten seconds."

Outraged at the rough manhandling, Gregory took a step forward with the intention of ripping Duncan's arm from its socket. Acheson was closest to him and saw the murderous look on Gregory's face. With his good arm, Acheson reached out and put a restraining hand on Gregory's shoulder.

"Ah, Acheson, I'm glad to see that at least one person here tonight has some good sense. Now, if you would be so kind as to call off your men." Duncan waved his gun toward the trees.

Acheson turned to Burnell and shook his head. The policeman didn't say anything.

"Chief Inspector, I'm getting rather impatient. Call off your men and their Special Branch counterparts or I pull the trigger."

Burnell trained the torch on her face, lighting two silvery tears tracing a crooked path down Emmeline's cheeks. With a sigh, he raised his voice so that it could be heard all the way down the footpath. "Stand down. Everyone put your weapons down."

"Chief Inspector Burnell, this is a mistake that you'll live to regret," Acheson hissed in his ear.

Finch groaned all of a sudden. He was starting to regain consciousness and had rolled onto his side. Everyone was momentarily distracted.

The shot shattered the silence.

# CHAPTER 30

Emmeline screamed. She felt some of Duncan's blood spatter on her cheek as he fell. The bullet had hit him in the center of his forehead.

Gregory was instantly by her side and folded her in his arms. He pressed her face to his chest and murmured soothing words against her dark curls. He felt her trembling and held her tighter.

She wept uncontrollably. "Gregory, I was so frightened. I thought I was going to die."

"Hush, darling. It's all over. He can't hurt you. I promise."

They heard footsteps running toward them. Soon, they were surrounded by officers from Special Branch and Scotland Yard. Chief Inspector Burnell took charge. Acheson spoke briefly to the leader of the Special Branch team to determine what had happened. He waved off suggestions about going to hospital. "It's superficial. I'll be fine. However, I think Sergeant Finch there is in need of some medical assistance. Please see to it that he is taken to hospital at once."

"Yes, Mr. Acheson. I'll have one of my men take him straightaway."

Burnell came up to them. "I've called Williams. He's coming down with a team from the Yard. They'll be here within ten minutes. The men here on the scene already are cordoning off the area. They have things well in hand."

Burnell glanced over at his young sergeant, who was now sitting up with the assistance of Gregory and Emmeline. He turned back to the Special Branch man. "I'll feel much better when a doctor has seen him. He's a good lad."

"Don't worry. He'll be in good hands. You have my word on it. But may I suggest that Miss Kirby and Mr. Longdon be transported as well. Miss Kirby has been through the mill tonight. They can give their statements tomorrow."

"Come on, Chief Inspector. We'll go back to my office," Acheson said. "It's fortunate Special Branch was here tonight and took down Redmond. Otherwise, more innocent lives could have been lost."

"I'm afraid Special Branch can't take credit for it. None of my men fired a single shot."

"Then your men are to be congratulated, Chief Inspector Burnell."

The chief inspector scratched his head. "I'm afraid my lads didn't fire either."

Acheson ran a hand through his hair. "You mean to tell me that some Good Samaritan just happened to be strolling through St. James's Park at midnight, came upon the scene, took matters into his own hands, and then disappeared into the night?"

"It looks that way, Mr. Acheson."

"That's insane. You don't believe it, do you?"

"Perhaps it was the Angel of Death and it was simply Redmond's time?"

Acheson stared at the Special Branch man, at a loss for words. The whole thing was bizarre.

"Ultimately, what does it matter, sir? Redmond is dead and he can't cause any more damage."

⋐⋑

Emmeline refused to go to hospital. Instead she sat on the claret-colored sofa with her head resting on Gregory's shoulder and her eyes staring at some unknown spot on the opposite wall. He was trying to clean the dried blood and dirt from her face with his handkerchief. She had hardly uttered a word since they had entered Acheson's office. Gregory tried to keep up a light patter of conversation, but he and Burnell exchanged concerned looks.

"Emmy, are you all right? Are you hurt anywhere?"

She shook her head and the silence enveloped them once more. Then she sat up. "Cold. I'm very cold."

Gregory pulled her closer to him and rubbed one arm to get the blood circulating. Acheson came over and handed him a tumbler of whiskey. "It's the shock. This will do her some good." He bent down on his haunches so that he was at eye level. "Come on, Emmeline. Drink it. It will warm you up."

She looked into his blue eyes for a long moment and started to cry. "I'm sorry, Philip. I'm sorry I doubted you. Can you ever forgive me?"

His whole face lit up in a smile. "There's nothing to forgive. Redmond was very good at manipulating people. Besides, the twins would murder me, if I banished Auntie Emmeline from the house."

This made her giggle. "Thank you. I don't deserve your kindness."

"Don't be silly. Now, drink this up. You'll feel better."

"I don't drink whiskey."

"You will tonight. That's an order."

She stared at the amber liquid in the tumbler and then took a small, tentative sip. She coughed and wiped her lips with the back of her hand. Her hand fluttered over her stomach as if the whiskey was burning a hole in it.

"That's better. Come on, love, another sip," Gregory coaxed.

"If I drink any more, you'll have to carry me home."

"Ah, the sacrifices we men have to make."

Emmeline sat up and swatted his shoulder. The color was starting to return to her cheeks and the glazed look had dissipated in her dark eyes. She took another sip and then pushed the glass away. "That's it."

Gregory drank the remaining contents of the glass in one gulp.

Acheson and Burnell smiled at one another. "Good girl," Acheson said.

Emmeline's brow suddenly furrowed. "Philip, your arm. Shouldn't you be in hospital?"

He dropped himself into the wing chair opposite the sofa and rubbed his injured limb. "It's fine. It's only flesh wound. However, I'd be grateful if you didn't tell Maggie how it happened. I wouldn't want her worrying."

"No, of course not."

"Thanks."

"I have a question."

For the first time that night, all the men laughed. "Only one, Emmeline?"

She smiled sheepishly. "Well, several actually. Let's start with how a Foreign Office official became involved in an international espionage drama. What are you MI5, MI6?"

The three men exchanged looks and Burnell tried to smother a smile. "Maggie always said that you were the

most perceptive one at university. Ostensibly, I work for
the Defense and Intelligence Directorate here at the Foreign Office and I do. But you're right, I am MI5. This
information does not leave this office. You will have to
sign the Official Secrets Act and none of this appears in
your paper. Maggie does not even know and I would like
it to remain that way."

"I suspected as much. Now, let's go back to the beginning. I think I've pieced some of it together in my
mind, based on what Paolo Talamini told me in Venice.
But both Charles and Talamini thought Giles Hayden was
Sergei Konstantin. Did you know it was Duncan?"

"That's what Redmond wanted everyone to believe.
And we did for a long time. He was Hayden's control officer. He was pulling all the strings. All along he was
planting evidence against Hayden to give himself an escape route, if we ever got too close." He went on to explain how MI5 had become suspicious of Hayden and
about Zobrinsky's dangerous balancing act to find evidence against him. "Unfortunately, he paid for it with his
life in the end."

"How did Charles get mixed up in this?"

Acheson sighed. "Charles was just being the good
journalist he always was. He smelled a juicy story and
was following up on a hunch. I tried to dissuade him from
pursuing it—like I did with you—but he wouldn't let go,
again like you. He became obsessed with unmasking the
Russian spy at the Foreign Office. I had someone watching him, but Redmond was too clever. He had Hayden try
to kill Charles in Venice and, when that failed, he took
things into his own hands here in London."

"How did Charles get away in Venice? He couldn't
have moved after he had been stabbed. I was there. I saw
him."

"That was Zobrinsky. After you got away, he called

me. We brought Charles to a safe flat in Lido, before you and Longdon came back with the carabiniere. A doctor we could trust treated Charles's wound. He had a high fever for a day or so. Then, he disappeared. Frankly, I think the forger we hired helped him. He was a funny little fellow. Nicolò Crespi."

Gregory's eyebrows shot up at the sound of this name. Nicolò Crespi was the old gentleman he'd had coffee with at Florian. He let his mind wander back to their conversation on that rainy afternoon in Venice. Was it merely a coincidence that Crespi was in the thick of things?

No one noticed his surprise and Emmeline merely nodded reflectively. "Forger? Oh yes, the one who painted that so-called Caravaggio for Talamini. But why the elaborate ruse? Why get Talamini involved at all?"

Acheson looked down at his feet and clasped his hands together. "We were hoping Talamini would get so enraged about the forged painting that he would kill Hayden and our problem would be solved."

Emmeline's eyes widened. "I see." Something didn't make sense about this whole forgery business, but she couldn't place her finger on exactly what it was that bothered her. "Instead, Giles somehow got wind that Talamini was talking with Charles and killed him, right?"

"No, it couldn't have been Hayden."

Emmeline looked at Philip in confusion. "What do you mean?"

"I don't know who killed Paolo Talamini, but it wasn't Hayden."

"How can you be so sure?"

"Because he was sitting next to me at a reception at the French consulate that night."

# CHAPTER 31

Emmeline and Gregory stared at one another. Even Chief Inspector Burnell appeared surprised.

"Then, who killed Talamini?" she asked. This was turning out to be an evening for unsolved murders.

"That's the question. In my opinion, the Venice police's conclusion that Talamini was killed by some of his Mafia cronies was the correct one. We'll never know, though."

"It doesn't feel right, Philip. There's something that we're all missing. Giles may not have done it, but I'm sure Talamini was killed because he got mixed up in this Sergei Konstantin business."

"It's not our problem. It's an Italian matter and they seem to be satisfied with their theory. As far as MI5 is concerned, the Sergei Konstantin case is closed. Just let it go, Emmeline. Be thankful that you're still alive."

"Well, of course, I am. But—"

"I think it's time I got you home," Gregory said as he glanced at his watch.

It was three o'clock in the morning. Lack of sleep and the remnants of raw tension were clearly etched on all their faces. He stood and gently drew Emmeline to her feet. He nodded and shook Acheson's hand. "Acheson."

"You know, Longdon, you were not half bad out

there tonight. If you weren't a thief, you'd make a good MI5 agent."

Gregory flashed him one of those smiles he used to charm even the most jaded of individuals. "Thief, Acheson? If I were you, I'd watch what I say. You could be sued for slander if you continue to hurl such accusations around." He took a step closer and lowered his voice. "I believe the term is *alleged thief.* Because, after all, nothing has ever been proven against me. It's been pure speculation on the police's part. Isn't that right, Oliver?"

"Chief Inspector Burnell."

"If you must insist on such formality, Chief Inspector Burnell, then. But you didn't answer my question?"

"Humph," Burnell grunted. "It doesn't deserve an answer. Everyone knows you're a thief. All of Interpol can't be wrong."

"Can't they? I wonder," Gregory said with a cheeky grin. "Well, gentlemen, I can't say that it's been a pleasure, but I wouldn't have wanted to work with any other chaps."

Emmeline's eyelids were starting to droop and she leaned heavily against him.

"Now, I must get this young lady home."

He put his arm around her waist and guided her to the door. They were in the outer office when Burnell caught up to them. "Longdon, a moment please."

"Yes, Oliver."

Burnell gave him a pointed look, but chose to let it go. "I just wanted—what I mean is—out there tonight," he stammered helplessly.

"Yes, Oliver?"

"Damn it, man." Burnell squared his shoulders and met Gregory's gaze. "I wanted to thank you for pushing me out of the way in the park. If it hadn't been for you, I wouldn't be here right now."

They were silent for a long moment. Then, Gregory reached out and put his hand on the policeman's sleeve. "No need for thanks. Anyone would have done the same, Chief Inspector Burnell."

The two men smiled and shook hands.

❦❦❦

In the following days, Emmeline and Gregory were debriefed, first by MI5 and then by Scotland Yard, and they were sworn to secrecy. The entire matter was quietly hushed up and soon slipped from the public's consciousness. The murder charge against Gregory was naturally dropped and slowly life began to return to normal. And yet, Paolo Talamini's murder remained a mystery. Emmeline didn't like loose ends. But this wasn't the only loose end.

Now that the dust had settled, she had to come terms with Gregory being back. Things could never be as they were before, but could she see a future for the two of them? She didn't think so. Too many things had happened. She was not the same person she was when he left two years ago. "And I can't go back. I won't go back," she said aloud to the kitchen.

The ringing of the doorbell interrupted her troubled thoughts. She dried her hands on a towel and went to answer it. On the doorstep was Gregory, looking more handsome than ever. He wore a short brown leather jacket. The zipper was open and revealed a cobalt crew neck sweater and dove gray corduroy slacks. Damn, he was particularly attractive in that shade of blue.

"The custom is to allow people to enter the house."

"What? Oh, sorry. Of course, come in."

"Thanks." He stepped inside the hall and shut the door behind him.

"Let me take your jacket." She hung it on a peg. "I was just going to put the kettle on. Would you like a cup of tea?"

"That would be lovely. Here these are for you." He extended a large bouquet of coral-colored roses. Her favorites.

She took the flowers and buried her nose in the middle of the bouquet, taking a deep breath of their heady scent. "They're absolutely beautiful. Thank you."

Her eyes found his and they were silent for a moment. Then, she looked away and hurried down the hall to the kitchen. He smiled and followed her. He sat at the table as she moved about the kitchen trying to regain her composure. She could feel her cheeks burning. How did he always manage to unnerve her like this? How?

She filled a vase with water for the roses and placed it in the center of the table. Golden strands of sunlight streamed in through the window, caressing the velvety petals and enhancing their seductive aroma. *Even the flowers are on his side.* The kettle whistled and she went over to make the tea. As she readied the pot, he went to the cupboard and took out the delicate Lady Carlyle cups and saucers. The set was a long-ago gift from Gran.

Once they were both settled, Emmeline said, "I've been thinking."

"I hope you haven't hurt yourself in the process."

She made a face and stuck out her tongue at him. "Ha. Ha. Be serious. I think Philip and the Italian police are wrong. In fact, I'm sure of it."

The smile vanished from his lips. "You mean about Paolo Talamini's murder?"

"Yes. Their theory doesn't make sense. The Mafia is an easy way out. Everybody's washed their hands of the matter."

"I happen to agree with you, Emmy, but the case is closed. There's nothing we can do about it."

Her eyes widened in surprise. "You do?"

"Do what?"

"Agree with me."

"About Talamini, yes. But for all intents and purposes, the case is 'officially' closed."

"I could get it open again."

"Emmy." The tone in his voice cautioned her against such a move. "That would be unwise."

"Who said anything about wise? I want the truth."

"Does the truth really matter in this instance? Talamini probably got what he deserved. After all, he was not the most noble of the world's citizens. I think you should let sleeping dogs lie."

"I don't understand you, Gregory. You just said that you agree with me. Now, you're trying to put me off. Why?"

He squirmed a little under her gaze, but said nothing.

"You know something, don't you? Something you haven't told the police. I'm right. I can see it in your face."

"Then you need glasses."

"No, I don't. I have perfect vision. Don't lie to me." She put her elbows on the table and leaned toward him. "What do you know?"

Gregory wanted to laugh. She looked as eager as a child trying to wheedle out a secret. "I think—"

"Yes?" she pressed.

"I think the two of us should go back to Venice."

She straightened up and pushed her cup away from her, sloshing some tea onto the saucer. "We are no longer together and I am not taking any trips with you."

"Not even if it means discovering the truth about Paolo Talamini's death?"

# CHAPTER 32

*Venice*

A sharp wind was blowing off the Grand Canal as they ambled down the Riva degli Schiavoni toward Piazza San Marco. However, it was a glorious day. The sun sparkled as wispy clouds scudded across the cerulean sky. The crowds of Carnival had disappeared and the city's rhythm had slowed to its usual relaxing pace.

Once again, Emmeline was struck by how much she loved Venice. She cast a sideways glance at Gregory. He seemed preoccupied. He had been very mysterious about where they were going this afternoon. The only thing he told her was that she would find all her answers.

They entered the square, passing beneath the lions of St. Mark's, the city's guardians. She stopped for a minute to admire the delicate cream-and-rose façade of the Doge's Palace. They also stopped in front of the Basilica. She would have liked to linger longer, but he glanced at his watch and propelled her along the arcade toward Florian. They passed Tomasso's shop, but didn't stop.

"What's the rush?" she asked.

"I don't want to miss someone."

"Who?"

"If you hurry, you'll see."

They entered the famous café and she immediately felt as if she had stepped back in time to another era— one of elegance and romance. Her eyes delighted in the plush red banquettes, the intricately carved gilt mirrors, and the medallion paintings on the ceilings and walls.

Gregory saw him immediately. He was sitting at a tiny corner table reading *Corriere della Sera* and sipping espresso. He seemed to sense Gregory's eyes upon him and looked up.

The older gentleman smiled and put down his paper on the banquette beside him. He stood up and waved to them to come over. He extended a hand. "Ah, Signor Longdon, I knew you would come. And you have brought Signorina Kirby with you. How marvelous."

He bent and kissed her hand. She blushed at the gallant gesture.

"Emmy, allow me to introduce you to Signor Nicolò Crespi."

They shook hands. Her eyes narrowed and then recognition finally dawned in her mind. "But this is—"

Crespi took her hand and tucked it into the crook of his elbow. "Please, signorina, signore, sit down and I will explain everything."

She hesitated for a second and Gregory looked at her askance.

"Please," Crespi begged.

"Yes, of course."

She sat down on the banquette and the two men took the chairs. Crespi called the waiter. Emmeline and Gregory ordered cappuccino, while Crespi signaled for another espresso.

They made small talk until their drinks arrived and the waiter tactfully disappeared. They were silent as they took sips of their coffees.

Crespi cleared his throat. "Signor Longdon, we all have our secrets."

Gregory and Emmeline exchanged looks, but they allowed him to continue.

"What the signorina was trying to tell you just now is that I am not Nicolò Crespi. Since I retired fifteen years ago and came back to Venice to live out my final years, I have been known as Nicolò Crespi. But I was not born with this name, nor was I born in Italy."

"I don't understand."

"His name is Spiro Panagiotakos. He was born on Crete in 1935. And he was one of the world's greatest forgers. Purportedly, he died fifteen years ago."

Crespi raised his cup to her and smiled. "Thank you for that very flattering description, Signorina Kirby. I must tell you that I very much enjoyed your series last year in the *Times* on forgery. It was very thorough. Naturally, I was extremely proud that you chose to make me the centerpiece of your articles. It also brought me up to date with what some of my old friends and rivals are doing today."

She couldn't believe she was sitting here drinking coffee, while he nonchalantly discussed his life of crime. She could see that Gregory was amused. He had unexpectedly found a soul mate.

"But you did not come here to talk about my past exploits, entertaining though they are. You want to know why I murdered Paolo Talamini and Duncan Redmond, alias Sergei Konstantin. Isn't that so?"

Emmeline was too stunned to respond. Meanwhile, Gregory had suspected the truth about Talamini's death, but despite what had been said that night, they all thought either Special Branch or Scotland Yard had killed Redmond.

"The sins of the father should never be visited upon

innocent children," Crespi began. "With the benefit of hindsight and maturity, I will tell you that I was very arrogant as a young man. I was a handsome devil and I knew it. Women simply fell at my feet. Then I met my lovely Marina." His voice softened and a faraway look entered his brown eyes. He sighed as he remembered the past. "She was the most beautiful woman I had ever seen. We met in Rome, the Eternal City, and immediately embarked upon a passionate affair. I was besotted. There was no other woman for me. Those first few months in Rome were a slice of paradise. We found a little apartment near the Spanish Steps. I painted. She taught singing.

"Then, as things naturally happen, Marina found herself pregnant. I was happy about the baby, don't get me wrong. But I started to worry about money. With a baby on the way, we would need more money. Babies need so many things.

"My paintings were not selling and this only strained our relationship. It's not that we didn't love each other anymore. We did, with the same intensity as when we first met, but Marina was having a difficult pregnancy. The doctor's visits were getting expensive. I desperately had to make some money. I was prepared to start prowling around the streets at night to steal just so that I could provide for my family.

"One day, as if by the hand of God, a man knocked on our door and said that he had heard that I was a painter. I did not know from where he came nor was I terribly curious. He had a job for me, if I was interested. *Interested?* I would have taken anything. And that's how I started my career as the 'world's greatest forger.'"

"What does all this have to do with Talamini and Redmond?"

"Bear with me, signorina. It is a long, painful road of

shame. Please allow an old man to take his time and atone for a lifetime of sins."

"I'm sorry. Do go on. I promise I shan't say another word."

"Thank you. Now, where was I? Oh, yes. The baby came. A beautiful girl. We called her Francesca after Marina's mother. We were a family and we were happy. Soon, though, I realized I was not ready for the responsibilities of fatherhood. The apartment became claustrophobic. Marina and I started to quarrel. Finally one day, I could take no more and I left. We were never married, so there was need for a divorce. I simply took my things and left one night. To my dying day, I will regret turning my back on Marina and Francesca."

Crespi stopped his story at this point. He swallowed the lump in his throat and reached out to take a sip of espresso. He shuddered at its bitterness

Tears pricked Emmeline's eyelids, as the story brought memories of the baby she had lost flooding back.

"Ah, the folly of youth. There are some things we can never get back." He sighed and shook his head. "But life goes on, does it not, my friends? I traveled. I painted. I pulled off some of the biggest hoaxes in the greatest capitals of the world. I reveled in the fact that my paintings could fool the 'experts.' I had all the money I could want. I had a villa on Lake Maggiore. I had apartments in London, Paris, and New York. The only thing I did not have was love. Yes, there were women—I was not a monk, of course—but they were not Marina. No one could replace her and Francesca in my heart.

"As fate would have it, their paths crossed mine. It was 1977. I came here to Venice for a 'job' and who do I see not five feet ahead of me in the *mercato* near Rialto, but Francesca. I knew her immediately. She was like my Marina, when she was young. Francesca must have been about seventeen at the time. I couldn't take my eyes from her. At one point, she looked straight at me and I had to pretend I was buying something at another stall. Soon, she was finished with her shopping. Marina was nowhere in sight. I decided to follow Francesca home. I told myself I would have one look at my Marina and then I would go. I just wanted to see her one more time.

"What I discovered broke my heart. Marina was dead and Francesca, sweet little Francesca, had a baby of her own. A girl. She had been abandoned by her boyfriend and was now struggling to take care of the baby without anyone to help her.

"When I saw this, I decided to stay in Venice. My daughter and granddaughter were here. They needed me. Of course, I could not appear on their doorstep and declare myself. That would be too cruel for Francesca after staying away for so many years. So I bought a palazzo on the Grand Canal and started keeping watch over them. I sent Francesca money anonymously each month. I would slip the envelope under her door personally. It assuaged my conscience a little.

"But this paltry effort was not enough in the end. The situation was too much for Francesca and one day she decided to give the baby up for adoption. It all happened when I was away from Venice for two months. On a job. I will never forgive myself for being away. If I had been here, I could have stopped it. By the time I returned, Francesca had vanished. I pretended I was an uncle from Milano and asked her neighbors if they knew where she had gone, but no one knew anything.

"It took weeks, but eventually I found out who was the loving couple who had adopted Romina."

Gregory turned his head sharply. "Romina? Tomasso and Sylvia Morelli's Romina?"

"Yes, Signor Longdon. Now you understand why I

had to kill Paolo Talamini. I had to avenge my granddaughter. He seduced her, got her hooked on drugs, and
then abandoned her. The poor thing was so miserable that
she killed herself. I could not allow such scum to walk
the earth, while my Romina was lying cold in her grave."

Crespi struggled to choke back a sob. "I waited for
him that night in the alley and I plunged a knife into his
heart. Just as he did to my darling Romina. I made sure
he knew who had killed him. My face was the last thing
that he saw in this world."

Emmeline was crying softly. Gregory squeezed her
hand. "Go on, Signor Crespi. Tell us the rest of it. You
can't stop now. We need to know all of it."

The old man swallowed hard. "I know you stole the
diamond necklace at the Talamini's ball, Signor Longdon. And I know you gave it to Tomasso. I thought to
myself, 'Ah, here is a man who despises Talamini as
much as I do. I must contrive another meeting.' You intrigued me. I had to know more about the man who
helped the parents of my granddaughter. I followed you.
Naturally, this led me to the signorina. I saw how much
you loved her."

Emmeline glanced at Gregory and then looked down
at her hands.

"But yes, Signorina Kirby, you cannot doubt that he
loves you. It is obvious to anyone with eyes. Just as it is
obvious that you love him."

"I do not," she asserted emphatically. "I did once,
but not anymore."

"Well, the two of you must resolve this between you.
But do not allow circumstances and stupid pride to take
away your happiness as it happened to me. I beg you.
Please do not let history repeat itself."

They were all quiet, each lost in his or her own
thoughts.

Gregory broke the silence. "Finish the story, please."

"By now, I'm sure you have learned that Signor Acheson and Zobrinsky hired me to paint the Caravaggio. I also helped them that night to bring Signor Latimer to the safe flat in Lido. He had a high fever and had lost a lot of blood. I sat with him. He was babbling about Signorina Kirby and the danger he had put her in. He muttered something about a photo and Russian spies. It was a little difficult to understand everything he was saying, but it was enough. From that moment on, I was determined to see that the signorina was not harmed. It was for you, Signor Longdon. For what you did for Romina.

"I became concerned when Signorina Kirby's hotel room was ransacked. I called you that day. Do you remember? To try to warn you and to tell you to trust only Signor Longdon."

"That was *you*? Yes, and the other day at the house when I was with Giles. That was you too, wasn't it?"

Crespi smiled. "Yes, I had seen Redmond and Hayden together at your house. Then Redmond left and Hayden pretended that he had just arrived."

Everything was suddenly clear. "And you followed us that night when Zobrinsky came to the house."

"Yes," Crespi said modestly. "You were in no danger. You did not see me, but I was nearby the whole time that Hayden was dragging you all over London. Until, finally, when Redmond showed up at the park and killed him. That was when I became alarmed. I hoped I could get close enough to shoot him without harming you. Well, you both know how it all ended. I am quite willing to tell my story to the police. I feel no shame for what I have done. And I would do it all over again. Please allow me to finish my espresso and we can go."

A tear dripped from her eyelash and splashed onto the table. She reached out and touched Crespi's hand.

"No, signore." Her voice was of full of emotion. "There's no need. I cannot thank you enough for watching out for me. You are a very dear man." She leaned over and kissed his wizened cheek. "Now, I think it is time for Gregory and me to go. To allow a little peace to enter your life."

She slid out from the banquette and Gregory rose as well. He extended his hand. "Thank you, Signor Crespi."

The old man put his other hand over Gregory's and squeezed it hard. "You are an intelligent man. Don't let her slip through your fingers."

Gregory smiled. "I did once. But I've been given a second chance and I don't intend to squander it."

"*Bene.* Then, everything will be all right." His gaze flicked over to Emmeline, who was waiting at the door. "Yes, I can see that everything will be all right. It does an old heart good."

Emmeline and Gregory wandered aimlessly through the warren of crooked streets for a couple of hours. They discovered hidden canals, each with its own secret. They soaked in the peace and serenity, allowing Venice to work her ancient magic upon their drifting souls.

They stopped on the little humpbacked footbridge just before they reached the quiet campo where Hotel Ala stood. Emmeline closed her eyes, making a mental picture she could take out from time to time on rainy afternoons in London.

"Venice is beautiful, but there are too many painful memories here at the moment. Perhaps, I'll come back one day. After the dust has settled a bit first."

"Yes, love. We all need some time."

She opened her eyes and he bent down to brush her lips with a soft kiss. His mustache nuzzled her cheek as he pulled away.

"We are not getting back together, Gregory."

"We'll see."

The insufferable arrogance of the man was astounding. Little did Emmeline know that the next time they met, it would be murder.

# About the Author

Daniella Bernett has wanted to be a writer since she was nine years old. She graduated summa cum laude with a B.S. in Journalism from St. John's University. She is a member of the Mystery Writers of America NY Chapter. *Lead Me Into Danger* is her first novel. She also is the author of two poetry collections, *Timeless Allure* and *Silken Reflections*. In her professional life, she is the research manager for a nationally prominent engineering, architectural, and construction management firm. Bernett is currently working on the next adventure in the Emmeline Kirby and Gregory Longdon mystery series. Visit her at www.daniellabernett.com or follow her on Facebook.